The
Sommelier

A Zachary Taylor Thriller

Daniel Llewellyn Shaw

ISBN: 9798313010151

Prologue

Hurtling through the air at one hundred miles per hour in the Cessna Caravan, Zachary Taylor felt that familiar rush. The small, single-engine aircraft was cramped and noisy, but he was used to it. After all, he'd done this some forty times before, so he was an old hand. Skydiving gave him a thrill that few other activities still could, a break from his normal routine. It did not, however, sit well with his wife of twenty-seven years, Sophie, who had on more than one occasion said things like "Are you serious?" and "Act your age," sarcastically nicknaming him *The Flying Sommelier*.

In the beginning, he patiently explained to her the whole sequence of events: from climbing to fourteen thousand feet in the plane, to jumping out and free-falling for one euphoric minute, then pulling the parachute and drifting to a gentle landing. How the parachutes were meticulously packed, checked, and rechecked, and how to deploy the secondary chute in the unlikely event the main chute failed.

Sophie never seemed convinced, however. As time went by, and their marriage fell into that functional disrepair that so often arises from the contempt only familiarity can bring, they eventually stopped talking about it. Silence became their unwritten agreement: he jumped and she looked the other way. Sometimes she found herself wondering if an accident might break the logjam she felt trapped in.

Zach shifted uneasily on the hard bench, acutely aware of the cold metal of the gun pressed against his temple. The man holding it, a slab of muscle named

Vinny, wore a sardonic grin as if daring him to flinch. A bead of sweat traced a cold line down Zach's temple, disappearing into his collar and making him shiver. Vinny leaned in closer, his breath reeking of garlic and cheap cigars. "We know you've been lyin' to Mr. Salvatore. You're one of them rats, ain't you?"

Zach knew the cover he used to infiltrate their criminal alcohol trade was paper-thin, held together by little more than luck. Vinny's finger hovered near the trigger, and for a terrifying moment, Zach wondered if his first undercover assignment would also be his last. The plane hit a pocket of turbulence, jostling them violently, and the gun wavered before Vinny steadied it. Had Salvatore sent this brute to tie up loose ends? Every instinct screamed at him to act, but he was paralyzed by the cold metal pressed against his temple.

"Get ready to jump!" The sharp voice of the skydiving instructor jolted Zach back to the present. The gun, the goon, Salvatore's bootleg operation – all of it vanished, replaced by the five other jumpers sitting on the benches of the stripped-down Cessna. Zach exhaled, unclenching his muscles as he checked the straps on his parachute. The dampness under his collar reminded him that some memories lingered, waiting for the right moment to resurface, like sharks beneath calm waters.

As they neared the jump site, they assembled near the open door, which the instructor was blocking in order to prevent anyone from unintentionally stumbling out. Zach, standing first in line, turned back to reassure himself that Vinny wasn't lurking somewhere behind him, waiting to shoot him as he jumped. Thankfully, all he saw was a mixture of eager novices and experienced thrill-seekers, who looked back at him expectantly.

"Go, go, go!" barked the instructor over the noise

of the engine and the wind. Zach took a deep breath, steeled himself, and leaped into the void. Tumbling through the sky, the rush of the wind pushed against him with relentless force. For those first few seconds, he allowed himself to fall freely before he arced downward. Belly down, arms and legs spread wide, the feeling of floating belied his rapid descent and the inherent danger.

"I've never felt so alive," he thought as he counted down the seconds. Below him, the patchwork of Napa Valley's green vineyards and the tiny clusters of buildings were rapidly growing larger. Just seconds ago they had seemed so far away.

At three thousand feet, Zach reached for the ripcord and pulled. For a brief moment, nothing happened. Then, with a jolt, the chute deployed, but something was wrong. Instead of catching the air and spreading out above him, the lines twisted, causing the parachute to tangle.

He started to spin uncontrollably as he struggled to regain control. He spread his legs to slow his descent, keeping his head up and his back arched, and reached for the breakaway handle to release the chute. He yanked it, hard. Nothing. It remained tangled, and he continued to spin as the ground rushed up to meet him.

Flying at one hundred and seventy-six feet per second, Zach had now descended to two thousand feet, with eleven seconds left before impact. He fumbled for the secondary chute and deployed it with a swift pull of the ripcord, the violent spinning ceasing as he felt a sudden deceleration. Fortunately, it didn't tangle with the main chute, but he was too close to the ground, too fast. He hit it hard, and everything went black.

The next thing Zach knew, he was lying in a hospital bed, white walls and the scent of disinfectant replacing the open sky. He looked to his left and saw Sophie seated by his bed, her arms crossed as she studied him with disapproval written across her face.

"Where am I?" he managed to say through the fog of the morphine.

"San Francisco General," Sophie replied in a voice that betrayed both concern and resignation. She leaned forward. "You were very lucky, flyboy."

"What day is it?" he asked.

"What day do you think it is?"

"Last I remember it was Sunday, September 4." He noticed a slight relaxation in her expression.

"Okay, you don't have a concussion. That's something. How do you feel?"

"Like a truck hit me."

"Well, the bad news is you have a broken pelvis and a fractured right ankle. The doctor says you'll be up and about on crutches in a week and, with physiotherapy, able to walk with a cane in a few months.

"I've told you before, Zach, you're not a kid anymore. You're fifty-seven years old. A man your age has no business skydiving." She paused for a beat as if deciding where to take her onslaught next. "Why this reckless compulsion to risk everything for a few seconds of extreme danger? Think of your family."

Sophie continued to lecture him about anything that came to her mind until Zach's nurse entered with his next shot of painkiller. As the new morphine kicked in, he drifted off into a welcome oblivion where he could no longer hear his wife.

Part I
The Sommelier

A sommelier's job is normally straightforward:
keep the wine flowing, the glasses full,
and the trouble just a sip away.

UCLA - 1986

They first met in French class at UCLA in February 1986. Zach was a sophomore majoring in History with a minor in French. Sophie was also a sophomore whose parents were French, making her much more proficient in the language than Zach was or ever hoped to be.

Zach had arrived late to class just as the professor was introducing the intricacies of the subjunctive mood. Scanning the room for an empty seat, he found one next to a beautiful girl with shoulder-length blonde hair. As he settled into his chair, he couldn't help noticing the delicate handwriting in her notebook. They exchanged polite smiles, but that brief interaction was enough to spark his curiosity.

After class, he mustered the courage to introduce himself. "Hi, I'm Zach," he said a little shyly.

"*Bonjour*, Zach, I'm Sophie," she replied with a musical accent that was definitely not Californian.

"Do I detect a French accent?" he asked.

"Very good. Yes, I grew up in Paris."

"So, you're a sophomore like me. Are you a French major by any chance?" he asked, anything to keep the conversation in play.

"How did you possibly guess that?" she replied, giggling. "And you? What's your major?"

"History, with a minor in French. I'm from here. With your background, I doubt I'll ever speak French as well as you. *Quel dommage*," he sighed.

"Don't pity yourself. I heard you in class. You talk just fine... for a guy from California that is." They both laughed, and decided to go for coffee. Over the next hour, they discovered a mutual passion for all things French, and perhaps for each other.

Soon they became inseparable and could be found together in their dorm rooms, eating meals, drinking espressos, and occasionally at French class. They spent hours exploring Los Angeles, from the beaches of Santa Monica to the eclectic neighborhoods of Silver Lake. The city became a playground for their young love, and their laughter a common soundtrack.

They frequently talked about their future together, what they would do, where they'd live, how many children they'd have, and travel and career plans. It was amazing and reassuring how in sync they were. They were soulmates who could tell each other anything, secure in the knowledge that their ideas would be heard, considered and accepted on their merits.

Sophie was beautiful, smart and slim, with emerald green eyes and that intoxicating French accent from her upbringing in France. She'd been born in California while her parents were teaching at UCLA for five years, and raised in France until she returned for college. To Zach, she was sophisticated and intelligent, always willing to listen and engage him in discussing life's endless mysteries, as university students do. She also had a keen eye for fashion, effortlessly blending Parisian chic with California casual. Her presence was like a breath of fresh air, invigorating those around her.

To Sophie, Zach was handsome, witty and clever. She'd never encountered a boy who knew classical music and philosophy. He took her to concerts at the L.A. Philharmonic and to dinners at swanky restaurants. His entertainment budget exceeded hers, as her parents were academics in Paris, and that sometimes bothered her a little. She had a scholarship to help pay her tuition, while he was on a full ride courtesy of his well-to-do father who was a successful financier from Beverly Hills. Despite their differences, they complemented each other well. Sophie's spontaneity and zest for life brought excitement and adventure into Zach's orderly existence. She taught him to embrace the unexpected, to find joy in the little things, and to appreciate the beauty of the present moment. Zach, in turn, provided Sophie with a sense of stability and security. He was her rock, grounding her flights of fancy with his unwavering support and rational perspective.

In June, the day before the Spring term ended and they'd go home for the summer, Zach took Sophie to a candlelight dinner at a French restaurant, complete with starched waiters and the scent of fresh bread wafting through the air.

As the waiter refilled their glasses, he stopped fidgeting with his napkin and took a deep breath, his pulse quickening. He glanced at Sophie, who was sipping her wine as her eyes scanned the paintings in the room. "Sophie," he began, his voice close to faltering. "There's something I need to tell you." She looked at him, her brows slightly raised. Zach swallowed, his mouth suddenly dry. "I think I'm in love with you."

Sophie's expression didn't change immediately, which made his heart pound even harder, as she set the wineglass down carefully. "That's sweet of you to say," she said slowly, her voice so calm it was as though he'd commented on the weather.

Zach felt a rush of heat rise to his face. "Sweet of me to say?" His voice cracked, betraying a vulnerability he was trying hard to hide. "That's it?"

Sophie hesitated, searching for the right words.

She could feel his frustration mounting. "Zach, I care about you deeply. I just wasn't expecting this so soon. I need more time."

"Time." He exhaled in frustration, shaking his head. "We've been seeing each other for months now, Sophie. How much time do you need?"

She pressed her lips together, feeling a tightness in her chest. "I don't know," she admitted, her voice small.

Zach pushed his plate away, his appetite lost. "So, what? I just wait around for you to decide whether or not you love me back?" His words were harsher than he intended, but he couldn't help it. His heart was exposed, and her response felt like rejection, even if she didn't mean it that way.

Sophie winced. "That's not what I'm saying."

"Then what are you saying?" he interrupted, his voice louder than he intended. He looked around, embarrassed, then leaned in, lowering his voice. "It feels like you're waiting for some perfect moment that might never come."

"I just need to be sure of what I'm feeling," Sophie said firmly, her tone steady. "I don't want to rush something that's supposed to mean everything."

Zach fell silent, his shoulders slumping. This was supposed to be a happy moment where they confirmed their love for each other. Instead, he felt like he'd opened his heart, only for her to take a step back.

The rest of the dinner was a blur of awkward pauses and half-hearted conversation. When they left the restaurant, Zach's mind was buzzing with frustration, confusion and disappointment. Sophie walked beside him, quiet, her own thoughts swirling. When they parted on uncertain terms, Zach returned to his dorm and fretted while he packed. Then he stopped and reached for the small stash tucked behind his books.

Rolling a joint with practiced hands, he lit it, inhaling deeply. Instead of calming him, it only amplified the chaos in his head. What had she meant by those lingering silences? Was she slowly pulling away from him without saying a word? Was she seeing someone else? He paced the room, his thoughts a tangled mess. Each unanswered question morphed into a gnawing insecurity, making him feel small and stupid: was he missing something everyone else could see? Was Sophie just waiting for the right moment to leave?

The next day, they each flew home without saying goodbye, both distracted and deep in thought.

Finally, after about two weeks, she wrote to him and confirmed that she loved him too. It was undoubtedly the happiest day of his life. He read that letter many times over and walked on air for days. The events of their last evening together quickly faded from their memories as they wrote to each other every week that summer.

When you're nineteen years old, you can recover from life's shocks quickly, but you also tend to take a lot for granted. While Zach would make snap decisions based on instinct, Sophie was more contemplative and took time to consider the myriad facets of every situation. In the early days of their courtship, they patiently gave each other the benefit of the doubt, taking time to work out the kinks and reach a mutual understanding.

This essential difference in their young, barely formed personalities eventually became more and more contentious. Back on campus in their junior year, they found themselves arguing more frequently, their once harmonious conversations turning into heated debates.

The differences now seemed to push them apart, creating a growing rift that neither of them knew how to bridge.

Sophie dreamed of traveling the world, exploring new cultures, and living a life free from conventional constraints. Her future was an open book, full of possibilities. Zach, on the other hand, was focused on his academic and professional goals, driven by a desire to make his mark in the world, and secure a stable future for himself and Sophie. These conflicting visions of the future created tension and uncertainty between them, slowly casting a shadow over their relationship.

The breaking point came a year after they first declared their love for each other. Sitting across from each other in the campus coffee shop, Sophie took his hands in hers. "There's something I have to tell you, but I'm afraid to."

"You know you can say anything to me, *chérie*," Zach replied, oblivious to the warning sign of what was to come.

"I don't want to hurt the person I love."

"You know there's nothing you can say that will change my feelings for you," he said a little more cautiously.

"I've decided that we should break up," she said, avoiding his eyes. "There, I've said it."

Zach looked at her intently, unable to comprehend the implications of what he'd just heard. This was the woman he planned to marry.

"Why?" he asked after a few painful moments passed.

"You're a wonderful person, but you come from money, and you're too trusting of people. I worry that will get you in trouble someday. And I want a more

Bohemian life. I want to be able to pick up and go anytime I want. I don't want to be tied down to a traditional lifestyle. I know that you take work and success seriously, and you will want to pursue a successful career. That's just not for me."

"Fine," he said stoically. "Since your mind is obviously made up, there's nothing for me to say, is there?" He was focusing on all the arguments they'd had, rather than the good times. "You know, when I gave you my heart, I didn't expect you to give it back with a knife in it."

Sophie just stared at him with tears in her eyes. This was one of the hardest things she'd ever done, and she was overwhelmed with sorrow and his cold response. How could this man who said he loved her be so callous? She'd hoped for more empathy.

"How much you've changed over the past year. Well, I guess I'll see you in class someday," he said resentfully, and he stood up and left her weeping quietly at the table, his dignity intact.

In truth, he would never be able to fully work her out of his heart. She would always be there, a yardstick by which he measured all newcomers.

Sorbonne Université – Spring Term 1988

Now a senior at UCLA, Zach elected to spend his last two terms at the Sorbonne Université in Paris under the Education Abroad Program.

A blend of history and modernity, its grand lecture halls and libraries exuded intellectual dignity, and every cobblestone street and ancient facade whispered tales of past scholars. Stately buildings with diverse architecture going back to 1257 stood witness to the university's rich academic heritage, yet it remained firmly rooted in the present. The lively Left Bank, with its bustling cafés and vibrant student life, provided a dynamic backdrop to Zach's studies, while the nearby Seine offered a scenic escape between classes.

Like other American universities, UCLA provided one of its recent graduates to act as a liaison with the French staff. That year, it was a former student by the name of Peter Mosley. He'd graduated two years earlier and worked at a prominent wine store in Los Angeles, where he developed an expert knowledge of wine and its business. The store mainly concentrated on French and Italian wines, since California's wine industry was still developing, although it was on the move and would eventually rival the best in the world.

It was early in the term that Peter approached Zach and other students with a proposition: would they be interested in doing a not-for-credit wine appreciation course after dinner for two hours a week? Their reactions were pretty easy to read: "You mean you're offering me the opportunity to learn something new and get wasted on French wine at the same time?"

Soon he'd corralled a group of a dozen students wanting the chance to drink alcoholic beverages while away from straitlaced California. Although some of them were twenty-one years old, none had much drinking experience. They knew little about wine, beyond that it came in red, white and rosé, and could be had in Paris for a few francs a bottle. A whole new world was about to open for them.

The first step was to have everyone purchase Hugh Johnson's *World Atlas of Wine* which, since its first publication in 1971, was the authority on all things wine. Now in its third edition, the introduction covered basic topics such as the history of wine, grape varieties, *terroir*, diseases, appellations, labels, and so on. It then proceeded country by country, starting with France – *naturellement* – with photos and maps that gave a comprehensive review of the wines from each country.

At seven o'clock on the following Monday evening, they assembled enthusiastically in one of the lecture halls for their first lesson. Peter was already there, with six bottles of red wine which he'd opened to let them breathe.

"Welcome, everyone. As some of you know, I graduated from UCLA two years ago. I then worked at Stanley's Fine Wines in Santa Monica, where I spent my time buying and selling French wine, meeting with distributors and winery representatives, and tasting a fair amount of wine," he said with a glint in his eye. This elicited a few sporadic chuckles.

"Robert Louis Stevenson once wrote, 'Wine is bottled poetry.' What did he mean by that? I'm here to take you on a voyage of discovery from wine drinking to wine appreciation. Anyone can drink wine, but until you understand the basics, what is it? If you're only looking

16

to alter your state of consciousness, wine will get you there; but if you want to learn how to enjoy the journey as well as the destination, this course is for you.

"Each of these sessions will be divided into two parts. The first will be from Hugh Johnson's introduction, covering topics such as wine growing, winemaking, grape varieties, and so forth, and the second part will be tasting the different wines, which will be grouped by region or grape variety.

"Tonight, we'll start with how to taste wine, and then taste six red wines from the Margaux region of Bordeaux, which lies three hundred miles southwest of us. Bordeaux is generally considered to be the leading wine region, or *appellation*, in the world. So, we're starting tonight at the top."

Zach put his hand up. "Yes, Zach?" Peter said.

"Why is a Bordeaux wine superior to a Burgundy, such as Nuits-Saint-Georges?" Last term, he'd shared a five-year-old bottle of Nuits-Saint-Georges at a fancy local restaurant. Being the only fine wine he'd ever tried, all he knew was that it was way better than the stuff you got for five francs.

"That's due to a combination of factors, that the French like to call *terroir*, which is the soil, climate, topography and the surrounding plants. Then there's the winemaker, although many argue his job is not to screw it up, that it's the quality of the fruit that makes great wines.

"In each wine region you will find different qualities of wine, from *vin ordinaire*, which I'm sure most of you know well, to first growth wines such as Château Margaux. So, while I may say that Bordeaux wines are the best, I'm talking about their best wines. There is a government rating system that ranks the different qualities, which we will get into in a subsequent session.

"One word of caution though: never tell a Frenchman from Burgundy that Bordeaux wines are superior. Assuming you want to live long enough to leave the country! Did that answer your question?"

"Yes, thanks," replied Zach, who still had his doubts about why Nuits-Saint-Georges was not as good as the vaunted Bordeaux. He would keep that question in the back of his mind as he learned more.

"Before we turn to the elements of tasting wine, I want to say a bit about how to read the label. Tonight, we have six Bordeaux wines, all with labels that tell you the essential information about the wine. Each label is composed of six parts: first, the name of the wine. For example, I'm holding a bottle of Château Palmer 1983. In this case, Château Palmer is both the name of the wine and the producer.

"Next, we have the year, or vintage, in this case 1983, which makes the wine six years old, and puts it in the sweet spot of five to seven years for red, and three to five years for white. This is a third-growth wine from Margaux, which can last for twenty years or more. When opening a prestigious wine that is six years old, let it breathe for at least one hour; I prefer two, to allow it to open up before drinking."

Another student raised her hand and asked, "What does 'third growth' mean?"

"That refers to the classification in 1855 which ranked the Bordeaux châteaux into five categories, from *Premiers Crus* down to *Cinquièmes Crus*. Third growth is *Troisièmes Cru* in French.

"When you look at the Château Palmer label, it does not show the classification; it only shows the region

– Appellation Margaux Contrôlée – which is one of the elements that must be on a wine label. Where the wine comes from.

"Next you have the size of the bottle and the amount of alcohol. Many labels include the grape variety, but Bordeaux red wines are blends of mainly three grapes – Cabernet Sauvignon, Merlot and Cabernet Franc – so it's not usually shown on the label."

The class continued with a lively discussion of the different aspects of wine labels, and the bottle of Château Palmer was passed around, in anticipation of the tasting to come. Finally, Peter poured one-ounce servings of the Palmer into Bordeaux-style wine glasses, which were passed around.

"First, hold your glass up to the light and look at the color. This is the first step to actively tasting wine, as opposed to simply drinking it. Anyone can drink wine, but it means so much more when you pay attention to it, just like you do when eating superb food."

They sampled the six wines, each time cycling through a routine of color, aroma and taste, noting the variations in each wine. They learned that Palmer was an equal blend of Cabernet Sauvignon and Merlot which gave it a supple, full-bodied and velvety character. Other wines were different blends, some lighter, some heavier in taste. They were all delightful, and the students were positively inspired.

Their journey into the wonderful world of wine had begun. Zach was beside himself with excitement. He comically resembled J. Thaddius Toad from *The Wind in the Willows* with his new motorcar: "O bliss! O poop-poop! O my!"

Near the end of the semester, Zach approached Peter in his tiny windowless office (more like a broom closet actually). "I've been thinking about a career in wine, but I'm not sure how to go about it," Zach said to Peter, who waved him to a seat in front of his desk.

"Which end of the business appeals to you?" Peter asked. "Growing the grapes, making the wine or selling it?"

"Quite honestly, I've never seen myself as a farmer, so growing is out. As for the other two, I could see doing both."

"There are many different components and skills involved in the wine business. One is all the information regarding the types of grapes, the effect of *terroir*, viticulture, viniculture, the regions, and history. Another is developing your palate by tasting the wines and remembering them.

"You could start by working at a wine store as I did, or at a winery, or you could pursue the more formal route and enroll in the Enology Department at UC Davis. There are prerequisites to getting into that program; one of them is chemistry."

"Thank you," said Zach. "I'll look into both options, and find out what courses I may need for UC Davis. You've given me a direction that I think will influence the rest of my life."

Zach and Peter became good friends through their time spent together, starting with the course and expanding with a trip to Burgundy in Peter's little car, for a long weekend of wine tasting and a gourmet dinner in a one-star Michelin restaurant. The dinner was another first for Zach as he'd never experienced such an exquisite five-course dinner, each course paired with a different wine.

The trip was thrilling as well as educational. Peter used his connections from the wine store to take them behind the scenes, where ordinary tourists didn't go. He showed them the caves of the famous producer Joseph Drouhin in Beaune, and introduced them to the proprietors of some of the prominent labels. Zach was able to taste some raw wine from the barrel, which was extracted using a pipette. It was very acidic, and Zach didn't like it. Later, when he was eating, he noticed that his teeth felt furry and were extremely sensitive. Where had all the enamel gone?

The French have a relationship with wine that can best be described as passionate. It's intertwined through their society, showing up in everyday life. Such as when Zach visited a small wine shop near the Sorbonne to buy a bottle of wine. When he entered, the proprietor was studying four wine glasses with different shapes sitting on the counter. He didn't look up or greet him, instead waving him to come forward.

"Which design do you think is better for a red Bordeaux?" he asked in French. Zach was immediately taken aback, since he'd never thought about it. The shape of the wine glass? At that point, a glass was a glass; it was simply a means of conveying drinks to your lips.

"I really don't know," he replied, which was true as he didn't have a clue what to say. This didn't discourage his host, as he held them up and examined them closely one by one. He was completely preoccupied with his quest, causing Zach to feel completely out of his depth. Eventually, as the man prattled on about the different aspects of appreciating wine, spouting theories that Zach had never heard or considered before, he felt comfortable enough to participate.

"I think I would choose that one for a Bordeaux," he said, pointing to a large Burgundy balloon glass, "because it provides the most space to savor the aromas."

"That's what I think too," came the surprising reply, making Zach feel quite proud that he'd weathered his first outing in the wine world with an expert, and done it in French! When their conversation ended, he chose two modestly-priced bottles which, due to his newfound knowledge from the course, were a significant improvement over the usual *vin ordinaire*.

Nowhere else would he experience the same passion as he embarked on his wine journey that would come to dominate his life.

Café du Chat Noir – May 6, 1988

By coincidence, Sophie was also at the Sorbonne for six months studying the French Impressionists, her favorite subject. She and Zach had stayed in touch and occasionally met for coffee. Their former bond was such that they could still talk openly, as if no time had passed. Toward the end of the spring term, they agreed to meet for coffee at the nearby Café du Chat Noir.

Zach was excited, but also nervous about seeing Sophie again, especially in Paris of all places. He'd spent the last year thinking about her more often than he cared to admit. As he approached the café, a jolt ran through him when he saw her sitting outside at a round, white marble-topped table. She was seated in a bentwood chair reading a paperback, the sight of her still taking his breath away. He sat down, and they fell effortlessly into that easy pattern of speech that comes naturally between two young people who were once intimate. Soon enough they were interrupted by their Parisian waiter.

"*Qu'est-ce que vous voulez?*" he asked smoothly, expecting a reply in English as he'd pegged them for Americans.

"*Je voudrais un croque monsieur, un citron pressé et un espresso*," replied Zach first, with an accent that was unmistakably foreign to the French ear.

"*Oui, Monsieu*r, and do you want milk and sugar with your espresso?" came his patronizing reply in English, which served only to annoy Zach. Shaking his head, but before he could return the favor, Sophie jumped in with her flawless Parisian French, and placed her order. She also engaged in a little French chit chat with the now fawning waiter, which only irritated Zach further.

After the waiter left, and they resumed talking about their studies, people they'd met, places they'd visited, and friends back on campus. Zach couldn't contain his enthusiasm about the world of wine that he'd discovered, and that he had applied to study Enology at UC Davis. He may have oversold the subject judging by Sophie's reaction.

"You've always had a passion for things you love," Sophie remarked, a hint of nostalgia in her voice. Zach smiled, appreciating the warmth of her words.

"And you, Sophie? How is the French boy you mentioned last time we talked?" Zach asked, trying to keep the conversation light despite the underlying tension he felt.

Sophie's expression changed, a mixture of joy and sadness playing across her features. "His name is Jacques," she began. "He's wonderful, really. But... well, it's complicated. His family is very traditional, and they don't approve of him dating someone who isn't French."

"That's tough," Zach replied, feeling a pang of jealousy he tried to ignore. "I hope it works out for you."

Sophie smiled, but there was a hint of sadness in her eyes. "Thank you, Zach. That means a lot."

As they continued talking, they realized that they had matured and changed, even though they were only twenty-one years old. Suddenly, Sophie began to cry, and Zach's protective instincts kicked in.

"Sophie, what's wrong?" he said, clasping her hands.

"I'm sorry," she replied, wiping her eyes with her napkin. "It's my father. He told my mother that he's thinking of leaving her for another woman."

"Why?"

"Her name is Madeleine. I met her a few times at parties that my parents hosted. She was recently divorced from her husband, who's another professor at the university," Sophie said through her sobs. "She's just a socialite but, according to my father, she's vivacious and witty and worldly – everything *Maman* isn't. I can't believe he's doing this to her."

Zach's heart ached for Sophie. He'd always admired the closeness of her family, but this news shattered that image. He found himself sharing her sense of utter despair, and all the distress she'd caused him last year melted away. There was nothing he could do of course, except be there for her while she talked it through.

"My mother and father have four children, they've been married for twenty-five years, they've built a life together!"

"What did you say to him?" Zach asked.

"I told him to grow up, act his age and stay with his wife! He's obviously infatuated with this Madeleine and flattered by her attention."

Zach was surprised, never having heard Sophie talk about her father this way. He was a senior professor that Zach had met a few times, and found seriously intimidating. When she needed to, Sophie could marshal an intense focus on a problem, and this was one of those times. She'd clearly thought this through, and Zach was getting her conclusions.

"What's your father going to do?"

"I don't know." More sobs.

"I'm studying the French existentialists in one of my classes; authors like Jean-Paul Sartre, Albert Camus, Simone de Beauvoir. They witnessed firsthand the horrors of World War II, and argue that life is absurd, that the answer lies in the bonds we form with each other. Someday, I hope your father will realize that what he has with your mother is all he needs because she loves him, takes care of him, has dedicated her life to him, and should be the most important person in the world to him. It's that relationship that gives meaning to an otherwise absurd existence."

"I'm sure he knows all about the existentialists," she replied, "but I doubt he ever applied their wisdom to understanding his marriage or appreciating my mother. That would be expecting too much."

They continued to hold hands like confused children whose parents had gone astray, then finished their lunch and agreed to call each other. They didn't. Instead, they completed their studies and returned to the home campus where they reacquainted themselves with their mostly different friends. They did, however, think of each other often. In particular, Sophie found herself considering Zach's words about existentialism and the bonds we form with others.

After they graduated the following month, they didn't talk or meet again for five years while they busied themselves with further studies and embarked on their careers. Zach went onto study Enology for two years at UC Davis, during which he learned virtually every aspect of winemaking, from growing grapes to turning them into wine. He embraced the well-worn edict, first introduced to him in Paris in 1988 by Peter Mosley: great winemaking begins in the vineyard.

One evening in the spring of his first year there, Zach visited UCLA to attend a reunion of the Paris overseas class. Also in attendance was Peter Mosley, which was an unexpected pleasure. "Peter!" Zach almost yelled when he spotted his old friend and mentor across the room. Threading his way through the tight crowd, glass of wine in one hand and a canapé in the other, he quickly had him all to himself.

"How are you, Zach?" he asked, sipping his wine.

"Great. Loving Davis. Learning lots. Soon I may know as much about wine as you," he said flippantly.

"I'm sure you already do," replied Peter with his usual modesty. "What will you do after graduation?"

"That's still undecided, but I'll probably work in a wine store for a while, like you did, and keep my eyes peeled for opportunities."

"Sounds like a plan," he replied, before they were split up by other students wanting their turn with Peter. The evening was a roaring success, as these types of events tend to be when old friends reunite.

During his time at UC Davis, Zach's passion for winemaking grew. He spent countless hours studying and learning about soil composition, grape varieties, and the meticulous care required to produce high-quality wine. He absorbed everything he could from his professors and fellow students, eager to make his mark in the industry.

Afterword, he worked at a couple of liquor stores doing everything from unpacking product to advising customers on the floor. He thought about Sophie often after their last meeting at the Café du Chat Noir. They'd shared something special, a bond that had never truly been broken despite the years and distance. As he moved on with his life, his graduate studies and new career provided a convenient distraction from his thoughts about the past. Although they were both in Los Angeles, it was a large city and an easy place to avoid an ex-lover.

Santa Monica – September 1993

Zach was having a great time. He was making enough money to afford his own car and an apartment without a roommate. He was doing what he loved, and always learning something new. The customers were loyal and knowledgeable, which allowed him to learn from them too. He was too busy to think about anything, or anyone, else.

He'd been with Stanley's Fine Wines in Santa Monica since April 1992. Armed with his UC Davis Certificate, two years of practical experience at other wine shops, and a reference letter from Peter Mosley, Zach was welcomed with open arms. Over the next four years, he would acquire an extensive knowledge of the wines that they carried, giving him a solid foundation for the next steps he planned to take.

The store was a wine lover's paradise, with an extensive array of French, Italian and Californian wines organized by country and region. A blend of cozy library and wine cellar, the earthy scent of oak barrels and the faint aroma of wine helped to transport visitors straight to the vineyards. This ambiance reflected its generous and friendly proprietor, who'd built a reputation for his knowledge and love of sharing it with others. A connoisseur who delighted in helping customers discover interesting new wines, Stanley offered regular tastings and gave an extra discount to customers looking for a special bottle.

One afternoon in September, while Zach was buried in paperwork, Sophie walked in. She was dressed in a cotton summer dress and sandals, her blonde hair tied back to reveal that gorgeous face and green eyes. No makeup required.

"Hello, Zach," she said. "How have you been?"

He looked up from studying today's list of deliveries, pen in hand. *Of all the gin joints in all the towns in all the world, she walks into mine...* "Pretty busy, right now," he replied without thinking, his brain still in analysis mode. He immediately regretted it. *Let's try again.* "Sophie! How nice to see you after all this time. What brings you here?"

"Someone told me you were working here, so I decided to drop by to see you."

"How have you been? What have you been up to since UCLA?"

"I'm okay. After grad, I returned to the Sorbonne for my PhD in art history, and now I'm a Teaching Assistant at UCLA. How about you?"

"As I predicted at our last meeting in Paris, I did the Enology Certificate at UC Davis, and eventually ended up here selling wine," Zach replied, looking at his watch. "Do you have time for a coffee? There's a neat café just down the street."

"Sure, let's go," Sophie said, noticing how easily they lapsed back into their familiar ways.

They walked down Santa Monica Boulevard to Bean & Co., which was a funky coffee shop that looked like it belonged in the sixties. The interior was dark wood with stamped tin ceilings. Mixed in with the small tables and chairs were leather club chairs and coffee tables, grouped to encourage thoughtful dialogue, like a good coffee house does. All that was missing was the cigarette smoke, which had been banned a month earlier. There was still a slight smell of tobacco that lingered, which held nostalgic memories for the regulars.

They ordered their cappuccinos, and carried them to a small table by the window, where they continued to tell each other about their adventures over the past five years. They'd each had relationships, but none of them had developed into anything memorable.

"This is really nice," Zach said. "I'm glad you decided to come by. How we've both changed, and haven't, over the years. You're on a path to becoming a University Professor, while I am... well, I'm not exactly sure where I'm headed. We're sort of the opposite of what you said we were when we broke up."

"Do you see yourself doing this forever?" Sophie asked.

"I think so. There are so many aspects of this business that could keep me occupied, and interested, for a long time. I don't see myself working in a wine shop forever. I might go to Napa and work in a winery for a while, get myself more deeply involved in the winemaking part."

"That sounds exciting," Sophie said, her eyes shining bright. After all, she was French; wine was in her blood. "I was thinking of applying for a teaching position in San Francisco."

"That would be fantastic," Zach replied, at the same time warning himself not to sound too enthusiastic. "There's this new winery in Napa called San Pancho, and if they'll have me, I would be getting in on the ground floor. Maybe I'll give them a call. When were you thinking of moving north?"

"That could take a while. You know how it goes. My first choice is Berkeley. I'll start sending out applications next month and see what happens."

Before long, they realized they'd been talking for almost an hour.

"I've got to go," Sophie said suddenly, checking her watch. "When shall we meet again?" she asked, referencing Vera Lynn's famous song in a nod to his tendency to quote war films and songs at the drop of a hat.

"How about dinner tomorrow, or whenever you're free?"

"Tomorrow I can't. I'm teaching a seminar from six to nine. But the day after works."

"Great. How about we meet at Alonzo's in Malibu at seven o'clock? They have terrific pasta," suggested Zach.

"Let's do that. Wait, I don't have your phone number." Sophie dug into her purse and retrieved a pen and a small notepad. They exchanged numbers and went their separate ways, looking forward to their next rendezvous.

Later, Zach found himself thinking about Sophie while in the shower, in the car, at work – constantly, actually. He worried that he shouldn't anticipate or expect anything, just let whatever this might be take its course. On the other hand, they were twenty-seven years old now, so who knows? Their stars might finally be aligned.

They arrived at Alonzo's Ristorante Italiano at the same time. Located on the Pacific Coast Highway, it was legendary for its cuisine and sought out for its stellar view of the beach and ocean beyond. Black-and-white photographs signed by famous personalities covered the walls, and large Tiffany chandeliers hung from the ceiling.

Their window table was draped in a red-and-white checkered tablecloth, with a candle in a wicker-wrapped Chianti bottle that was covered in multicolored wax. The rays of the setting sun danced on the glassware and chandeliers, enhancing the romantic atmosphere.

Soon, their waiter, looking very Italian with his dark hair and mustache, and wearing the continental uniform – white dress shirt, black bow tie, vest and pants, and white apron – brought them menus and the wine list, and lit their candle.

"*Buonasera e benvenuto ad Alonzo's,*" he said with a flourish as he unfurled and placed their cotton napkins on their laps, then departed with a solemn promise to return. This made them immediately feel at ease. The evening was off to a promising start.

"Shall I order the wine?" Zach asked, perusing the wine list while Sophie studied her menu.

"Naturally," she replied. "What's good here?"

"I've had luck in the past with their specials, but they're best known for their pastas. When the waiter returns, we'll see what he's recommending tonight."

As if by magic, their waiter rematerialized at their side.

"If I may *Signore e Signorina*, tonight's pasta is wild game meat cannelloni baked in a béchamel and tomato sauce. It is the chef's specialty from an old family recipe." He put the fingers of his right hand to his lips and, in the universal gesture of Italian food lovers, smacked his lips as he spread his fingers outward and looked heavenward.

Giggling, Zach and Sophie looked from the waiter to each other, and nodded their heads vigorously in surrender.

"Shall we share a Caesar salad to start?" Zach asked to Sophie's affirmative answer. "For the wine, I'm thinking this Villa Antinori Chianti Classico Riserva 1985 will work well."

"*Si, Signore*; an excellent match for the dinner," said their waiter, who left them alone to more important matters.

"So...," said Zach across the table.

"So," replied Sophie, sizing him up. "I thought you preferred French wine."

"Since working at Stanley's, I've expanded my repertoire to include Italian wine. I now like to think of myself as an equal opportunity drinker. Also, I didn't have much choice, as the wine list only has Italian wines on it."

Just as they were about to start talking more seriously, the sommelier arrived with their wine, dressed like the waiter but minus the apron. Around his neck he wore a silver *tastevin* on a chain, the universal sign of sommeliers.

"*Buonasera*. I have this Chianti Classico Riserva for you," he said as he presented the bottle in both hands, label forward so Zach could verify it, which he did. Then he produced his corkscrew, and removed the metal cap and cork.

"May I sample the wine?" he asked.

Receiving an affirming nod from Zach, he poured a small bit into his upraised *tastevin*, swirled it around and sipped. Satisfied, he poured Zach a taster in his wine glass.

As Zach went through the tasting ritual of looking, swirling, gurgling and finally swallowing, the sommelier shared some interesting points about the wine.

"This wine is made by the famous Antinori family in Tuscany, Italy, who've been in business since 1385. The Riserva is made from the Sangiovese grape, resulting in vibrant flavors of red berries, plum, spice and earthy mushroom. It is medium-bodied with soft tannins, and represents excellent value. The 1985 vintage was superb. Is it to your liking, *Signore*?"

"Very nice," replied Zach. The sommelier filled their glasses and poured the balance into a decanter, which he placed on the side of the table with the empty bottle.

"What is that little silver dish you're wearing?" Sophie asked.

"Thank you for asking, *Signorina*. Three hundred years ago, wine was stored in barrels in dark cellars and served in pitchers. Quality was an issue, and wine was judged by its clarity and color. But this was difficult in the dim candlelight, as there were no electric lights then. So, the winemakers of Burgundy had their silversmiths create the *tastevin*, with these shiny facets to refract the light and highlight the wine. Now we wear them as a symbol of our trade. *Prego*, enjoy the wine."

With that, he was off in search of more customers to serve, leaving Zach and Sophie to resume their conversation.

"So...," said Zach again.

"So," replied Sophie again with a broad smile. "Here we are again."

"You know, when we were talking at Bean & Co., I was struck by how parallel our life paths have become. We're both headed to San Francisco in the next few years and settling into careers, something I recall you once said you didn't want to do."

"I wasn't very practical five years ago," Sophie admitted. "Time passes, people change. I'm focused now on art history, as you are on wine. There's an idea. Why don't you become a sommelier? Wouldn't that look good on your application to the winery?"

"I'd actually come to the same conclusion. It would be easy for me after the UC Davis Certificate. There is a course offered by the American Institute of Sommeliers here in L.A. which starts in January."

"I think you should do that. You obviously love it, and you have a talent for it. If it feels right, go for it. You can always do something different later." There was the old Sophie, the one who didn't want to get tied down.

"All right, I will. How are your parents? Are they still together?" Zach asked, remembering their distressing conversation at the Café du Chat Noir in Paris five years ago.

"In the end, they stayed together. My father realized that leaving my mother was not the right thing to do, whether due to pressure from us, or because he figured out that his infatuation would eventually turn into the same relationship he already had with my mother. In any event, they seem like they're happy together now."

"I'm happy to hear that. You were very upset."

"Yes, well, I was, and I let my father know it in no uncertain terms. So did the rest of the family. We basically ganged up on him. Even so, he still wasn't very interested in giving her up, almost as if he wanted to keep both of them. That's when I went home to make sure everything was okay."

"What happened to Madeleine, I think you said her name was, the *femme fatale*?" At this, Sophie's expression darkened.

"Quite tragic, actually. She died of a drug overdose a few months after we read my father the riot act. It was ruled an accidental death."

"That's awful. I hope she didn't end her life because of your father."

"Let's not talk about it anymore," Sophie replied, avoiding eye contact. "I'd rather hear more about your plans."

As the evening progressed, they began to realize their feelings for each other were still there. It was as if no time had passed, and they were still in college.

Perhaps Zach was afraid of being rejected again, but he could not quite bring himself to push things forward. As it turned out, it was Sophie who took the initiative. She had made up her mind. He didn't stand a chance.

Napa – 1995

Six months later, Zach and Sophie were engaged to be married. Their wedding took place in August on the lawn at Zach's family home in Beverly Hills. Sophie's parents flew in from Paris and got along with Zach's parents as well as could be expected. At least everyone behaved themselves. Then they were on their way to San Francisco – Sophie to teach art history as an Assistant Professor at UC Berkeley, and Zach to join San Pancho Winery as a junior winemaker.

Zach had taken the sommelier course in 1994 and was now a member of the American Institute of Sommeliers. His dedication to the craft had earned him a reputation for having an exceptional palate and a keen understanding of wine pairing, which led to a raise and more responsibility at Stanley's Fine Wines. They were sad to lose him but wished him well and promised to carry San Pancho wines in the future.

Arriving in San Francisco with their worldly possessions in a U-Haul trailer, their first order of business was to set up house in their new rental apartment. With limited funds, they'd chosen a one-bedroom walk-up in Haight-Ashbury, famous for the hippie movement in the sixties but now gentrified, and affordable, which was the main thing.

The suite was in a three-story Victorian building. It had plenty of afternoon light from its western exposure, dark hardwood floors, tall ceilings, lath and plaster walls that could use some paint, and a laundry room in the basement. It wasn't perfect, but it was theirs, and they settled quickly into their new life together.

Their first day of work arrived in early September. Zach was the first to leave at seven o'clock in his silver Volkswagen Rabbit for the one-and-a-half-hour drive to San Pancho Winery in Napa. Sophie left later in her little green Peugeot 205 because her trip to Berkeley was less than an hour. It wouldn't be long before Zach had them studying a map to figure out a better location to shorten their commutes.

Navigating the early morning traffic, Zach's anticipation grew with each passing mile. He arrived a little after eight-thirty to find a magnificent sand-colored winery, built in the Californian adobe-style on the outskirts of Napa. Founded four years earlier, San Pancho Winery was already producing wines from mature vineyards that it had purchased, as well as with grapes from other nearby producers. So far, it had seven labels focusing on Cabernet Sauvignon and Chardonnay, two grape varieties that typically showcased Napa Valley.

The winery was owned by the Torres family, which traced its winemaking roots back fourteen generations in Rioja, Spain. They knew a thing or two about making wine, and wanted to create the next generation of great wine in the New World. Given their roots, their priority was to produce wines using the Tempranillo grape, which they had brought from Rioja and planted in Napa. The first vintage was set to be picked this year, and bottled two years after that.

On his first day, Zach met Rodrigo Torres, the thirty-something second son of the family, tasked with the New World expansion. He was charismatic and passionate, exuding a confidence that was both inspiring and intimidating. As Zach was shown around, Rodrigo reminded him that Tempranillo had been in California since the early 1900s. Called Valdepeñas, it did not fare well as it was planted in the hot and dry Central Valley. The grape's worth had since been confirmed by other producers in the cooler climates and higher altitudes of Napa.

"Napa has ideal growing conditions for Tempranillo," Rodrigo remarked as they meandered through the winery. "Warm summer days are cooled by evening fog from the Pacific Ocean, preserving the grapes' flavor and boosting acidity. Rocky, well-drained soils create intense flavors and tannins.

"Our first harvest began in August and will be completed early next month. We pick the grapes by hand at night and bring them directly to the winery, where they're put in stainless steel tanks to ferment for twenty-two days. After that, the wine is aged for twenty-four months in those fifty-nine-gallon French barriques over there to add the subtle oak notes.

"We want our Tempranillo to retain the character of Old-World Rioja, but with a New-World Californian style. Something old, something new. A marriage of both worlds, expanding an old family tradition into new markets."

Rodrigo's tour was comprehensive, with a running commentary on the five-thousand-square-foot winery – from the laboratory and offices, to the crushing, fermentation, bottling and shipping rooms , the extensive underground barrel room that could also host private dinners, and finally, the tasting room open to the public. Wine flowed in Rodrigo's veins, and his enthusiasm was infectious. Zach felt completely at home, and could see himself staying a while.

He was impressed by the state-of-the-art facilities, and the attention to detail in every aspect of the winemaking process. At the end of the tour, he was assigned a desk in the communal office space and introduced to other members of the staff. The next day, his work would begin in earnest.

When Zach arrived home, it was eight o'clock, and he was exhausted. Not from hard labor, mind you, but from the mental overload of all the information he'd absorbed on his first day. Sophie wasn't home yet. The blinking answering machine signaled a message, presumably from her.

"*Coucou, chéri.* Don't wait up for me. Too many people to meet, too many things to discuss, and too many policies to absorb. *Ciao.*"

It was past midnight by the time they crawled into bed, after a weary discussion about their day. Too tired for sex, they were asleep in minutes.

The following weeks were a blur, as Zach worked in the crushing and fermentation rooms, where he learned how to process the grapes into wine. Making wine had progressed a long way by 1995. Grapes were no longer crushed manually with people's feet, at least not in the New World. The winery used a crusher-destemmer, which crushed the grapes and removed the stems. From there, the juice was then pumped into large oak barrels to ferment for up to three weeks.

Zach was assigned the new guy's job, which was to punch down the cap in the fermentation barrels. As the yeast produced alcohol, it also created carbon dioxide, pushing the grape skins and pulp, or "cap," to the surface. The punch down was done by hand with a plunger three times a day.

Once the sugar turned into alcohol, the skins were pressed to create more wine, and the lot was then transferred into smaller oak barrels for its second fermentation. Here it sat for up to eighteen months, depending on the grape variety, before bottling in another room.

Time flew by in that first year as Zach and Sophie worked long hours to get a foothold on their career ladders. They were both energized by their work and were happy together. Their shared passion for their careers and unwavering support for each other created a solid foundation for their young marriage. Pretty soon, they moved into a two-bedroom rental apartment in Vallejo, which was halfway between San Pancho and Berkeley, and a thirty-minute drive for each of them. Sophie quickly claimed the second bedroom as her study.

In 1998, their son, Lucas, was born, followed two years later by Emma, their daughter. Their growing family required larger accommodation, and with help from Zach's parents, they bought their first house in Vallejo. Here they would stay and thrive for ten years, before moving back to San Francisco.

Those years were Zach's happiest, filled with the joy and contentment that raising children brings. When asked how many kids he had, he often replied "Three, one of each." Then he'd break the awkward silence that followed by explaining there was also Ralph, their furry canine child who was two.

By the time Zach left San Pancho Winery, he was their marketing manager with a staff of four, responsible for every aspect of selling their wines. After thirteen years, he gave his notice and went out on his own as a wine consultant. It was the scariest thing he'd ever done, but he had Sophie's support, who was now a tenured professor at Berkeley. They were now forty-two years old, the kids were ten and eight, and Ralph, their Airedale Terrier, was still two.

In March, Zach, Sophie and family moved into their forever home on Valencia Street, in San Francisco's Mission District. With three thousand square feet, there was plenty of room for everyone, including Ralph, who, as soon as Zach opened the door, bounded past him and proceeded to closely inspect every room on every floor. Eventually, he returned, wagging his tail to signify his approval.

The house was a quirky Victorian built in 1900. Painted a bluish gray, the wooden structure was twenty-five feet wide with three floors. As they wandered around, listening to the kids argue over which bedroom would be theirs, they realized that it needed some fixing up – cracks in the plaster, faded paint, worn wooden floors. None of that mattered; it was theirs, and they would grow into it.

While Sophie went upstairs to mediate the bedroom choice, Zach went down to scope out the basement and figure out where to put his new wine cellar. He was in luck: the previous owners had left behind a fully equipped, temperature-controlled room with professional wooden racks for fifteen hundred bottles. This was a bonus he hadn't expected, as they hadn't toured the basement during their first whirlwind visit.

Zach ran his consulting business from home, which grew organically to the point where he was in high demand. He curated and appraised wine collections, designed wine lists for restaurants, and provided lectures, tastings, wine-paired dinners and guided winery tours. He published articles and tasting notes on his website, and in December 2010, he started posting about wine and food on a new social networking service called Instagram, which had launched two months earlier, and rapidly gained in popularity. In its first year, it had ten million users; ten years later, it would have a billion.

He also joined the ranks of the California Department of Alcoholic Beverage Control, known as the ABC, to supplement his income and also learn more about the regulatory side of things. There, he underwent rigorous training that included counter-surveillance tactics, advanced firearms handling, situational de-escalation techniques, and covert operations skills to combat illicit activities in the alcohol industry. It wasn't long before his instructors realized he was ideally suited to be an undercover agent in the fight against the criminal booze trade, a job he would do part-time for six years.

Two years later, Zach served one year as President of the American Institute of Sommeliers, an organization that trained sommeliers in the expanding aspects of their trade. While anyone could call themselves a sommelier, it was instrumental in formalizing the certification process. Wine waiters and others flocked to their courses, which offered three levels of accreditation, the highest being master sommelier. For that, students needed not only an encyclopedic knowledge of all things alcoholic and ten years' experience, but also the ability to identify twelve wines in blind tastings by type, quality and region.

Sophie found herself traveling more frequently. Her career in art history took her mostly to Paris, where she gave lectures. As an expert in her field, she enjoyed the attention and the opportunities it brought, but also sensed that she and Zach were growing apart. "That's to be expected," she would say to console herself.

"What's your lecture about in Paris next week?" Zach asked her, looking up from the novel he was reading the night before she was to depart, after a superb dinner of coq au vin, one of their specialties.

"Frédéric Bazille. The Impressionist painter who never was," Sophie replied, looking up from her book.

"Do I know his work?"

"You could be forgiven for not. He only painted for seven years before dying at twenty-eight in 1870 during the Franco-Prussian war. Too bad. He shared studios with Renoir and Monet, and would have been as famous as them."

"Forgive me, but it sounds a bit bloodthirsty." In response, Sophie just grimaced, and they returned to reading their respective novels.

It was in May 2014, that Luke and Emma approached their father to have a serious conversation about their future. They were in the family room, and Sophie was listening from the adjoining kitchen.

"Dad, I don't want to go to college," fifteen-year-old Luke said, with thirteen-year-old Emma nodding her support behind him. Was he detecting a conspiracy in the making?

"Why not?" Zach replied, tentatively.

"College doesn't do anything. Everyone says it's a waste of time and money."

"Really. Tell me, what would you like to do instead?"

"I want to go to acting school," Luke said. He had been taking acting lessons since he was ten, and had been in a few bit parts and advertisements.

"I don't want to go to college either," Emma

chimed in, emboldened by her brother. Zach could see he had a full-blown rebellion on his hands.

"Are you listening to these kids?" Sophie shouted from the kitchen. "We're going to be supporting them for the rest of our lives!"

Facing down the pitchforks, Zach said calmly, in his sternest fatherly voice: "College is the best time of your life. That's where your mother and I met and fell in love. We also made lifelong friends and had the best time of our lives. We were free to make our own choices and have fun.

"College isn't designed to teach you a job. Instead, it teaches you how to think, and exposes you to new ideas that expand your understanding of the world and life. You have no idea of what you'd be missing if you skipped it. How about this: you'll both go to college and major in whatever you want. Luke you can major in acting. Emma, what do you want to do?"

"I want to be an actor too," she replied.

"All right, you can both study acting as your major, provided you study business as your minor. The big thing you need to do is decide which school you want to attend. They're difficult to get into, so Luke, make a list of at least three to apply to. Also, you need to figure out the deadlines for applying to each place, and when to write the SAT or that other exam."

Zach looked at Sophie for support. She looked dubious, but didn't voice any objection, which was something. In her opinion, Zach was a soft touch when it came to the children. They seemed satisfied, however, and life in the Taylor household returned to a semblance of normalcy.

Before they knew it, they were in Zach's car headed to Los Angeles and the University of Southern

California, where Luke was starting as a freshman in the recently renamed School of Dramatic Arts. Emma was in the car too, so she could visit USC and other nearby campuses to see if she liked them.

Luke's research determined that for acting, Los Angeles was *the* place for him. Staying in California made sense since local students received a tuition discount on their tuition. While Berkeley enjoyed high rankings for its drama department, he preferred to move away rather than carpool with his mom, who was still a professor there. He also wanted to be in Hollywood, having set his sights on film and television acting.

The business of getting into college had been long and complicated, requiring a sustained and methodical approach which Luke managed splendidly. First, there was selecting the colleges, then getting all the reference letters, writing the SAT, filling out the applications, and writing the countless essays. All of these were daunting tasks, but Luke had done it: USC, which was both the most difficult to get into and his first choice, accepted him as a freshman.

All of the hard work was punctuated by amusing moments. A question in the USC application asked, "What is the most important invention?" Zach and Luke discussed inventions like the wheel, the computer, the printing press, and the like. Eventually, Luke threw up his hands in defeat, saying, "What about the treadmill? I think I'll put the treadmill." A hilarious discussion ensued about its contribution to society and hamsters. In the end, he wrote "the computer." Coward.

During those twenty years, Zach and Sophie were very busy, focused on their careers and raising their family. As time passed, Zach and Sophie's marriage evolved into a working partnership that functioned fine but lacked passion. They didn't touch each other anymore, and sex was only a memory. After the kids left for college, and Ralph to a different dimension, they were left eating quiet dinners together, followed by television and bed, to be repeated day after day. Zach didn't realize it yet, but he was lonely.

In 2018, Zach was introduced to Lilith by a mutual friend. A single woman about his age, she was tall, thin and bony, with straight red hair and severe black glasses. When she spoke, she showed considerable intellect, and when she was excited about a subject, she became positively bubbly. She wasn't athletic at all, a bit clumsy actually, and seemed to prefer sitting, reading, dining and gossiping.

Originally from Ohio, where she worked in the restaurant trade, Lilith moved to San Francisco when she was twenty-eight. There, she entered the art world, initially doing anything and everything in various art galleries around town. She married an affluent gallery owner and divorced four years later without any children. With her share of his money, she was able to buy her own art gallery selling contemporary art. She also had an abiding love for fine food and wine.

Lilith and Zach became friends, although they only saw each other twice a year for wine-inspired lunches. Theirs was an intellectual relationship, with no sexual chemistry between them. They simply enjoyed each other's company and the chance to exchange ideas. Lilith had a firm grasp of all things art-related, even though she hadn't gone to college. She seemed to be fascinated by Zach's knowledge of history and philosophy, which caused his mind to operate differently from hers. He, in turn, basked in the attention she gave him.

Their favorite place to meet was Ernie's Bistro on Polk Street on Nob Hill, where they always chose a secluded table that allowed them to talk freely. Today, Zach was curious about her extensive art knowledge.

"Tell me about investing in art," he said, sipping the 2018 La Nerthe Côtes du Rhône Villages Les Cassagnes he'd brought. "How do you know what to buy?"

"Through a combination of research and intuition," she explained. "You have to know the different artists and movements, understand what makes a piece valuable. Sometimes it's the artist's reputation, other times the historical significance or the uniqueness of the work. Think of it like a treasure hunt."

"What about the financial side? How do you determine if a painting is a good investment?" he asked next.

"That's a bit trickier," Lilith admitted. "You have to consider the artist's career trajectory, the condition of the artwork, its provenance and market trends. Sometimes, emerging artists can be great investments because their work is still affordable, with potential to increase in value."

"I don't know," Zach said. "I've always thought the art world was a dark place, filled with con men and forgeries. Just thinking about it scares the hell out of me."

"You mean to say, Zachary Taylor, that the art world is riskier than your world of wine, with all the scandals I read about? Sometimes I wonder where you get such ideas from."

"Fair point. I guess 'fools rush in where angels fear to tread' applies everywhere. Neither are for naive beginners if you're investing serious money."

"I know how to assess the provenance of an

expensive painting. How do you do that for rare wine?" Lilith asked.

"Pretty much the same thing. You start by examining the bottle. If it's extremely rare, you try to trace the owners back to the original sale. The winery's reputation is important too. As you can imagine, it's very time-consuming and only done for the rarest bottles."

While Zach and Lilith found they had plenty to talk about, Sophie and Lilith did not take a liking to each other. They shared a negative telepathy that Zach could sense, which only served to remind him further of his faded marriage. Perhaps it was because Lilith was single, confident, and threatening. More likely it was because Lilith saw that Zach's marriage had become cold and distant, worn down by the years of routine, endless compromise and conflict. It was almost as if Lilith had decided that Zach deserved a better mate.

Zach's friendship with Lilith would significantly affect his life in a few years.

The air in San Francisco held a rare June warmth as Zach walked through the doors of the California Department of Alcoholic Beverage Control headquarters on New Montgomery Street. Finally, after twelve months of training, today marked his first day working undercover. The courses had been comprehensive, covering everything from liquor license law to advanced surveillance techniques, and how to blend into the often-chaotic world of bar owners and distributors.

On weekends, Zach had supplemented his skills with Brazilian Jiu-Jitsu classes, knowing a split-second grapple could mean the difference between neutralizing a threat or becoming its victim. Though the ABC training had sharpened his instincts and given him a keen eye for spotting criminal enterprises, it was on the mats where he truly honed his ability to stay calm under pressure, learning to leverage technique over brute strength.

BJJ taught him how to control opponents without causing severe injury. Ideal for handling unarmed suspects and de-escalating confrontations effectively, it emphasized technique over strength, enabling him to subdue larger or stronger individuals without having to use excessive force.

With his gut coiled tight, Zach wore a half smile that concealed his nerves as he strode through the lobby. The chief had called him into his office for a briefing, and he didn't want to keep the man waiting.

"Agent Pruno," Mitch Adams began, pulling a file from his desk and handing it over. "Ready to get your hands dirty?"

"Yes, chief," Zach replied with a slight nod. He opened the file and skimmed the documents inside. There was a picture of a burly man in his seventies with slicked-back silver hair and a cigar clenched between his teeth. The name below the photo read Angelo Salvatore. Zach glanced up, raising an eyebrow.

"Salvatore? The crime family? That's our target?"

Adams leaned back, crossing his arms. "Angelo Salvatore. He's a big fish in the bootlegging business. They're smuggling large amounts of grappa from Italy and running their operation from a warehouse in the Mission District. The job's simple: get inside, find out what they're up to, then report back."

Zach looked up from the file. "What's my cover?"

Adams handed him a small leather wallet with an ID. "You're Jason Prentice, a sommelier from Napa. You were in fine dining, lost your job, you're pissed off, now you want to break into the underground liquor scene."

Zach inspected the ID, nodding. "Jason Prentice. Got it. Anything else I need to know?"

Adams pushed a small black phone across the desk. "Burner phone. Keep your personal one in your locker here. If you need anything, call me on this. Remember your counter-surveillance training – don't let yourself be followed, take different routes home. Above all, stay alert."

Zach pocketed the phone, his face a mask of confidence, but inside, his heart hammered. This wasn't just a quick bust; it was infiltration. He'd need to play his cards right or he might become a target himself.

Adams' eyes bore into him. "One last thing, Pruno. Salvatore's men? They don't trust easily. They'll test you, try to catch you off guard. You've got to be ready for anything."

Zach met his gaze and nodded. "Understood."

Salvatore's warehouse was in the back alleys of the Mission District, blending into an eclectic landscape that had seen its share of reinvention and intrigue. Inside, the place was cavernous, filled with crates and barrels stacked high and the faint, sour smell of alcohol. As Zach approached cautiously on foot, he spotted a few men milling about, their hard faces looking suspicious as they took stock of the new guy.

One of them stepped forward, a man with a thick neck and a permanent scowl. He eyed Zach up and down. "You Prentice?" he asked, his tone more accusation than question.

"Yeah, that's me," Zach replied, keeping his posture relaxed. He extended a hand. "And you are?"

The man ignored his hand. "Vinny. Angelo's right hand. Follow me."

Zach followed Vinny through the maze of crates, catching snippets of conversation and the occasional glance from other workers. They stopped in front of a group of men gathered around a table. "Mr. Salvatore, this is the new guy."

Salvatore glanced up, his sharp eyes appraising Zach in silence. After a moment, he spoke, his voice low and dangerous. "You have quite the reputation, Mr. Prentice. Heard you were the best in Napa. Shame what happened up there."

Zach shrugged, feigning nonchalance. "Things change. I'm here now, and I know my wines."

Salvatore's eyes narrowed in the manner of one who expects loyalty. "We'll see about that." He nodded to a man at his side, who grabbed a small glass bottle and poured a clear liquid into a glass, sliding it across the table to Zach. "This is the finest grappa in Italy. Try it."

Zach picked up the glass, his face impassive as he brought it to his lips. The liquid hit his tongue with a fiery burn, harsher than anything he'd ever tasted. He swallowed, feeling the alcohol scorch his throat as he forced himself not to cough. He took a breath, nodding appreciatively.

"Smooth," he said breathlessly, while his throat burned. "Good heat, not too much bite."

Salvatore watched him closely, his expression deadpan. Then he burst into laughter. "I like him. He knows how to treat the boss," he said to his men. Turning back to Zach, "Let's see how much you know about *good* liquor."

Zach felt the air around him tense. He'd expected something like this, but not in the first ten minutes. He kept his face neutral as Salvatore continued. "We need you to catalog the goods, make sure everything is in order. Vinny here will take you to one of our stashes. If you're as good as you say, you'll know how to spot the real from the fake." He leaned back, his gaze unrelenting. "And if you mess it up, well..."

Zach nodded, quelling his nerves. "Lead the way."

Vinny grunted, gesturing for him to follow. They went back to a small storeroom, filled with more barrels and cases. Vinny stopped in front of a row of open grappa bottles, crossing his arms. "All right, sommelier. Tell me which of these is real, and which is the cheap knockoff. I'll give you two minutes."

Zach started examining them, their labels almost identical. He picked one up, holding it to the light, his mind racing as he examined it for clarity and viscosity. The seconds ticked by, and he felt Vinny's gaze scrutinizing his every move.

"Real," he said, setting one bottle aside. He

picked up another, turning it slowly, and placed it beside the first. "Real. This one," he said, picking up the last bottle, "is fake."

Vinny frowned as he inspected the bottles. He looked back at Zach, his expression confused. "How did you know?"

Zach shrugged. "The label's off by a millimeter, which is a classic sign of a counterfeit job."

Vinny grunted, clearly dissatisfied but unable to dispute the results. "Okay, Prentice. You passed the test. Let's get back." In light of the man's negative IQ, Zach was impressed he managed to string so many words together in one go.

When they got back to the table, a grizzled man with a deep scar across his left cheek motioned for Zach to step closer. Standing, he reached into his jacket and pulled out a hefty Colt automatic. The gun gleamed in the dim light, its cold metal catching the eyes of everyone in the room as he pressed the barrel to Zach's temple. He forced himself to remain calm, steadying his breath as the older man began to question him.

"So, you know your grappa, but do you know your guns?" the man sneered, his voice low and laced with menace, as he held the gun steady. "I don't care much for sommeliers. I care about loyalty. Tell me, Prentice, if that's your real name, how do I know you're not a cop?" Zach felt the chill of the metal against his skin and took a deep breath, thinking fast.

"Loyalty isn't just a word to me, and while guns are not my thing, I do know that if you pull that trigger, three things are going to happen: first, you'll have a body to get rid of, and that's a lot of work; second, you won't get the benefit of my extensive knowledge; and third, you'll have to find someone else to keep track of your stock. Now, if you don't mind," he said, slowly reaching up and guiding the gun away from his head. He could see the men around him watching, waiting for the slightest crack in his armor.

Finally, after what felt like an eternity, Scarface put the gun away, giving a slight nod. The others seemed to accept it, though their eyes lingered on him. Zach was dismissed with a warning glance, but he knew they weren't done testing him. They'd be watching him like hawks, especially Salvatore.

When the day finally ended, Zach slipped away, his heart still racing from the close call. As he walked back to the patrol car parked five blocks away, he took a circuitous route, doubling back twice to make sure no one followed him. A flicker in the reflection of a storefront window caught his eye – a man in a dark jacket, keeping far enough back to avoid suspicion. Zach felt his pulse quicken. He couldn't lead them to his car, so he ducked into a narrow alley, disappearing into the shadows. After a few moments, he stepped into a doorway, pressed against the wall, and held his breath.

The man entered the alley, scanning the area with a furrowed brow. Zach saw his chance. He slipped out of the alley and darted into a small crowd on the sidewalk, blending in seamlessly. He circled back, emerging a few blocks over, where he watched the tail searching the alley in vain before finally giving up. Zach continued on, not slowing until he was sure he was alone again, his heart pounding as he reached the car.

Two weeks later, as the late afternoon sun dipped below the skyline, the dull roar of engines shattered the tense silence inside the warehouse. Salvatore's men had no time to react before the doors burst open, and a swarm of ABC agents poured in with their guns drawn.

"Hands in the air! Nobody move!" Zach raised his hands, moving slowly to avoid suspicion. He'd supplied a stream of information about the operation, and this raid was the culmination of his first assignment. While the *capos* and soldiers were there, Angelo Salvatore wasn't. No matter, they knew where he lived.

In the blur of the next few hours, Zach was cuffed and loaded into a van with the others, and the smuggled grappa was seized as evidence. As they were being processed, Salvatore's men remained eerily calm, exchanging quiet smirks and half-hearted protests. What did they know that he didn't?

Salvatore's well-paid lawyers, the best he called them, went to court and had the charges dropped based on a technicality. According to the judge, their rights had been infringed because nobody knocked on the door or announced themselves as law enforcement before entering the warehouse.

"Don't let it get to you, Agent Pruno," Chief Mitchell Adams said in his office after they heard the bad news. "The first time's always the hardest."

Zach sighed, running a hand through his hair. "Feels like we just handed Salvatore a free pass," he replied, his voice tight with frustration.

Adams clapped him on the shoulder. "Never mind. There'll be other opportunities. We'll get him eventually."

Sutter Street Auctioneers – June 5, 2018

On a rainy afternoon on June 5, Edward Pavlov found himself at Sutter Street Auctioneers in the financial district. The stately building, adorned with Corinthian columns and stone carvings, provided Old-World elegance amid the modern skyscrapers. Inside, the scent of mahogany mingled with the faint aroma of antique parchment, creating an atmosphere steeped in history. The spacious auction room was filled with rows of chairs facing a raised dais, where prized artifacts awaited their turn to be claimed by motivated buyers.

Edward was there on an exploratory mission to find a source of rare wines he could resell as a business venture. His initial idea was to offer them to his circle of well-heeled friends, who he was certain would be serious collectors. He had the buyers; now he needed the wine.

He was a big man who weighed just under 300 pounds, a presence that filled any room he entered. At sixty-one years old, his once dark hair was now peppered with gray, a subtle betrayal of his age that he dutifully touched up in an effort to retain a semblance of youth. Raised as an only child in Palo Alto, an affluent enclave south of San Francisco, he was the product of a household emblematic of the Silicon Valley boom. His father was a high-tech wizard, immersed in the throes of the burgeoning technology sector, while his mother devoted her life to homemaking.

Edward's upbringing in Palo Alto was marked by privilege. His childhood home was filled with the latest gadgets, a byproduct of his father's industry connections, but it often lacked the warmth of human interaction. His father, perpetually busy with his career, effectively left Edward to forge his own path. His mother, though loving, was often overwhelmed by the responsibilities of managing their home and her husband's demanding schedule. This environment instilled in Edward a strong independence and a relentless drive for success.

Palo Alto was an incubator for his ambitions, leading him to the University of Southern California, where he studied business management. The energy of USC, and the competitive spirit of Los Angeles, were the perfect breeding grounds for Edward's ambitions. He graduated *magna cum laude*, then cut his teeth at various established firms, honing his skills and learning the intricacies of the corporate world. His hard work paid off, and twenty years ago he'd ventured out on his own. Things had worked out so well that he could now afford to look for new opportunities. The wine business intrigued him, but he needed a way in.

At two o'clock, the auctioneer called for everyone to be seated in the large auction hall, which could hold one hundred people. There were about forty there today, each registered and holding a paddle for bidding, including Edward, who'd seated himself at the back in the tenth row. This was the first time he'd attended an auction of rare wine. He assumed it would be like the less formal charity auctions he knew, and he was not disappointed.

There were thirty-one lots of rare wine to be auctioned. The first consisted of three bottles of Chambertin 2015 from a producer he didn't recognize. The auctioneer opened the bidding at $300. Paddles went up all around Edward, and after three minutes of frenetic bidding, the auctioneer announced, "Sold to paddle number fourteen for $1,650."

Edward could see paddle fourteen was a middle-aged man sitting near the front in the second row to his right, who was talking intensely to a woman sitting beside him. "Who knew what they were arguing about; perhaps his wife doesn't approve?" he mused, reminding himself that he was now single and free of that particular hindrance.

The process was straightforward enough, but he realized that he was woefully unprepared, as he hadn't researched the catalog beforehand, and so had no idea which wines to buy or what to pay for them. Today, he would just have to observe and take notes, then do his homework and figure out how he could turn a profit later.

As the session progressed, Edward noticed an Asian gentleman dressed in a gray designer suit was the most prolific purchaser of what seemed to be the finest wines. He was seated to Edward's left in the third seat of the third row. Edward noticed how smoothly he handled his paddle in sync with the bidding rhythm. He clearly knew his way around an auction house and had come prepared, as evidenced by his decisive bidding. While he didn't bid for everything, he was mostly successful with the wines he wanted.

The auction came to an end just before four o'clock, and the successful bidders lined up to pay for their wines. Edward decided to approach the snappy dresser in the payment line.

"Excuse me, I thought I should introduce myself. I'm Edward Pavlov," he said, extending his right hand.

"James Wong," the stranger replied with a placid smile that Edward found hard to read. They shook hands.

One could be forgiven for thinking James Wong was much younger than his thirty-eight years. Athletic and lean with jet black hair, he cut a handsome figure when out on the town in his Armani suits and Bally shoes. He clearly came from money, was cultured and polite, and not to be trifled with. Black horn-rimmed glasses added to his austere appearance.

"I have to admit I'm new to this, James," Edward continued. "I want to learn more about it. The wine that is, not the auction part. Would you be interested in joining me for a drink when you've finished?"

"I'd be delighted, and please call me Jimmy. What brings you here today?"

Edward hesitated before answering. He did not want to seem like an amateur or too eager, or divulge too much of his plan, which quite frankly was more of a concept than a plan at this stage. "My business interests are far-ranging, which have led me to consider investing in fine wine. I'm looking for a partner who can help me find rare wines like the ones auctioned here today."

"To buy or to sell?"

"Both actually. I mean, to buy low and resell higher to my contacts." Hearing this, he had Jimmy's full attention.

"I might be able to help you with that," Jimmy replied ambivalently, as they reached the payment counter, where he paid for his purchases. "There's a bar a few doors down. Let's go there now, and I'll come back for my wine afterwards."

They entered the dimly lit bar, found an isolated table and ordered two double Johnnie Walker Blacks on ice. When their drinks arrived, Jimmy shifted the conversation from the usual pleasantries to more serious matters.

"You wish to get into the wine trade," Jimmy said, taking the initiative. This stranger across the table had no idea about how useful he could be to him.

"Yes. I'm well-connected in the city with collectors who will pay handsomely for rare wines that they'd have a hard time finding on their own. I'm looking for a source that can supply them over the long term. These are serious people."

"How do you know this?"

"It comes up from time to time in conversations. I know they're buying, and comparing notes with each other about what they've found. The common complaint is they can't find the wines they want."

"How many collectors are we talking?" Jimmy asked.

"As many as twenty I would think."

"If I could provide you with a reliable supply, how would you sell them to these people?"

"We're all members of the same men's club, so I was thinking that I would host dinners there which they'd attend, and conduct mini auctions, much like today," Edward replied.

"Did you have any particular wines or vintages in mind?"

"Not really. As I said, I'm new to this and figuring it out as I go. I've heard the big labels mentioned, like Château Lafite Rothschild. I could ask around and see what interests them."

"That won't be necessary. I already know what they want, and I can find them."

"Do you buy them at auctions, like I saw you do today?"

"Yes, that, and also from private sellers in Asia. Like you, I am also connected, but in my case with people who want to sell their collections. I'm sure I can provide you with as much wine as you can handle."

Edward could not believe his luck. He had gone

from a vague concept to what promised to be a lucrative business in one afternoon! "How would we price them?" Edward asked.

"The wines I have in mind will be exceptionally rare and very old. Through smart buying, I'm able to buy them at favorable prices. In order to cover my costs, I would propose that we split the prices that you get at auction seventy to me and thirty to you. That way we won't have to do all that dreary accounting and, most important, we'll keep the details between us. Would that be acceptable?"

"Most acceptable," replied Edward, still struggling to believe his good fortune.

They exchanged business cards, and agreed to put their new venture into action immediately. Jimmy would obtain at least two cases, and let Edward know what they were, along with the reserve bids for each. Edward would start identifying potential buyers and set up the first dinner auction at his club.

Back outside on Sutter Street, they shook hands once again. Jimmy returned to the auction house to pick up his wine, and Edward went in search of his parked car to return home, where he would start making phone calls. As they walked, they were both calculating the enormous profits within their grasp.

Hong Kong – October 12, 1990

Jimmy Wong's tenth birthday party was a lavish affair, marked by the fragrance of sweet and savory dishes wafting through his family's mansion on Victoria Peak. The living room was filled with silver streamers and a banner that read "Happy Birthday, Jimmy!" in colorful letters. The cook had prepared a feast that included dumplings, longevity noodles, roasted duck and a cake with bright red icing, the color of good fortune.

Born in the Year of the Monkey, which represented cleverness, versatility and innovation, Jimmy was smart and quick-witted, with a mischievous and playful nature. He was the youngest of five children, and his mother's favorite. His parents had high hopes and expectations for their most excellent boy.

Jimmy's nannies, his three older brothers and his sister, May, busied themselves with last-minute preparations, setting the table and organizing the pile of presents. Jimmy, however, was not interested in the party arrangements. His energy was frenetic, like a firecracker lit at both ends. He darted around the room, chasing his little friends with wild, uncoordinated movements, shouting at the top of his lungs.

"Jimmy, slow down!" his mother, Cecilia, yelled, her voice edged with frustration. "Behave yourself. Your friends are here to celebrate with you, not to run wild."

Raymond Wong, a stern man with jet black hair and a perpetually furrowed brow, watched his youngest son's antics with growing irritation.

"Jimmy, enough!" he barked. But he was beyond

hearing and crashed into the table, sending a plate of dumplings skittering across the floor. The room fell silent, the cheerful atmosphere gone. His friends, their eyes wide with excitement and fear, looked to their own parents, unsure whether to laugh or run.

His father's patience snapped. He grabbed Jimmy by the arm, dragging him away from the chaos.

"You are a disgrace," he hissed, his voice low and controlled, the words slicing through the air like a knife. "Don't you understand how embarrassing this is for us?"

Cecilia hurried to pick up the fallen food, her cheeks flushed with a mix of anger and shame. May and her brothers stood by with expressions of sympathy and annoyance. They'd all endured their father's rage before, but Jimmy's behavior was beyond anything they had ever experienced.

After all the guests had left and the house was quiet again, Jimmy sat on his bed, his eyes red and puffy from crying. His mother entered the room, her stern expression softened slightly by concern. She sat down beside him, smoothing his unruly hair. "Jimmy," she said quietly, "why do you behave this way? Don't you see how it hurts our family?"

He looked up at her, tears brimming in his eyes. "I don't know, *Māma*," he said somberly. "I don't know why I do these things. I can't help it."

Weeks later, after many visits to doctors and specialists, Jimmy was diagnosed with bipolar disorder and placed on a cocktail of antipsychotic, antidepressant and mood stabilizing drugs, which would be his new normal for the rest of his life. The news was a blow to the Wong family, especially his parents. To them, mental illness was a failing they refused to accept. His father withdrew further into his stern silence, while his mother struggled to reconcile her love for her son with her confusion and disappointment.

"You are our son," she told Jimmy one night, her voice trembling. "We will always love you, but you must try harder to control yourself. Do you understand?" Jimmy nodded, but deep down he felt the weight of their disappointment like a stone on his chest. He wanted to be the son they could be proud of, but the battle within him was one he did not know how to fight.

He had been born into a family whose name was synonymous with success in Hong Kong. The Wongs, once mere shadows in the alleys of Kowloon, had evolved into titans of industry and vice, building their fortune on the lucrative foundation of gambling. Raymond Wong was a man of steely resolve and cunning, traits that had propelled him from a penniless street vendor to a kingpin of Macau's gambling empire. His wife, Cecilia, was his perfect counterpart – ruthless in business, exacting at home, and uncompromising in her expectations of their five children.

The Wong mansion, perched on Victoria Peak far above the sprawling city below, stood in testament to their swift rise. Here, luxury was the norm, but so was discipline. Raymond and Cecilia believed that each of their children was a project, an investment to be sculpted into perfection. Their first three sons – Ronald, Thomas and William – were models of this doctrine, each excelling in academics, sports, and business from a young age. Their daughter, May, was groomed to be the perfect blend of elegance and shrewdness, expected to marry well, and extend the family's influence through a strategic alliance.

Jimmy, the youngest of the Wong children, was different. From an early age, it was clear he did not fit the mold his parents had achieved with his siblings. While his brothers and sister thrived under the pressure of high expectations, Jimmy wilted. He was a sensitive child, prone to mood swings that baffled and frustrated his parents, and his struggles in school were dismissed as laziness. His hypercritical tiger parents' solution was a regimen of strict training and harsh reprimands, believing tough love would forge him into what they desired.

When Jimmy's erratic behavior culminated in his bipolar disorder diagnosis, for his parents it was not a medical condition as much as a criminal accusation. For them, the diagnosis was a stain on the family's reputation, something to be corrected rather than treated. Therapy was imposed not as a means of understanding or support, but as another form of control, a way to mold Jimmy into their vision of the ideal son.

Isolated and misunderstood, Jimmy's childhood was one of loneliness and rising resentment. The mansion on Victoria Peak became a gilded cage where every corner reminded him of his inadequacies. Therapy sessions, which were supposed to be sanctuaries of understanding, felt like interrogations designed to root out his weaknesses. His parents' disappointment was a constant shadow, an ever-present reminder of his perceived failures.

Yet, despite his despair, Jimmy found a flicker of resilience and independence. He began to understand the complexities of his family's business in a different light. Unlike his siblings, who saw the darker family enterprises as stepping stones to power, Jimmy viewed them as a means of survival. Over the years, he learned the intricacies of the casino floor, the subtleties of currency exchange, and the veiled operations of the escort services. He absorbed these lessons not out of ambition, but out of necessity; a way to carve out a place for himself in a family that had rejected him.

The casino in Macau, with its world of flashing lights and calculated risks, became his sanctuary. Here, he discovered a different kind of education; one that valued cunning over conformity, where the ends justified the means. He watched and learned as fortunes were won and lost with a roll of the dice or the turn of a card. He saw how a well-placed bribe or a subtle threat could shift the balance of power. This world, so different from the rigid confines of his parents' expectations, offered him a sense of control and purpose.

By the time he reached his late twenties, Jimmy had carved out a niche within the Wong Empire. He became the go-to fixer for problems that required discretion and a certain moral flexibility. His bipolar disorder, once a source of shame, became a wellspring of creativity and resilience. The manic phases fueled his audacious gambles and rapid-fire decisions, while the depressive episodes, while debilitating, gave him a depth of introspection that his siblings lacked.

One night, after a particularly harsh reprimand from his father, Jimmy slipped out of the mansion and made his way to the harbor. Standing at the water's edge, he looked out at the boats bobbing gently in the moonlight. The cool breeze and sound of the waves calmed him. In that moment, he realized he needed to solidify his own path, away from the expectations of his family.

He relocated to Macau, immersing himself in the world of gambling. He found himself captivated by the strategic thinking required to outsmart the odds. It was a world where he felt alive, where his restless mind found focus.

This newfound obsession did not go unnoticed by his parents. Ever vigilant, they saw his move to Macau as a potential threat to their carefully curated image. They called a family meeting, a rare event that Jimmy would rather have avoided.

"Jimmy," his father began, his tone severe, "We have noticed your increasing involvement in the casino. This is not your place. You must shift your focus and prepare for your role in other areas of the family business."

"I've been working hard, father. I'm learning, and I'm helping the casino grow," Jimmy protested. "I understand the games and the players. I contribute to the casino's success."

"Your place is not at the tables," his mother interjected. "You have responsibilities elsewhere. Do not shame us with this gambling habit."

The word "habit" stung. At that moment, Jimmy realized they viewed his passion as a vice, not a legitimate interest. Frustrated and hurt, Jimmy felt the familiar tide of anger and despair rising within him. He forced himself to remain calm, knowing any outburst would only confirm their worst fears about his condition.

"Yes, Mother; yes, Father," he said quietly to placate them, but he remained in Macau in defiance of their wishes.

Ernie's Bistro – March 23, 2022

It was past noon as Zach drove to Ernie's for his lunch date with Lilith. He didn't like to arrive late for their infrequent encounters, which always included interesting conversations accompanied by excellent food and wine.

They enjoyed Ernie's, due to its convenient location on Nob Hill, easy parking, menu selections, friendly waitstaff, and especially Ernie himself. Simply being in his company lifted you up. He always had a kind word and a funny story that you'd never heard before, even if you had.

The restaurant, with its blue and white striped awning, had an eclectic décor. Pine green walls with framed photos covered its forty years in business at the same location, and linen-covered tables with wicker chairs complemented a long mahogany bar that ran along one wall from front to back.

Zach spotted Lilith seated at a table for four in the back. She was with another woman and waved as he approached. He waved back and limped his way with his cane to one of the empty chairs, where he parked himself opposite them.

"Sorry I'm late," Zach apologized. "I lost track of time."

"Don't be. Fifteen minutes is not late," Lilith replied.

"I try to be punctual, unlike my wife who considers half an hour late to be on time. One year, the kids and I gave her a T-shirt for Christmas that read 'Always late but worth the wait.' She thought it was hilarious while we thought it was accurate. At any rate, it didn't make any difference. She wears it with pride and she's still always late."

"First things first," Lilith said. "Zach, I'd like you to meet my friend Barbara. Barbara, Zach."

"How do you do, Zach," said Barbara, extending her hand across the table.

"What an unexpected pleasure," replied Zach, a little unnerved since he wasn't expecting this. Barbara was about the same age, with natural gray hair and blue eyes that sparkled when she spoke. She wore a wedding ring, but the subject of her husband never came up. It was not long before Zach noticed she seemed very interested in him – much like a tiger eyeing its next meal – which only heightened his rising discomfort. He would have preferred a little warning and background about Barbara before meeting her. Lilith had an annoying habit of springing things on him.

"What wine are we drinking today?" asked Lilith, who looked forward to his choices at their lunches.

"I brought this 2017 Gigondas. Ernie allows corkage and charges a very reasonable fee," he explained to Barbara. "Speaking of which, here he comes."

"Hey guys, how're you doing today?" Ernie asked in his typically friendly manner as he approached their table.

"Not too shabby," Zach replied, warmly shaking Ernie's outstretched hand.

"A blonde walks into a library," Ernie said next, completely out of context. "In a loud voice she says to the librarian, 'I want a Big Mac, fries and a Coke!' The shocked librarian shushes her, and says, 'Madam, don't you realize you're in a library?' The blonde pauses, then whispers, 'In that case, I'll take a Big Mac, fries and a

Coke.'" Everyone laughed, while rolling their eyes at the same time. "Today our special is Rigatoni Bolognese, made with beef, pork and veal. What wine did you bring today, Zach?"

"It's a Gigondas from France's Southern Rhône region. A poor man's Châteauneuf-du-Pape, but don't say that to anyone in Avignon. The quality is superb, reminiscent of its famous neighbor. Its soft floral qualities will go well with lunch."

Lilith caught the waiter's eye, and he came over with glasses, including a fourth for Ernie. After he'd poured the wine, everyone took a sip and Zach declared the wine satisfactory. Then Ernie was off to greet another table.

"Zach is a sommelier," Lilith explained to Barbara, as they perused the lunch menu.

"That sounds fascinating. I've never met a sommelier before. What's it like?" she asked.

"That's a big subject. I like to think 'sommelier' is just a fancy term for someone who knows how to boss around grapes in liquid form," he replied, to polite laughter. "In my case, I consult, I teach, and best of all, I drink. I'm sounding like Julius Caesar describing his victory in 67 BC over Pharnaces in Turkey," Zach said with a chuckle. He was not sure they understood the joke. "I came, I saw, I conquered... No? Forgive me. I was a history major in college."

"Could you teach me about wine?" Barbara asked next, moving right along. Nope, they didn't get it.

"Of course I could. For that, we would need to determine your level of knowledge and interest. My first teacher taught me that the purpose of wine appreciation is to make the experience more meaningful, just like understanding the different aspects of fine food."

"I tend to drink what others order, but I don't like red wine; it gives me a headache."

"Past studies have said that your headaches are caused by sulfites, tannins or histamines. However, there is a new one that looks at a plant flavanol called quercetin which is in red wine. They think the problem comes from the combination of quercetin and alcohol. That's an overly technical way of saying we don't know the cause but we may be closing in on it. We do know that red wine's a bigger headache than white."

"How interesting," Barbara said, but Zach could tell she'd moved on. He changed topics, but as lunch progressed, he noticed they were asking all the questions and he was giving the answers, much like in an interview. *An interview for what?* he wondered, and decided to reclaim the initiative.

"Are you familiar with the quotation about intelligent women by Leo Tolstoy?" Zach asked as they finished their meals.

"Tell me," Barbara replied enthusiastically, leaning forward, which emphasized her ample bosom.

"He said, 'Nothing is so necessary for a man as the company of intelligent women.' I just wanted to say how much I appreciate being able to spend this time with you."

"What a nice thing to say, and *so true*," Barbara gushed, and was about to say something more when Lilith suddenly interrupted and announced it was time to go. As Lilith always generously allowed Zach to pay at these occasions, he asked for the check, paid, and they went their separate ways.

He never saw Barbara again, but thought about her from time to time. He was intrigued by what it might have been like to get to know her. He didn't like to miss an opportunity to meet someone new, but in this case, he sensed it might have led to unwanted complications.

Something else occurred to him: Lilith's way of dealing with him was always abrupt and unpredictable. He couldn't help but wonder if it was designed to give her some advantage, to keep him off balance, as if she had a predatory nature. What was her game? The image of the tiger came to mind again.

City College - November 16, 2022

In the early years of his consulting business, one of the ways Zach supplemented his income was by teaching about wine at City College of San Francisco, located on Frida Kahlo Way in Ingleside. Founded in 1935, its main campus featured notable Spanish Colonial Revival buildings built in the early twentieth century. In its Diego Rivera Theater was one of his largest murals, *Pan American Unity*, a masterpiece that draws admirers from around the globe. Having a wide array of academic programs, it welcomed Zach's proposal to lead its inaugural course on wine appreciation.

His class, modeled loosely on Peter Mosley's in Paris all those years ago, was located in one of their seminar rooms with a conference table that seated twelve. As his students straggled in, Zach couldn't help but notice the diversity of the group. They were seven women and four men, aged twenty-two to seventy-one, all wanting to learn more so they could enjoy more. Their occupations ran the gamut as did their backgrounds. His class was a melting pot in a microcosm.

Zach arrived early so he could hobble in with his cane and seat himself at the head of the table. Six weeks after the skydiving accident, he was starting to wean himself off the opioids and was regaining his confidence in moving around.

Today's lecture was on wine value and price inflation, which he figured would appeal to everyone. Who doesn't want to get the best value for the best price? In researching his topic, there were some surprises in store which he built into his lecture. With everyone seated and cell phones turned off, the murmur died down and they turned to look at him expectantly.

"Good afternoon and welcome everyone. As you know, in this course, we are exploring the many aspects of wine in order to expand your appreciation of it. Wine has been an integral part of society for thousands of years, and for good reason. In the words of one of my heroes, Robert Mondavi, 'If you go back to the Greeks and Romans, they talk about all three – wine, food, and art – as a way of enhancing life'. This was a continuing theme throughout his life. My personal experience is that the more you know about it, the more you'll like it, and the more expensive it becomes.

"We'll come back to that in a minute. First, a little history: Robert Mondavi lived from 1913 to 2008. He graduated from Stanford and Berkeley, and, in 1943, convinced his father to buy the Charles Krug Winery in Napa Valley. After a fight with his brother, he left the winery to start his own. In 1966, Robert Mondavi Winery became the first new winery in Napa since the 1930s, with the goal of creating world-class wines.

"Known as the godfather of American wines, he tirelessly promoted them throughout the world. In 1979, he started Opus One with Baron Philippe de Rothschild of France, a Bordeaux blend that sells for five hundred dollars a bottle. In the words of Robert Parker, 'He had the single greatest influence in this country with respect to high quality wine and its place at the table.'

"Today, we're going to examine the price of wine over the last fifty years, and how to find the best value. The cheapest wine is rarely great, nor is the most expensive always the best. There is a sweet spot between twenty and forty dollars where the knowledgeable shopper can find the best values. In other words, when you look at the price of wine, the challenge is to find quality at a reasonable price. There are a few things to consider in order to make that happen. Before we go there, let's have a brief look at the history of wine prices.

"Some people say that the price of wine has increased dramatically since the 1970s, when the baby boomers reached drinking age and, as with everything else they touched, defined the sophisticated industry as we know it today. But that would be an over-simplification.

"Wine has been part of civilization for thousands of years. Consider the price of Italian wine in 50 BC. Before Julius Caesar conquered Gaul, Italian merchants were selling wine there. Tom Holland wrote in his book *Rubicon: The Last Years of the Roman Republic*, 'By Caesar's time the exchange rate had stabilized at a jar of wine for one slave, which, at least as far as the Italians were concerned, made for a fabulously profitable import-export business.'

"Fast-forward to the 1970s, when French wines were well-established, but California wines were just getting started. A bottle of Château Mouton Rothschild, a renowned Bordeaux blend since 1853, could be purchased for around twenty dollars. Today, the 2020 vintage is selling at $1,300! Now, contrast that with Robert Mondavi's Napa Valley Cabernet Sauvignon, that sold for about ten dollars. Today, the current vintage can be had for fifty dollars. Mouton 6,500% increase; Mondavi 400%. Which one represents the better value today?

"Both are what we call Bordeaux blends. The Mouton is 84% Cabernet Sauvignon, 13% Merlot, 2% Cabernet Franc and 1% Petit Verdot, and the Mondavi is

80% Cabernet Sauvignon, 11% Merlot, 5% Petit Verdot, 3% Cabernet Franc and 1% Malbec. Adding the Malbec gives the Mondavi an up-front creaminess which distinguishes it from the Mouton. Is the Mouton the better wine? Definitely. Is it worth the price? Do the math. What would you rather buy for $1,300 – one bottle of Château Mouton Rothschild or two cases from Robert Mondavi Winery?

"These price increases are due to a number of factors, starting with inflation, which has had a major impact on the prices of goods and services in the last fifty years. As the cost of living has increased, so has the cost of wine. In addition to this, reputation, production size, cost of land, and the increasing popularity and quality of wine have all left their mark.

"In order to calculate today's price in 1970 dollars, I used the Consumer Price Index, or CPI, to adjust for inflation. The CPI in 1970 was 38.8, while the CPI in 2022 was 292.7. For example, the Mouton Rothschild at twenty dollars in 1970 would be $150 today using 1970 dollars. As I said earlier, today's Mouton is now an eye-popping $1,300, more than ten times its 1970s price. In contrast, the Mondavi should be seventy-five dollars, but its price only fifty dollars.

"Enter supply and demand: Mouton Rothschild has a strong reputation, a long history, and is thus in high demand. Mondavi, on the other hand, is a relative newcomer, and its price has not kept up with inflation. Another reason is Mouton Rothschild produces about twenty thousand cases per year, whereas Mondavi makes about one hundred thousand cases.

"Returning to the Rubicon, Sassicaia was the first Super Tuscan to be introduced to the world in 1968 at ten dollars per bottle. Using 1970 dollars, it should now cost seventy-five dollars, but its price is $375. This premium is due to its superb quality and its limited production of only ten thousand cases per year. Like the Mondavi example, there are other Super Tuscans in the twenty-to-fifty-dollar range.

"Which brings me to my last point: there are new wines being introduced every day which, together with improving wine-making techniques, provide stiff competition to the established labels. They offer comparable quality at bargain prices. Argentina has many reds with scores of ninety and ninety-one points in the twenty-to-thirty-dollar range. British Columbia, in Canada, is one of the youngest wine regions, and now boasts over three hundred wineries. I predict its trajectory will mirror that of California, which has a forty-year head start.

"So, here's my conclusion: to find quality wine at a reasonable price, try newer labels that are not established. This is an ongoing process since, as they gain in reputation, their prices will inevitably rise. But that's the fun of it: you can go out and, as we say, kiss a lot of frogs to find the princes.

"I want to close by touching on the subject of unicorns. Are any of you are familiar with that term? (Nobody raised their hands.) No? A unicorn is a wine that's so rare that it's hard to believe it exists. They're the holy grail of wine experts and are sought out by collectors everywhere. Competition for them is big and so are their prices. For example, a bottle of 1947 Château Cheval Blanc, one of the top Bordeaux châteaux, is currently $28,000. They can fetch much higher prices in the right circumstances. In 2010, a 47 Cheval Blanc sold for $304,374 at auction, and that's not the highest price that's been paid. That prize goes to a 1945 Romanée-

Conti from Burgundy that sold at auction for an eye-watering $558,000.

"At these high prices, unicorns are rarely bought to drink. Instead, they're investments that collectors expect will appreciate in value, much like rare art. That's it for today. Does anyone have any questions or points they'd like to discuss?"

"Yes, Marcello," Zach said to the thirty-three-year-old plumber who raised his hand.

"My family is Italian, and we make wine at home. We get together in the fall and divide up the bottles. It's not the best wine, but at fifty cents a bottle, I don't hear anybody complaining," he said to chuckles from the class. "Anyway, what Italian red wine should I buy for special occasions?"

"Why don't you try one of the Super Tuscans we discussed? Village Wine Traders on Folsom has them, and they'll give you ten percent off if you buy a case. Next? Mary."

Mary was a forty-one-year-old nurse practitioner who'd never given much thought to wine before this course. Given her medical background, she brought with her a visible skepticism toward alcohol that Zach noticed had softened as the course progressed, and the romance of wine gradually seduced her.

"In our house, we normally buy two buck chuck from Trader Joe's. What budget California wines do you recommend for an everyday wine?" she asked.

"The wines from Paso Robles offer good value. I'd check out the lower-priced labels from DAOU. Also, Coppola Diamond Cabernet Sauvignon is good, and Beringer in Napa has some good values. Try their Founder's Estate line."

At four o'clock, Zach was back in his car and on

his way to Ernie's for a bracer with Lilith before heading home. He texted her to confirm he'd be there at four thirty, and hoped she wouldn't spring another one of her friends on him. Did she intentionally like keeping him off balance? It occurred to him that she might be a narcissist, or maybe even a mild sociopath, but since they only met twice a year, he'd probably never know her well enough to say for sure. Still, he had his doubts, and remained cautious about her.

"Will it be Scotch or a vodka martini today?" he thought as he sped along Highway 280. "Probably a Scotch."

Part II
The Swindle

Imitation may be the sincerest form of flattery, but counterfeit wine is flattery without sincerity.

In the basement of his Laurel Heights Home, Jimmy Jin-Hie Wong was concentrating on his newest creation – a believable 1946 Pétrus from a blend of wines he'd acquired. He was dressed down from his usual chic apparel in a black polo shirt and khaki chinos, Ferragamo loafers, and disposable plastic gloves. He avoided jeans as much as possible; they were not really his thing.

Living alone in his grand house suited him just fine. He endured weekly visits from his Mexican housekeeper with whom he had only rudimentary communication, since his Spanish was non-existent and her English was limited at best. He allowed her free rein of the house with the exception of the basement, which was strictly off-limits. He kept the key to that door in his pocket at all times.

The house was modest in comparison to his family's mansion in Hong Kong, built on their gambling fortune made through tenacity and cunning. In one generation, they had gone from nobodies to vast wealth. Having spent his formative years working in his family's casino in Macau, he'd learned the value of hard work, how to cut corners to get ahead faster, and, most important, not get caught.

He was still an angry, lonely boy who suffered from recurring bouts of depression and anxiety, having grown up in therapy craving the attention denied by his tiger parents. When Mei-Ling, his first love, died suddenly from a brain aneurysm, he realized that he needed to get away. At age thirty-six, he proposed to his father that he try his luck in California, to which he reluctantly agreed after many tense discussions.

Armed with lots of money and a mandate to increase it, he'd come to San Francisco eight years ago on a visitor's visa that allowed him to stay for six months. The renewal process did not bother him as it allowed a dutiful son, who still yearned to please his parents, to return home twice a year to reunite with them and his family. It also allowed him to make semi-annual reports about his progress in person to his father who, at seventy-four, still maintained an iron grip on the family.

It was now twenty-five years since China took Hong Kong back from the British and reneged on its promises to maintain its civil liberties and freedom. In many respects, his adopted home offered better opportunities than Hong Kong, which was slowly succumbing to domination from Beijing. So, here he was, self-exiled to California as a hedge against China's threat to his family's wealth.

Seated at a long, unfinished plywood bench covered with empty bottles, labels, and corks, he was writing in his black book which contained the recipes for his "vintage" wines. On the floor was a wine bottle corking machine, and against the opposite wall of the large room sat a multitude of cardboard boxes with empty wine bottles waiting silently for their rebirth.

Finding the right bottles was time-consuming, but with perseverance he managed to do it. Part chameleon, he'd go to recycling depots dressed in shabby clothes to source empty bottles, then attend expensive wine events as a well-dressed connoisseur. He knew what he was looking for, and over time he amassed five hundred empty vintage bottles. He had enough for the Pétrus that he was making today.

Next came the labels, which he recreated using the proper label paper, modern scanning and printing methods, then lightly baking them in the oven to age them. He also distressed and tore them to show typical wear and tear from handling the bottles over the years.

Since the wines were so old, and the corks needed to be replaced after thirty years, buyers didn't expect the original corks or lead caps. They could be new and nobody would be the wiser. Sometimes he dipped the recorked bottles in molten red wax for effect.

The wine was the real trick. Buyers today were smart and experienced; he had to get the details right in case someone actually drank it. What he had going for him was most of them would not have direct knowledge of how a 1946 Pétrus should taste. The best they could do was to compare its taste to more recent Pétrus vintages they might know.

In the four years since his first meeting with Edward Pavlov at Sutter Street Auctioneers, their wine business had flourished. Edward was finding buyers at the rate of two cases each month, which Jimmy supplied with ease. Today his task was to fabricate a wine that tasted like a vintage Pétrus. For this he relied on his cultivated palate, achieved over many years of tasting and drinking fine French wine, first in Hong Kong and Macau, and now in San Francisco.

It was elementary that Pétrus was made from Merlot grapes, which was typical for the wines of the Pomerol region of Bordeaux, and that exposing wine to air aged it. All he had to do was achieve the right wine mix, and then age it to create the aromas and flavors that could pass for a 1946 Pétrus. This was more art than science. Even he did not know what it should taste like, but he could make an educated guess.

The right formula required hours of experiments using the real thing and other lesser wines to extend the volume. Today, he had four real 2018 Pétrus for the base that had cost him $4,700 per bottle. For blending, he had another eight less expensive Bordeaux bottles, also from Pomerol, which had been breathing for eight hours.

From his pocket, Jimmy pulled out a small glass vial and a rolled-up hundred-dollar bill. He tapped out a neat line of cocaine on a small mirror and leaned down swiftly, inhaling with a sharp snort. The familiar rush hit him almost instantly, electrifying his nerves and sharpening his focus. His pupils dilated as his heartbeat quickened, and for a few moments he just sat there, basking in the dizzying clarity that came with the high. He felt invincible, ready to blend like the master he was.

With his senses heightened, Jimmy got to work. He opened the four bottles of 2018 Pétrus with a flourish. His hands moved deftly as he poured the first bottle into a large decanter, then set about mixing in some of the lesser Bordeaux. He swirled the blends together in his large crystal glass, the rich aromas rising in waves. His tongue flicked over the rim as he took careful sips, judging the smoothness, the balance of tannins, the complexity of flavor, then spat each mouthful into a plastic cup he kept on the bench.

Confident he'd achieved just the right taste after many critical sips, he poured the wine into a dozen bottles. Leaving an inch of air at the top to account for natural evaporation since 1946, he inserted corks without any markings using his corking machine. He took extra care to make sure he used a few different types of cork in case some inquisitive fellow wanted to compare bottles, since they would have come from different collections.

From this blend that cost him an average of two thousand dollars a bottle, he now had rare wine worth twenty-two thousand and likely fifty thousand after his partner, Edward, talked them up to his select buyers at his men's club. They wanted only the best, and could be expected to pay accordingly. With more money than they would ever spend, they competed with each other for the finest things it could buy, including wine. They cared more about the bragging rights associated with having the rarest wines, which they treated the same as their investments.

Of course, Jimmy was aware of the risk of being found out, especially given the publicity about fake wine and the rise of anti-counterfeiting companies out there that offered to authenticate rare wines. He was relying on Edward's close relationship with his buyers, and the reputation of his exclusive men's club, to sell the wine without too much scrutiny.

It was time to move the goods.

"Ed?" Jimmy said when Edward answered, "I've assembled a case of 1946 Pétrus. When can you pick it up?"

"That's excellent news, Jimmy. They'll be of great interest to my group, who I'm sure will pay the regular premium for them. I'll include a bottle or two at my next dinner auction with the other wines I have at the house. May I drop by tomorrow before noon?"

"That will be fine," Jimmy replied disconnecting the signal, satisfied that his *Gweilo* partner was none the wiser about the provenance of the rare wines he provided to him. While Edward sometimes asked where they came from, Jimmy only gave him vague explanations about Asian collectors, omitting details like names and dates that could be verified. He also

86

knew nothing about his family and its source of wealth; only that he was a rich Hong Kong businessman.

Their symbiotic relationship, like that of the rhinoceros and the egret in the wilds of Africa, worked remarkably well. Each brought something to the partnership that the other lacked. Edward had the respectability which Jimmy did not that gave him access to well-heeled buyers; and Jimmy had the expertise and provided the finest wines that Edward could only dream about finding without devoting a huge amount of time and effort. He had an uncanny knack for finding extremely rare, unicorn wines that occupied a mythical status in the fine wine world, and could be sold for astronomical prices.

Their partnership, now in its fourth year, was a lucrative one for both of them. They still split the money seventy/thirty, using the faulty logic that Jimmy paid handsomely for the wines. If they sold the twelve bottles of the 1946 Pétrus for fifty thousand dollars each, well, let's just say the effort would be well worth it for Edward, and significantly more for Jimmy. Just thinking about it always brought a smile to his face. While Edward was becoming rich, Jimmy was becoming richer and, most importantly, pleasing his father.

"This is as it should be," thought Jimmy, given that Edward was inferior to him in every way that mattered. In time, he would no longer need him. Then he would return triumphant to Hong Kong and a proud family that always thought he could never achieve such a level of success and fortune.

Jimmy put the twelve bottles in a box against the wall, and labeled it. Then he returned to making another rare vintage, this time from Burgundy. He took great care to keep his winemaking equipment in the basement, away from prying eyes. Only the finished bottles were ever seen on the main floor.

At eleven o'clock the next morning, Edward arrived at Jimmy's stately home on Commonwealth Avenue. Built in 1916, it was an imposing example of colonial architecture in pale yellow stucco with white wooden windows. With his eyes looking down, he ignored the surroundings as he wheezed his 289 pounds up the path to the front door.

"Ed. Please, come in," Jimmy said inscrutably as Edward brushed past him into the grand foyer. They adjourned to the living room, as was their custom.

Seated in one of two silk brocade wing chairs, Edward said, "I brought you the ledger of our sales and distributions so far this year, and here's your check for last month." Edward handed the sheet and check to Jimmy, who quickly looked it over while he placed the check in his pocket. He'd seen previous versions, so it only took a few seconds for him to absorb the numbers.

"This appears to be in order," Jimmy said, looking up from the document. "You're to be commended for the excellent job you do. Not an easy task, finding all these private buyers."

"And you too, for sourcing all these wines," replied Edward. "I always worry that someday soon I will saturate my network and need to locate new buyers. I may need to start consigning some wine to an auction house. I have one in mind." This was not the first time he'd raised this issue, but more so lately.

"As we've discussed before, my strong preference is to keep our affairs as private as possible," replied Jimmy. "It's my training, I guess. Not that I have any particular objection to auctioning the wine; it's just that I'd prefer to maintain a tight control over the process."

"I'm just saying we may need to involve an auction house someday." Edward reminded himself that Jimmy wasn't like him. He only trusted him because he controlled the money. His gut told him that this partnership wasn't going to last forever and he should watch his back. He worried that beneath the polished veneer was a snake that might strike at any moment.

"Now for the wine," Jimmy said as he rose from his chair and walked over to the wall where the case was waiting. He placed it at Edward's feet, who immediately began inspecting the bottles.

"Very nice," Edward said, holding up each bottle one at a time and closely examining the Pétrus labels. Each shared the same design and type of paper, but bore unique gouges and tears from years of handling. "Did you acquire these at auction or from a private seller?"

"I put this case together mainly from two sellers in Asia, one who was getting on in years and wanted to reduce his collection, and the other who found himself in financial difficulties. They are both longtime friends of the family, and appreciate that discretion is desirable. You understand how these things are. They will be a source of more rare bottles in future."

"We are just middlemen helping to transfer expensive wines from one collector to another."

"Highly knowledgeable middlemen," Jimmy corrected him gently.

"Yes, that is true enough. Well, I shan't keep you any longer. I should be on my way."

The two men parted company at the front door. Jimmy returned to his work in the basement, while Edward drove to his house in Russian Hill to store the new case.

Macau – October 12, 2008

On a cloudless autumn evening fourteen years earlier, Jimmy wandered into the casino intending to celebrate his twenty-eighth birthday in style. As he approached the tables, his eyes caught sight of a stunning dealer, her fingers deftly handling the cards. "She must be new," he thought. "I've never seen her before. If I had, I definitely would have remembered." Her name tag read simply "Mei-Ling".

"Welcome," she said softly, looking up at him with large brown eyes. "Care to try your luck?"

Jimmy hesitated, then nodded, taking a seat. "Why not?" he said nervously, an unusual reaction for him. She apparently didn't know who he was; that was good.

As the game progressed, they exchanged glances and smiles. After a particularly lucky hand, Mei-Ling leaned closer and whispered, "You have a natural talent."

Jimmy chuckled, a genuine smile spreading across his face. "Or maybe it's just beginner's luck," he replied playfully.

Over the following weeks, their conversations became more intimate. Mei-Ling's kindness and patience were a balm to his erratic emotions. One night, as they walked along the waterfront, he opened up about his struggles. "Sometimes, I feel like I'm drowning," he confessed, looking at the dark water.

She took his hand, her touch reassuring. "I'm here, Jimmy. You're not alone. Would you like to talk about it?"

Their relationship blossomed in the shadows of

Macau, hidden from his family's expectations. Mei-Ling became his confidante, an anchor in his turbulent world. With her support, Jimmy began to see a brighter future.

One evening, as they sat in Mei-Ling's small apartment, the conversation turned serious. "Do you ever think about leaving?" she asked, her eyes searching his.

"Every day," Jimmy admitted. "With you, I feel like I finally can."

Their moment was interrupted by the shrill ring of Jimmy's phone. He answered, and his face paled. "Hong Kong? What happened?" Mei-Ling watched with concern as he listened, the news from the other end of the line causing a storm of emotions on his face. He hung up, his hands trembling. "My mother... it's her heart. I need to go to Hong Kong right away," he said, his voice barely above a whisper.

Returning to the mansion, the air was thick with fear and uncertainty. The family was in denial. Nobody would talk about what happened, as if refusing to acknowledge it somehow meant it didn't happen. Jimmy went to his mother's bedside and sat with her for a week.

Cecilia Wong survived her heart attack, but the incident marked a turning point for the family. With his mother's health in decline, Jimmy was forced to stay in Hong Kong and take on a more active role in the business under his brothers' watchful eyes.

The transition was anything but smooth. Jimmy's mental health deteriorated under the relentless pressure, his moods swinging more wildly than ever. Seeing her brother's distress, May took him aside and spoke to him with uncharacteristic gentleness. "Jimmy," she said softly, "You don't have to do this. Don't destroy yourself trying to please them. Find your own path. Be who you are meant to be." Her words resonated deeply with him. For the first time, someone in his family acknowledged his pain, his struggle. It encouraged him to take a step back, to reevaluate his life and his choices.

With Mei-Ling's support, he began to distance himself from the family's grip. He moved back to Macau, where he was once again in the world he loved. His relationship with Mei-Ling flourished. She remained his foundation, helping him through the highs and lows of his condition, as they began to build a life together.

But fate, as it often does, had other plans.

As Jimmy sprinted through the opulent casino, he ignored the flashing lights and cacophony of the casino floor. All he could focus on was the pounding in his chest, and his silent prayer that Mei-Ling would be okay. His phone call with the security chief, detailing her collapse, still echoed in his ears.

He burst through the double doors of the casino's medical room where Mei-Ling had been taken, his breath coming in short gasps. Mei-Ling lay still on a stretcher, her face ashen, her chest rising and falling faintly with each labored breath. A nurse was adjusting an IV drip and a doctor was speaking in hushed tones to one of the security guards.

Jimmy rushed to her side, grasping her hand. "Mei-Ling," he whispered, his voice cracking. Her eyes fluttered open for a moment, a flicker of recognition and pain crossing her face before her lids drooped shut again. The doctor approached him, his expression grave.

"Mr. Wong, she may have suffered a brain aneurysm," the doctor explained, his tone professional but laced with the empathy of someone who had delivered such news too many times. "We have stabilized her as best as we can, but her condition is critical. We're going to transfer her to the hospital for testing, but her chances of survival are unknown at this time."

Jimmy's world tilted. Mei-Ling? A brain aneurysm? His mind raced. This couldn't be happening, not to her. Not now. He had seen tragedies unfold in the casino – people losing fortunes, lives crumbling under the weight of addiction – but this was Mei-Ling, the woman who'd stood by him despite his struggles. The thought of losing her was unbearable.

The ambulance arrived, and the medical team moved efficiently. Jimmy followed, his mind swirling with memories and fears. The ride to the hospital was a blur, sirens wailing, lights flashing. He held Mei-Ling's hand the entire way, whispering reassurances, though he wasn't sure if they were for her benefit or his own.

At the hospital, time seemed to stretch and contract in a disorienting dance. Doctors and nurses worked tirelessly, but the sense of impending loss hung heavy in the air. Jimmy was ushered to a waiting area, where he paced like a caged animal, his thoughts racing. He tried to recall every detail of their time together, clinging to memories like lifelines.

Then came the moment he'd been fearing most. A doctor approached, his face a mask of compassion. "I'm sorry, Mr. Wong," he began, and Jimmy felt the words like a physical blow. "We did everything we could, but the damage was too extensive. Mei-Ling passed away peacefully."

On hearing those words, Jimmy suddenly felt as if the air had been sucked from his lungs, leaving a void where his heart should be. The spirited woman who'd helped him navigate his tortured world was no more. As he walked back through the corridors of the hospital, he felt a profound emptiness. The lights of Macau, once so dazzling, were now only harsh and cold.

Back at the casino, the opulence was suffocating. Jimmy stood at the entrance, looking out over the gaming floor where Mei-Ling had spent so many hours. His mind was a tangled mess, racing and plodding all at once. Mei-Ling was gone. The only person who'd ever truly understood him was now just another face fading into the shadows of memory. He thought of her smile, the way she'd tuck her hair behind her ear, her fingers dancing deftly as she dealt cards.

It was all too much to bear, and the emptiness within him seemed to stretch infinitely. He needed to forget. The thought surfaced suddenly as he stood amidst the neon-lit chaos of the casino floor. He felt for the pack of cigarettes in his pocket, but it wasn't enough. He needed something stronger to blast through the void and burn away the gnawing grief that threatened to consume him.

Jimmy spotted Victor near the high-stakes tables. A longtime dealer with a sideline in procuring whatever vice his clientele craved, Jimmy steered clear of him, but tonight he didn't care. He made his way over, forcing a casual nod as he met Victor's eyes. Victor glanced around before leaning in, voice low and greasy, "What can I do for you, Jimmy?"

"Mei-Ling..." he replied, a haunted look in his eyes.

He didn't have to explain; the news was already on the floor. Victor's lips curled into a knowing smile. Without a word, he led Jimmy down a dim corridor off the main floor, away from the glittering lights and prying eyes. He reached into his jacket and pulled out a small baggie of white powder. "This will help," he murmured, his tone both friendly and transactional. Jimmy took the bag, knowing Mei-Ling would have been horrified, as he indulged his despair.

Finding a quiet alcove, he poured a small amount of the powder onto his hand. The rush of adrenaline mixed with an overwhelming sadness as he leaned down, inhaling deeply. The sting hit instantly, and within moments, a numbness began to spread through him, blotting out the pain. He closed his eyes, letting the drug seep into every crevice of his mind, pushing back the memories that clawed at him.

He stumbled back onto the casino floor, now a blur of lights and sound, his senses heightened. The noise crashed over him, waves of laughter and clinking glasses, but it all felt distant, like watching a film on mute. He realized he didn't care about the consequences anymore. He didn't care about anything. All that was left was the hollow echo of Mei-Ling's absence, and the fading warmth of a love that had been the one bright spot in his turbulent existence.

Back at the bar, he ordered a drink he didn't need, which he downed in one go. The burn of the alcohol mixed with the sharp edges of the cocaine still tingling in his veins. He'd let the dragon into his life, hoping it would swallow him whole, just as the loss of Mei-Ling had swallowed his heart.

The dinner for his wine cronies was set for seven o'clock. Edward Pavlov arrived at The Redwood Private Men's Club of San Francisco at five so he could set up and decant the wines they'd be drinking this evening. He'd brought the wines for dinner, along with three cases of Jimmy's rare wines, which he expected would fetch a handsome sum. As these wines sold better as individual bottles, he'd broken up Jimmy's boxes to restrict tonight's offering to one or two bottles of each label.

"Edward the Large," as his soon-to-be ex-wife called him, was dressed impeccably in a black silk suit imported from his Hong Kong tailor. A maroon and navy tie with a thin gold stripe added a touch of elegance, while the crisp white shirt beneath it highlighted his broad shoulders and ample frame. His dark hair, peppered with gray, was carefully styled to mask thinning strands, a small vanity he allowed himself.

Physically, Edward had begun to show the signs of his sixty-one years. He rarely exercised, preferring the comfort of his office and boardroom to the gym. His approach to health was sporadic at best, relying on short-term diets that never yielded lasting results. Giving up smoking five years ago was his last significant health concession, a decision forced on him more by necessity than desire.

In short, Edward Pavlov was one of those men who was larger than life, a formidable presence both physically and in personality. He wielded his size and confidence like a weapon, using them to dominate business dealings and personal relationships. His imposing stature often meant he got his way, whether negotiating a deal or navigating the complexities of his marriage. Edward was a man used to being in control, and he thrived on power and respect.

He'd reserved the private Eucalyptus Room on the second floor, which was necessary as the club rules didn't allow commerce to be conducted in the public rooms. They also didn't allow cell phones; but they did allow drinking, which very much suited his purpose. He was counting on the consumption of copious amounts of alcohol to slow the group's wits and loosen their purse strings at the auction.

The Redwood Private Men's Club had been founded in 1911 and was still housed in its original five-story brick building situated on Nob Hill. Originally formed by unclubbable titans of industry who were barred from more established clubs due to their unseemly business methods or modest beginnings, it was now home to an eclectic selection of the San Francisco elite, nouveau riche, and up-and-comers. The building's entrance, marked by grand wooden doors with intricate carvings, opened into a lobby that transported all who entered back to the early twentieth century.

The décor was still Victorian and looked like it had been there since the club first opened its doors. Heavy velvet drapes in deep burgundy hung on the lobby windows, and mahogany furniture stood on Persian rugs worn down by a century of foot traffic. A huge crystal chandelier, with its myriad prisms, cast shimmering light across the ornate plaster ceilings.

The older members and staff also looked like they'd been there from day one. The former could be found in the reading rooms, scouring newspapers with the intensity of generals planning their next campaign, in one of the restaurants eating lunch or dinner, or in the bars in the afternoon, bracing themselves for the trip home. There was a bar on four of the five floors, each having a unique ambiance, but all sharing an aura of exclusivity. Only the offices on the top floor were spared their presence, reserved for the sober administration of the club's affairs.

Gossip, especially about business, was the mainstay of the membership. The club's hushed corridors and dimly lit alcoves were ideal for discreet conversations. Anything about anybody could be said in confidence, and it went without saying that nothing was ever written down. The walls seemed to absorb all those secrets, with their wooden panels and thick tapestries that muffled any sound. One naturally took care to discuss such matters only with other gentlemen of character and discretion. Consequently, there was a high level of trust among the members, based on a curious assumption that all of them could be counted on to do and say the right thing.

It was in this grand tradition of exclusivity that Edward presented and sold rare wines monthly in one of the private rooms of the Redwood Club. Known for his impeccable taste and deep knowledge of wine, he was well-regarded by the members. His presentations were much more than mere sales pitches; they were journeys through the vineyards of Bordeaux and Burgundy. Members would sit enraptured as he described the vintages, the *terroirs* and the stories behind each bottle. Then they would eagerly snap them up as they were offered for sale, mainly for the prestige of simply owning them.

It was now approaching seven o'clock, and Edward was ready for his guests, the first of whom arrived promptly at seven.

"Edward! Good to see you again," said Hugh Albright effusively as he made his way directly over to the counter to view the merchandise. Hugh was a sixty something banker in the city. Short and portly with wispy gray hair atop a puffy face from years of over-imbibing, he was dressed in the banker's uniform – a Brooks Brothers dark blue pinstripe suit and striped tie. He was a long-standing club member who loved to own rare wines. He loved the prestige associated with them, telling his friends about them, and highlighting them when he gave his guests tours of his otherwise modest home. He was one of those collectors who bought the label, not the contents. Edward didn't know if he had ever drunk any of the wines that he'd sold to him in the past four years, but he suspected not.

"Hello Hugh," replied Edward with a big smile on his face as he joined him at the sideboard. "You're looking well."

"That's a fact, dear boy. Tell me, which of these beauties are you personally recommending this evening?" he said, lowering his voice to a conspiratorial whisper.

Assembled before him were thirty-six of the rarest French wines that money could buy, including one bottle of the 1946 Pétrus. They'd been drawn randomly from Jimmy's cases which were stored in Edward's wine cellar at his home in Russian Hill. Edward was none the wiser about how or where Jimmy acquired these wines, beyond what he'd told him – that they came from Asian collectors and auctions. He believed him, especially after they attended a few auctions together where he observed his obvious expertise in choosing the best deals. The man from Hong Kong knew his way around and never overpaid. Another thing Edward didn't know was the extent of his guile, which he masked with a finesse that made his true nature almost impossible to detect.

"You know the rules, Hugh. I can't give you an advantage over our friends, now can I."

"No, no, of course not," Hugh replied with a wink. He was the type to always try his luck, then quickly retreat when there could be any suggestion of impropriety.

"Owoo, I see you have a 1946 Château Pétrus! This is simply excellent, just excellent," Hugh said, wringing his hands with glee.

"As you know, Hugh, all of these wines are extremely hard to find," said Edward. "I've gone to a lot of effort to bring you these examples of the finest that money can buy." He fixed him with his best *only serious buyers need apply* look.

The next to enter was William Baxter, a philanthropist who came from old money by San Francisco standards. He was tall and lean in his seventies, and kept his hand in managing the family office investments. Given his status, he didn't wear a tie with his black cashmere blazer and gray slacks. In a rare concession to the lax times, the club had reluctantly abandoned its rule that required ties be worn on the premises.

"Edward, Hugh," he nodded as he approached the wine to have a peek.

"Good evening, Bill. How's the golf game?" asked Hugh, hoping to engage him in conversation. He would very much like to have William Baxter as a customer, but so far had been unable to land him. Attracting the super-rich was always a tricky business, one that required a delicate touch.

"Can't complain," came his non-committal reply as he studied the bottles, being careful not to touch them as if they were precious works of art – which in many ways they were.

Soon they were joined by the others and their waiter, wearing an all-white uniform, who poured them flutes of Krug 2008 Brut Champagne sourced from the club's cellar. All the members knew each other well from Edward's monthly wine dinners, and their conversation was convivial as they stood around the sideboard, sneaking furtive glances at the assembled bottles. All told, in addition to Edward, there were three CEOs, three investment bankers, two philanthropists, one banker, a retired doctor, a dentist, and a corporate lawyer. The topics of conversation this evening would be wine and club politics.

The youngest of the group was Ryan Townhill who, at thirty-eight, was a mover and shaker, and a director of the club. A dashing young investment banker, he'd started, built and sold a software company for a fortune, and now ran his own family office where he invested in successful start-ups. He had dusty blond hair and blue-gray eyes, set in a chiseled face above an athletic body. His light gray Brioni power suit fit him like a glove, which he wore over a black silk Polo shirt. As he mingled with the group, he did his best to ignore Hugh Albright's signals to chat. He could barely tolerate the short, pudgy banker.

At seven thirty, Edward invited everyone to be seated. The chairs were arranged strategically, with six members on either side and him at the head of the table so he could control the process. Nobody seemed to notice or care that there were usually thirteen who attended his events.

Their waiter busied himself pouring two-ounce tasters for everyone of a 1945 Château Mouton Rothschild that Edward had drawn from Jimmy's wines to use as a teaser.

"As is our custom at these events, you're invited to try one of these exquisite wines that are available for purchase tonight. I think you'll be impressed with the quality and reassured to know you're not buying vinegar."

"Hear, hear!" said the lawyer. What followed were murmured conversations about the excellent quality that the Mouton still had after so many years. Edward picked up snippets like "impeccable", "proper storage makes all the difference" and "you can never go wrong at these events".

With the tasters drained, two new waiters brought in plates with a marinated shrimp salad, while the original waiter poured everyone a glass of 2019 Louis Jadot Bâtard-Montrachet Grand Cru. They moved seamlessly as if choreographed by Fred Astaire. The admiration of their skill was only overshadowed by the excellence of the cuisine from the club's renowned chefs.

The next course was followed by beef Wellington cooked to perfection, served with asparagus with hollandaise sauce and baby carrots. It was accompanied by four bottles of 2015 Château Lynch-Bages Grand Cru which, like the Montrachet and the Mouton, had been decanting for over two hours and was at its best.

Dessert was skipped in favor of coffee, espresso, teas, hazelnut madeleines, and Rémy Martin XO Cognac. The intended anticipation of what was to come was building nicely.

At eight fifteen, it was time to get the show on the road. Edward stood up and clinked his Cognac snifter with his spoon.

"Gentlemen, may I have your attention please!" he announced to a dozen turning heads. "Tonight, we have an exceptional selection of rare wines that are hard to find, to say the least. In front of you have been placed summary sheets on each of the twenty-two labels on offer tonight. There are thirty-five bottles in total, as we have two bottles of some of the labels. All of them come from private collections whose owners, as usual, wish to remain anonymous. I am confident that what we have here is the genuine article." He paused to let the implied guarantee linger.

"Without further ado, shall I start the bidding for the first item on your list, the 1991 Leflaive Montrachet Grand Cru? We have two bottles here tonight. As you can see on your sheets, this was an exceptional vintage for this wine. Can I have a bid of, say, $20,000?"

Ryan Townhill was the first to raise his hand. "I'll bid $40,000 for both bottles."

Not to be outdone, and considering the price a bargain, Hugh the banker bid $41,000, to be closely followed by the lawyer at $41,500. The bids came fast and furious until the price peaked at $90,100 in Ryan's favor. All went quiet for a few seconds until Hugh Albright raised his hand.

"It seems a pity that two such special bottles should be kept together. May I urge our friend to split them so the rest of us can have a shot?"

"I'm certainly willing to share with my friends, provided that I can keep one for $45,050," Ryan replied, looking around the table for reactions. "How do we handle this, Ed?"

"Who would like bid for the other Montrachet?" Edward asked. "Please raise your hand." Three hands went up.

"Then if there are no objections, I suggest we agree that Ryan may have the first bottle, and continue the bidding for the second." Nobody objected, and bidding among the three for the second bottle of Montrachet continued apace until the retired doctor was successful at $48,900.

"Next, we have two 1945 Château Mouton Rothschild. Do I have a bid of $15,000 for the first one?" Six hands shot up, which caused Edward to raise the bid to $16,000 and two hands were lowered. $17,000 and one hand was lowered; and so on until one hand remained at $21,500.

"Bill has bid $21,500. Is anyone interested at twenty-two?" Edward asked. The dentist, who was one of the original bidders, raised his hand, and the bidding continued among three members until Bill finally succeeded at $47,900. The second Mouton garnered less competition and sold to the dentist for $44,600, much to his delight.

Auctions are peculiar things, thought Edward. The bidding ebbed and flowed like an ocean tide, with waves of enthusiasm followed by periods of calm, only to start up again until the auctioneer finally declared the item sold. Both thrilling and unpredictable, the evening progressed in this vein for three hours until only one bottle remained.

"And now for the 1946 Pétrus," announced Edward as he moved over to the sideboard, where he picked it up and handed it to Hugh who was seated nearest to him.

"Hugh, please examine it, then pass it around for

the others to inspect. As you'll see, it's been around the block in its seventy-seven years." He was referring to the label which was stained, gouged and torn off at the lower right corner.

"As most of you know, Pétrus is from Pomerol and is not a château per se, although it's often referred to as such," he continued, glancing at Hugh. "It's also not a classified growth, unlike Lafite, Mouton and the others. Those great wines from Médoc were already well-established by the time it appeared in 1837. It was, shall we say, a Johnny-come-lately.

"The name Pétrus shot to fame when it won a gold medal at the 1878 Paris Exhibition. At the time it was only a small vineyard of seven hectares or seventeen acres. You can read more about it in your fact sheets.

"This is the most important estate in Pomerol and one of the best from Bordeaux. Often called the most expensive wine in the world, this vintage is exceedingly hard to find. Who will start the bidding at $30,000?"

Always one to bid at the start but rarely at the end, Hugh put his hand up to get things started. So far, he'd only managed to snag a Château Latour for $21,700, which he considered a bargain and a prestigious addition to his cellar.

The bidding was energetic as hands shot up in rapid succession, increasing to $69,600 when there was a pause. William Baxter, as the highest bidder, was looking determined to go the distance against all-comers.

"Bill has bid $69,600," said Edward, looking around the table. "Do I have anything higher? No? Then we have "69,600 going once; 69,600 twice; 69..."

"I'll bid $70,000," the retired doctor said. "Hell, it's only money, and this is a piece of history that's impossible to find."

"In that case, I'll have to go to $75,000," said William, staring at the doctor, who stared back with equal resolve. The bidding continued for another minute between the two of them until William was eventually successful at $97,000. Envious eyes rolled as he was congratulated and slapped on the back by his neighbor seated to his right.

The evening broke up quickly after that as the hour was late, and they wanted to get their prizes home and tucked away in their cellars. In all, almost two million dollars had been dropped tonight, and Edward had all the checks in hand.

These evenings brought in twenty million dollars per year, which was nothing to sneeze at; and this was the fifth year! The December dinners always brought in the most, as everyone was in a holiday and charitable mood. Tonight's haul was the most ever, which would please Jimmy.

"A splendid event, as usual Ed," said William, his hand outstretched. They shook hands and chatted amiably about the evening and the wines. "I've always been curious about how you're able to find them. You must spend an inordinate amount of your time searching high and low."

"That I do, Bill," Edward replied, "but, as you know, I'm well compensated for my efforts. It's satisfying and worth it."

"Where do you find them?"

"I have a source who buys them from wealthy collectors in Asia, people who are getting on in age or whose financial circumstances have changed. It's demographics really; collectible wine changes hands like rare art."

"Do you know anything about these sellers – who

they are, where they bought the wine, how long they've held it?"

"That I do not, but I'm assured by my source that they are legitimate collectors. I've also watched him buy wine at various auctions in town and was impressed with his expertise at spotting the right wines and paying the best prices. I expect some of the wines come from there."

"I'd be interested in any further information you might obtain since, as you know, they are very expensive. More confirmation would certainly be welcome."

"You'll be the second to know, Bill."

They continued their discussion for a few minutes, then William wished him the best of the holidays and took his leave, none the wiser about the provenance of Edward's wines. As he left, he made a mental note to do some digging into the rare wine trade.

Russian Hill – January 4, 2023

Zach navigated his blue 2019 Audi A5 sedan through the winding streets of San Francisco as night fell over the city. His destination was Russian Hill, one of the city's most picturesque neighborhoods. Known for its steep streets and historic charm, it offered breathtaking views of the bay and the iconic Golden Gate Bridge in the distance.

At Lilith's invitation, Zach had agreed to meet her friend Vanessa, since Sophie was out that evening for a university event. He was curious and slightly apprehensive, wondering what this new acquaintance would be like. Lilith had been mysterious about the details, simply insisting it was important that he meet her.

As Zach turned onto Lombard Street, famously dubbed "the crookedest street in the world," he marveled at the skill required to navigate its tight, serpentine curves. The street was lined with manicured flower beds fronting elegant homes.

He pulled up in front of a cream-colored, 1910 Spanish Colonial Revival home. The stately house, with its stucco facade and red-tiled roof, complemented the architectural heritage of Russian Hill. The arched windows and wrought-iron balconies added a touch of Old-World charm, and the well-kept property hinted at the pride its owners took in maintaining its beauty.

Zach stepped out of his car and took a moment to appreciate his surroundings. The air was crisp and carried the faint scent of sea salt from the nearby bay. The streets were relatively quiet, save for the distant hum of city life and the occasional sound of a cable car clattering along its tracks. This part of Russian Hill felt like a tranquil oasis amid the vibrant metropolis.

As he climbed the front stairs slowly, one foot at a time, leaning on his cane, the grand house seemed to promise an evening of intrigue and potential new beginnings. Lilith had been adamant that he'd like Vanessa, though she'd offered no further explanation.

He rang the doorbell and turned to catch sight of the expansive view behind him. From this vantage point, the city spread out like a colorful tapestry in the fading light. Then the door swung open, and Lilith greeted him with a warm smile. "Welcome to Villa Vanessa," she said, her eyes sparkling with excitement. Looking down at his cane with concern, she asked: "What happened to you?"

"I had a minor disagreement with a parachute; it didn't open when I wanted it to," Zach replied.

"When did this happen?" Lilith asked next, now looking positively shocked.

"In September. I was skydiving in Napa and fractured my pelvis and right ankle. It's fine; I'll be right as rain in another couple of months. Hello, I'm Zach," he said, looking past Lilith to her friend, who was hovering behind her.

Vanessa was about their age, and *very* attractive. At five feet seven inches, she was a few inches shorter than Zach, with brown eyes and shoulder-length brown hair. She was dressed in a bright silk blouse with black pants. He felt an immediate allure that he had not felt in a long time.

After the customary introductions, they led him through the hallway to the living room, where the two ladies settled Zach into one of the opposing couches in front of the fireplace. It's remarkable what a cane can do if you want to be fussed over. Zach was basking in the attention he was receiving.

Lilith poured Zach a double Dalwhinnie 12 on ice from a dozen excellent Scotches sitting on the silver drinks trolley. She stayed with the red wine that she was nursing while Vanessa, returning from the kitchen, also poured herself a Dalwhinnie and sat on the opposing couch. With Lilith sitting on the hearth to his left and Vanessa in front of him, he was surrounded.

Looking around, the interior of the home was just as impressive as the exterior, with its high ceilings, expensive furniture, and comfortable atmosphere. Zach was taking in the various Impressionist paintings, which included an original Degas and Manet, before Lilith brought him back.

"Zach, why don't you tell Vanessa a bit about yourself, starting with the skydiving," Lilith suggested.

"As Lilith may have already told you, I'm a sommelier. When I have a mischievous smile, it generally means I'm the most dangerous person in the room – especially if you're sober. My wife calls me 'The Flying Sommelier' because I skydive in Napa every chance I get, which is about once a month. Don't let the cane fool you; I'm really all right.

"Anyway, I did my undergraduate in history at UCLA in the late eighties, then studied enology at UC Davis. After that, I worked at some liquor stores, eventually landing at Stanley's Fine Wines in Santa Monica for four years where I was able to hone my skills and cultivate my palate. I then moved onto a winery in Napa where I was in charge of marketing. About fifteen years ago, I decided to strike out on my own and start my own consulting business. Oh, and I am a past President of the American Institute of Sommeliers."

"Which winery?" Vanessa asked.

"San Pancho, in Napa."

"I don't know it well," Vanessa replied, "but I have tasted some of their wines over the years."

"I haven't been marketing their wines since I left. Perhaps if I had, you would know them better," Zach said with a mischievous smile.

"What do you do in your wine consulting business?"

"A variety of things. I create and value wine collections for clients, cater wine-paired dinners, curate wines for a few restaurants. Help wineries market their wines. I also lecture on wine at City College. Basically, if it involves wine, I do it."

"Would you be interested in valuing my wine cellar?" Vanessa asked.

"I'd be delighted."

"But first," said Vanessa, "let's have some hors d'oeuvres." She went to the kitchen and returned minutes later with plates of three French cheeses, crackers, and seared foie gras with a citrus purée. Finding himself in such luxurious surroundings with such delicious food, Zach realized that Vanessa was something special.

"This is exquisite," he said as he ate some of the foie gras. "What's the purée made of?"

"It's fresh grapefruit, chardonnay and rosemary."

"Incredible."

During the next hour, Zach and Vanessa did most of the talking as they got to know each other. He found out she'd grown up in San Francisco and after high school joined Bank of America as a teller. She rose in the ranks to become a branch manager, married, left the bank, had two children and divorced at age thirty-six.

As they told each other their life stories, Vanessa revealed that she was currently going through a messy divorce with Edward, her common-law husband of twenty years, who'd moved out a year earlier.

"He's a successful businessman who sees no reason to part with half of his wealth. To him, it's simply bad business. As a result, my lawyer told me I need to value our fairly extensive wine collection for community property purposes since it's probably worth *mucho dinero*. Shall we go see it now?"

Vanessa led them downstairs to the wine cellar. It was fairly typical for a house like this: twenty by twenty feet, temperature-controlled, with high-end hardwood wine racks attached to three of the walls and a table and chairs in the middle for tastings. On the table were two crystal decanters, corkscrews and other accoutrements. Open wooden cases sat on the floor. Stacked against the empty wall were about thirty cardboard boxes of wine with handwritten labels identifying their contents.

As he looked around, Zach guessed there had to be six thousand bottles in all. He noticed the names on the boxes: Pétrus 1946, Musigny 1998, Mouton Rothschild 1945, Chambertin 2002, Romanée-Conti 1961, Cheval Blanc 1947, Montrachet 1991... If this trend continued, Vanessa's collection could be worth millions.

Feeling like a kid in a candy store, he moved over to the nearest rack and started examining bottles. The first thing he saw was the wines there appeared to be less rare than those in the boxes, but who's to say how people organize their cellars? He looked back at Vanessa.

"I see you've noticed that the bottles on the racks are not as special as the ones in the boxes. Edward allowed me free run of the cellar on the strict condition that only he was allowed to touch the boxes on this wall, which he regularly trades with his friends. The few I was ever allowed to taste were superb. Such a pity," sighed Vanessa, rolling her eyes to everyone's delight.

"*Quel dommage*," said Zach with a wide smile. "I can certainly value this cellar. Why don't I come back next week and start work? We can deal with the terms of my engagement then." They returned to the living room, where they talked some more about wine and art, and eventually about Vanessa's marriage and impending divorce.

"December before last, Edward had left me alone at our house in Lake Tahoe to return early to the city for business meetings. The next day he called me and told me to get out of the house, that we were finished, and to return here. When I got back, he'd moved into a rental house in Pacific Heights.

"He's been trying to talk me into selling this place and moving into an apartment. He wants to give me three million dollars to go away. My friends convinced me to hire an attorney, who told me to stay put. When I told him, he started yelling at me. I thought he might become violent. Eventually, the storm passed and he left, saying I was making a big mistake involving a lawyer, and that we should work it out ourselves."

"That's quite the story," Zach said. "Are you worried?"

"He can be very pushy when he wants something. He's been known to threaten people when he doesn't get his way. In the twenty years we've been together, I've always gone along and never crossed him. He's not used to my standing up to him. I think he believed that I'd go quietly like the good little wifey I've always been."

Looking at his watch and realizing the hour, Zach

bade them a hasty good night, and went home at eight thirty to a smoldering Sophie who was keeping their dinner waiting.

"Where have you been?" she asked pointedly. "You're late. Dinner's probably ruined."

"Hello dear. It's so nice to see you too after a long day. Lilith just introduced me to a new client, who hired me to appraise her extensive wine collection."

"Fine. Sit down, and let me see if I can rescue dinner," she replied a bit more calmly. "What's her name and why does she want her wine collection valued?"

Instead of sitting at the table, Zach went over to the wine cooler, which stood in a corner of the kitchen, and chose a nicely aged red. "Vanessa Cole. She lives on Lombard and is getting a divorce. Her lawyer wants the wine appraised as community property. As you know, under California law, she's entitled to half of just about everything in their estate, including the wine. At any rate, I have to spend some time in her cellar, cataloging her six thousand bottles."

"Wow, that's a lot of wine. How much is it worth?"

"You'll be the second person to know once I do the research and establish the values."

"Well, be careful. You know what Lilith's friends are like," she said as she served their dinner of reheated leftovers, which were overcooked as predicted. They ate silently with their eyes glued to their cell phones, which had become their habit ever since the kids had moved out.

Pacific Heights – January 8, 2023

Edward was making a sandwich while ads played during the PGA Sentry Tournament of Champions in Maui. The spacious kitchen was quite good for a rental home, with its stainless-steel appliances and marble island. Dark cabinets contrasted with the light marble countertops and expansive windows made it bright.

A year ago, Edward had told Vanessa he was done, and rented this house on Vallejo Street in Pacific Heights. A careful planner, Edward had found this place as soon as he realized it was time to move on. As it came fully furnished, he only needed his toothbrush and some clothes to move in. Anything else could be picked up from Vanessa as he needed it.

Built in 1905, the house was a three-story, gray brick building measuring a modest three thousand square feet. Despite its age, it had been well-maintained. The exterior, with its ornate cornices and large bay windows, hinted at its historical roots, while the interior seamlessly blended the old with the new. The one drawback was the walls and ceilings were all painted white. Thankfully, the wooden floors and tasteful furnishings countered the bland whiteness.

The living room was a functional arrangement, with a plush gray sofa, two wing chairs, a glass coffee table, and an impressively large flat-screen television mounted on the wall, which was ideal for watching sports. Large windows offered a magnificent view of the Golden Gate Bridge, its red towers framed perfectly against the backdrop of the shimmering bay waters.

Edward often found himself standing by the

floor-to-ceiling windows in the living room, a glass of wine in hand, gazing out at the bridge. The view never failed to soothe him, the vast expanse of the bay and the majestic bridge reminding him of the possibilities of his new life. All in all, for a furnished, short-term rental on short notice, he could have done worse.

Edward's sanctuary was the master bedroom, with its king-sized bed and high, tufted headboard. A large bay window, set in an alcove, looked out to the front yard and Vallejo Street beyond. From there he had a clear view of any visitors who might happen to drop by at an inconvenient time. He valued his privacy and didn't like to be interrupted.

An experienced businessman, Edward knew how to cut a deal and was attempting to negotiate a divorce settlement directly with Vanessa. At first, he'd convinced her that they should avoid using lawyers, expecting her to fall into line since they'd never actually married. She'd brought nothing much of monetary value when they started living together twenty years ago. His plan was to pay her a lump sum settlement of three million dollars. If he were feeling generous, he might throw in spousal support. He'd keep his business and investments and list their two houses for sale. Then she went behind his back and hired a divorce attorney, who was planting dangerous ideas in her head. Idiot lawyers. They were only money down the drain. Vanessa and her lawyer would soon learn why people did not cross Edward Pavlov.

Just as he was about to take his first bite of the ham and Swiss cheese on rye, the doorbell chimed. He crossed into the foyer and opened the front door. Before him stood two intimidating men the size of refrigerators. They were in their thirties, dressed in windbreakers, jeans and sneakers. Both sported gold chains around their necks and right wrists, and tattoos that peeked up from the tops of their T-shirts. Their appearance screamed trouble.

"Mr. Pavlov?" the fridge on the left asked politely.

"Yes," replied Edward. "What can I do for you?"

"We are here on a delicate matter on behalf of Angelo Salvatore."

"I'm sorry, but I don't think I know anyone by that name."

"You may not know him, but he knows you. Do you know a Mr. Hugh Albright?" giant number one continued, still politely. The second giant had yet to speak; he just stood and stared straight through Edward, making him feel decidedly unsettled.

"Of course I know Hugh; he's a member of my club and a respected banker in the city."

"It seems our Mr. Salvatore paid your Mr. Albright $460,000 for six bottles of wine that have not been delivered. When we visited Mr. Albright to collect the wine, he referred us to you. He said you have it."

"Did Mr. Albright happen to mention what the bottles were?" Edward asked next nervously. He knew where this was going. Damn Hugh anyway!

"Actually, I have a handwritten list here," he said, producing a small note from his right jacket pocket. "It says: 'Pétrus 46, Romanée-Conti 61, Montrachet 91, Mouton 45, Cheval Blanc 47 and Chambertin 02' Do you recognize them?"

"May I see that?" Edward fought to keep his hand from shaking as he took the list and read it carefully, playing for time. He hardly saw the words as his mind raced through the possible outcomes of this meeting. "When did he pay Mr. Albright?"

"Let's see; less than a month ago, I think."

"I don't know your client, but I do know Hugh. He's an upstanding person who will keep his promise if he made it. I'm going to have to call him to verify this transaction and see what involvement, if any, I have. You can appreciate this is the first I've heard of it."

"*No problema*. Why don't you see if you can reach him now?"

"I'll try, but it's Sunday and he's a banker, so I doubt he'll pick up." Edward took out his cell phone and dialed Hugh's number. It rang six times without an answer. "As I thought, he's not answering. Why don't I contact him tomorrow and then get back to you?"

"That won't be necessary, Mr. Pavlov. We'll be in touch, but don't take too long. Mr. Salvatore can become extremely irritable when things drag on. Enjoy the rest of your Sunday."

"What did you say your names were again?" Edward asked.

"We didn't. I'm Mr. Smith, and this is Mr. Brown." The two bruisers then abruptly turned and walked back to their silver Ram 1500 pickup truck. As Edward watched them go from the open door, he worried about how he was going to extricate himself from this situation in one piece.

Across the street was a nondescript gray Ford sedan with two FBI agents dressed in brown suits. They'd recorded the exchange between Edward and his new friends using a camera and a parabolic microphone.

"What do you make of that?" asked Special Agent Terence Morgan.

"It looks like we should either warn the gentleman of the house or open a new file," replied his partner, Special Agent Carlos Garcia.

"Our investigation is only Angelo Salvatore. After the boss reads the transcript, he can decide if he wants to run it up the flagpole." With that, they drove off without warning Edward about the very real danger he was in.

Meanwhile, Edward returned to the golf game but couldn't concentrate. Eventually he gave up and poured himself a Scotch to steady his nerves. They weren't about to accept his explanation that Hugh hadn't placed an order. More likely they'd keep pushing until they either had the wine or their money back, or maybe both. Great.

For the rest of the afternoon, Edward toyed with the idea of driving over to Hugh's house and confronting him then and there but decided against it. Better to approach this situation calmly and methodically, and fast, before it became a bloody disaster. After all, he had the listed wines in his cellar at the house. "*No problema*" the giant on the left had said. He could learn to hate those two words.

That evening was spent with a new female friend who provided Edward with a welcome distraction and allowed his nerves to settle down. After a superb dinner and several drinks, they retired to her apartment for a nightcap. He barely navigated his way home at one o'clock in the morning, relieved the day had ended on a high note. He reminded himself that he had adapted well to the single life. Edward Pavlov was back.

At nine o'clock Monday morning, he called Hugh on his cell phone. "Hugh? Edward. Listen, I received a visit yesterday from two unsavory characters looking for six bottles of wine they say you sold to an Angelo Salvatore. Do you know anything about this, by any chance?"

"Oh, that," Hugh replied with his characteristic aplomb. "I meant to call you about it but was distracted by this and that, and it must have slipped my mind."

"The two men representing this Salvatore fellow say he paid you $460,000 for this wine, but you haven't delivered it. They even gave me a list of the six bottles." Edward recited the names of the wines, so there was no doubt in Hugh's mind.

"Yes, that sounds right. I'm sure that's right. Can I buy them from you for, say, $400,000? Old Hugh has to make a living too, you know."

"Fine. I'll do it to help you out," replied Edward sternly. "Next time talk to me first. These are not the kind of people you want to deal with. What if I couldn't get all of these wines which, as you know, are rare and hard to find?"

"My sincere apologies, and thank you. You are too good to me. Shall I pick them up or will you handle the delivery?"

God, Hugh made it all sound so legitimate. Did he know who he was dealing with? "They're going to call me back. The wine is at the house, so I'll have to go get it. It'll need to wait until later in the week when I can arrange a meeting with Vanessa. Leave it with me."

"Not a problem, not a problem at all. One more thing. Once we settle up with Mr. Salvatore, I think he will be a steady customer. Will you be able to supply him with more of your exceptional wine?"

"Honestly, Hugh, I'd rather not think about that right now. Let me handle the situation at hand, then maybe we'll consider future dealings."

"Very good, old buck. I'll wait for your call... What do you want me to do with your payment?" Hugh said.

"That's another thing. Aren't you the least bit concerned about where the money came from? It's Angelo Salvatore we're talking about."

"In my line of work, we worry about that all the time. Don't worry, we'll be fine. Now, about your payment..."

"I just hope you know what you're doing," he said, giving up. "Credit my account for now while I sort this mess out."

Villa Vanessa – January 9, 2023

After an hour of physiotherapy, Zach arrived at Vanessa's house at twelve thirty, the afternoon sun casting a gentle glow over her magnificent home. She opened the door almost immediately, her warm smile inviting him in as if he were an old friend rather than a visitor.

"Well hello, Zach," she said, her voice an intriguing melody that instantly eased the lingering aches from his therapy session. Her brown hair was done up in a loose style that framed her face beautifully, highlighting her striking features. As she stepped aside to let him in, he caught a whiff of her perfume, a delicate blend of floral and citrus notes that was... what would he call it? Provocative. Yes, definitely provocative.

The soft rustle of her movement drew his eyes to her outfit. She wore a Ralph Lauren blue-striped Oxford shirt, which clung to her form in all the right places. Its unbuttoned top hinted at a daring playfulness. Her jeans hugged her hips and legs, emphasizing her figure, and she stood barefoot, giving the overall effect an air of relaxed confidence.

"Before we get you started," Vanessa said, "I thought we should have some lunch. Do you like chicken Kiev?"

"It's one of my favorites. How unexpected, and how nice of you to do this," he replied, following her into the kitchen, which was a harmonious blend of modern appliances and vintage charm. White cabinets contrasted with dark countertops, and a vase of fresh flowers added a splash of color to the room. Vanessa moved with an easy grace, her every action exuding a calm efficiency.

"While I finish the preparations, why don't you find us a suitable bottle of white wine in the fridge? I think I have four or five bottles that will do." Zach followed Vanessa to the Sub-Zero refrigerator and examined the choices: Greywacke Sauvignon Blanc 2022, Beringer Private Reserve Chardonnay 2019, Roserock Drouhin Oregon Chardonnay 2020, and a Jean-Marc Brocard Chablis Premier Cru 2020.

"You have a well-stocked fridge. Mind if I serve the Beringer? It's the oldest, it's ready to drink, and its rich, creamy body I think will go perfectly with the chicken," Zach said, still looking in the fridge, his back turned to Vanessa who was busy assembling the chicken, salad vinaigrette and a baguette.

"Whatever you want... you're the sommelier," she replied, concentrating on preparing the food.

"That said, I'll tell you the sommelier's greatest secret: half the time, we're just praying we opened the right bottle."

She laughed, then told him where to find the wine glasses. Together they carried the dishes onto the terrace, which offered a commanding view of the city and the bay to the north. When they were settled and the wine poured, she paused, and braced herself for a serious discussion.

"I'm worried Edward might do me harm," Vanessa said, trembling slightly. "I have no idea really, but he can be dangerous. Right now, he hates me because I hired a lawyer. He's capable of anything. I'm worried something's brewing, but I don't know what."

Zach reluctantly interrupted the delicious meal and sumptuous wine. "You should consider putting this down in a letter and give it to one of your friends and your lawyer, to be opened if something happens to you."

All right. I'll think about that."

"You mentioned it before, but I don't remember: where did you say he's living now?"

"He rented a house on Vallejo Street in Pacific Heights while we sort out our lives. He visits from time to time to pick up things he needs and deal with the wine, but lately he can't look me in the eye. I think it's finally registering that I'm not going to let him walk all over me. As I mentioned before, he thought I'd agree to take three million dollars and just go away. Now he's realizing that I'm entitled to fifty percent of pretty much everything, which is twenty million or more. When I say that, I'm assuming the wine collection is worth a few million."

"How long were you married?"

"We were never married; we lived together for twenty years," Vanessa replied. "We both have grown children from previous marriages and didn't see the point. We were good for a long time, but two years ago he started distancing himself from me. We started having stupid arguments all the time. Then one day, out of the blue, he told me he was leaving."

"It happens. Enough time passes, you take each other for granted, and contempt sets in. I'm so sorry."

"Don't be. Now I've met you, we're having a delightful lunch together, you're going to help me value the wine collection, and eventually, this nightmare will be behind me. What do you think of this wine?"

"Of course, I'm familiar with Beringer. Did you know it's Napa's longest operating winery? After one hundred and fifty years, they know what they're doing. It's rich, creamy and luscious, and the floral and peach aromas immediately draw you into the flavors of honey, pineapple and vanilla. A perfect complement to your exquisite cuisine. A fellow could get used to this."

"Well, I look forward to your company as you slave away in my wine cellar." As they clinked glasses, their eyes were locked in something both curious and undefined.

After lunch, Zach adjourned to the wine cellar with his iPad to record the collection, which consumed the rest of the afternoon. 5,932 bottles is a lot of wine, and with 219 different labels to research and value, he had his work cut out for him.

He was particularly intrigued with the 408 bottles of extremely rare wine in the thirty-four boxes against the wall. During his inspection, he examined a sampling of their labels, all of which looked genuine. Many were damaged, as one would expect after so many years. Still, how had Edward managed to acquire that many rare bottles? That would have required years of concentrated effort, not to mention the dollars involved. He supposed anything was possible, and he had not been hired to authenticate the wine, only to value it. When he emerged four hours later, Vanessa was lounging in the living room, reading.

"How'd it go?" she asked, putting down her book.

"I was able to catalog all the information into my spreadsheet. Next comes the research."

"Where do you find out how much a wine is worth?"

"There are various sources on the internet, some free and some I subscribe to, such as auction houses. The farther back the wine goes, the less reliable the information is, but I can triangulate the prices to come up with a value. You have some fairly old vintages down there that are worth a lot. I will pay particular attention to them as I expect the boxes against the wall will be worth more than the rest of the cellar."

"I can't tell you what a relief it is to have you helping me with this," Vanessa said, not getting up from the couch. "The stress of dealing with this divorce makes me feel so alone." She crossed her arms, looking as though she felt cold.

"I can imagine," replied Zach sympathetically. "Give me a couple of days to assemble a preliminary analysis, and I'll call you to schedule our next meeting." Looking down at Vanessa stretched out on her couch, he was trying hard to keep things on a professional level, sensing that he was being drawn into something he was afraid he might get used to and like too much. Which would not be the worst thing, would it? Then he reminded himself she was another one of Lilith's friends. What could possibly go wrong given his track record with Lilith and her friends...?

"That would be lovely," she said as she rose to her feet. "Is there anything I can get you before you leave?"

"No, thanks, I'd better get back. By the way, I noticed you have a number of bottles that are twenty to thirty years old, but they're not wines that are meant to be kept that long. You should drink them soon. I'll identify which ones and set them aside for you."

They walked to the door, where they hugged a bit longer than his wife would consider appropriate. That's when Zach realized how much he valued her presence, her kindness, and her ability to make him feel at home.

"Lunch was simply marvelous; thank you. I'll call you soon," he said as he exited.

"I look forward to it," Vanessa replied, and she meant it.

Edward's House – January 13, 2023

"Hello, Vanessa, how are you today?" Edward asked in his nicest, kindest voice.

"Hello, Edward," Vanessa answered flatly. "What can I possibly do for you?"

"I need to come over this weekend and pick up some of my rare wine. You haven't touched it, have you?"

"Of course not. You make that very clear every time I see you or talk to you. How could I forget?"

"Very good. What day would suit you?"

"Actually, never," Vanessa replied evenly.

"I beg your pardon? What does 'never' mean?"

"It means that my lawyer has advised me not to release or dispose of any community property until the divorce is finished. That includes the wine." Vanessa could hear Edward starting to breathe heavily, which he commonly did when he was stressed, and felt her lip curl into a slight smile.

"But... but..." he sputtered in frustration, "you can't be serious. I knew this was going to happen. I told you not to hire a lawyer, that we could settle this between ourselves. What on Earth were you thinking? Now look what you've done."

Vanessa decided to remain silent for a while to see what was coming next. She didn't understand what the big deal was with the wine. Maybe he was going through withdrawal.

"Are you still there?" Edward said after a few seconds. She could hear him take a puff from his inhaler.

"I'm right here."

"What do you propose we do about it?" he asked,

his voice on edge. He was defaulting to his more condescending self that occurred when he didn't get his way. Being a bully had worked for him throughout his life in his business dealings and was his default strategy with Vanessa.

"I don't propose anything, Edward. You left me high and dry, then tried to maneuver me into an unfair settlement. I agree that lawyers shouldn't be necessary, but in this case, you left me no choice. It is what it is."

"That's not true. I'm giving you eight thousand a month to live on until this thing is finished."

"That doesn't even cover the expenses of running this house. Look, if you want to speed up the process, tell your lawyer to agree to my lawyer's demands and start giving me more each month."

"Dream on, Lady!" Edward yelled into his cell phone before disconnecting. He was now pacing in his living room, wheezing, and his face was beet-red. If he were a cartoon character, smoke would be coming out of his ears.

"What the hell am I going to do now?" he asked himself, keenly aware that he would soon be visited again by Messrs. Smith and Brown looking for Angelo Salvatore's wines.

At eight o'clock the following Sunday morning, Edward was awakened by the doorbell and looked out his bedroom window to see who'd interrupted his sleep. He spotted the Ram truck and inwardly groaned. The goons were back. He put on his dressing gown and hurried downstairs. With a deep breath, he opened the door to find them blocking the morning light.

"Gentlemen, how can I help you today?" Edward asked, standing in their shade.

"Mr. Salvatore would like his wine," Mr. Smith

said politely but firmly so as to leave no doubt where this would go if he didn't get it.

"Are either of you married?" Edward asked. The two hulks glanced at each other, unsure of how to answer. "No? Well, if you were, you'd understand my predicament. You see, my wife has the wine at our house over in Russian Hill."

"I don't see how that affects anything. Go and get it, bring it back here, and give it to us."

"That's just it. My wife and I are separated; she's got the wine, and her lawyer has frozen it until the divorce is settled. I can't get Mr. Salvatore's bottles until that blessed event happens. If Mr. Salvatore would be patient for a little while, I'm sure I can deliver his wine within the next few months."

"Mr. Salvatore is not going to be happy about this, not happy at all," Mr. Smith said, shaking his head slowly from side to side while looking into Edward's eyes. Mr. Brown, as usual, stared through him menacingly.

"Please tell him I'm a man of my word, and I promise to deliver his wine to him as soon as I can. His wine is safe; it's not going anywhere."

"Give me a minute while I call him." The two men stepped down the stairs, out of Edward's earshot while Mr. Smith made a call on his cell phone. After a minute, they came back up the stairs.

"Mr. Salvatore's very disappointed in you," Smith said sullenly, blocking the light again. "He says you can have the two months, but he wants an extra bottle per month for his trouble, starting this month. You can choose which one, as long as it's one of the six he ordered. We'll be back on January 31 to get the first bottle and check on your progress."

"Understood. Please tell him I won't let him

down," Edward said to their backs as they walked away. He got out his cell phone and dialed. "Jimmy? It's Ed. Listen, can I come over? Something's come up that needs our attention. No, it's not a problem. Now? Okay, I'll be right there."

Realizing he wasn't dressed, Edward ran up the stairs, threw on some casual clothes, and went back down to the garage. He drove south, then west, in his dark blue 1961 Mercedes 220 SE cabriolet, careful to obey the speed limit all the way. The last thing he needed at the moment was any undue police scrutiny. In his agitated state, he didn't notice the silver Ram 1500 pickup truck that was two car lengths behind him or the nondescript gray Ford sedan that was another car length behind them.

Eight minutes later, the convoy arrived at Jimmy's house. Edward pulled up in front, the silver truck parked at the end of the previous block with the gray sedan at the beginning of the same block on the opposite side of the street. That way, everyone could see what happened without being noticed.

Edward walked briskly up the path and rang the doorbell. Jimmy opened the door, looked up and down the street, and ushered him inside. Sitting in their cars, Smith and Brown were wondering how this new player fit into the picture, while the two FBI agents were totally confused, but had a growing suspicion that another case was brewing.

"So, what brings you here in such a rush?" asked Jimmy warily as they stood in the foyer. He could see that Edward was upset. He had beads of sweat on his forehead, and his appearance was noticeably unkempt.

"One of my clients, the banker, sold six bottles of our wine for $400,000 to Angelo Salvatore," replied

Edward. "Do you know about him?" Jimmy shook his head. "I looked him up. He's seventy-one and the head of one of the local crime families. He's known for getting what he wants when he wants it. Long story short, Vanessa has the wine in my cellar but won't let me have it until the divorce is done. I am hoping that you have or can get the six wines by the end of the month."

"I see. How long will it take to finalize the divorce?"

"Who knows? Months for sure, and he wants one more bottle for every month he waits."

"That means you need seven bottles, not six."

"Correct."

"What are the wines?" Jimmy asked, growing less impressed with each passing second.

"Château Mouton Rothschild 1945, Pétrus 1946, Cheval Blanc 1947, Romanée-Conti 1961, Montrachet 1991 and Chambertin 2002. Plus, a second one of any of them for the delay. Can you help me?"

"You're telling me that you want me to find these unicorn wines in two weeks?"

"Or at least the one penalty bottle to buy us time to either find the others, or I'm able to get them from my cellar."

"Why don't you give him his money back?"

"I haven't asked him yet, but I'm pretty sure he wants the wine," Edward said sheepishly, looking down at his feet.

"Do you have a key to the house? Can you go there when Vanessa is out and take the bottles?"

"She changed the locks," Edward replied, rolling his eyes, "and the security system will record me."

"Why don't you simply settle with her? That way you could get the wine by the end of the month."

"There's a lot of money riding on this. I can't just walk away from half of everything I've worked for. I need to keep the pressure on until she gives in."

"Okay, you go and let me see what I can do, but I wouldn't hold my breath if I were you."

Jimmy saw Edward to the door. As he watched him drive away in his vintage Mercedes, he noticed a silver Ram 1500 pickup truck, followed by a nondescript gray Ford sedan, drive in the same direction. "That's a lot of traffic for this time of day," he thought.

Of course, Jimmy had the ability to create the seven bottles in the next two weeks, but that might create awkward questions about provenance that he didn't want to answer. He looked at his watch, almost midnight in Hong Kong. He decided to call his older brother anyway.

"*Wái?*" Ronald's sleepy voice answered.

"Brother, it's Jimmy," he said. "I need an introduction to our associates in San Francisco. I have a job for them."

"What time is it, little brother?" Ronald groaned.

Meanwhile, Smith and Brown drove carefully through the streets of San Francisco to Little Italy, their faces tense with anxiety. Their destination loomed up ahead, the fortress-like mansion of their boss, Angelo Salvatore, patriarch of one of San Francisco's notorious crime families.

Salvatore's home was a testament to Old-World opulence, with its high stone walls crowned with wrought-iron spikes. The imposing gates, flanked by stone lion statues, slowly creaked open. As the truck rolled by the soldiers standing guard on the cobblestone driveway, the grandeur of the estate became more apparent, with its blend of Renaissance and Baroque styles, ornate balconies, arched windows and intricate carvings adorning the facade.

Inside the truck, Mr. Smith glanced at Mr. Brown, whose knuckles were white from gripping the steering wheel. Both men knew the gravity of their situation. They had again failed to secure the six bottles of rare wine that Angelo had ordered, and now they had to face their boss.

The interior of the mansion was as grand as its exterior, with gilded mirrors and crystal chandeliers reflecting dim light on mahogany walls. The air was oppressive with the scents of aged leather and fine cigars as Smith and Brown reluctantly climbed the carpeted stairs past another guard, to the second floor where they would find their grumpy boss.

Entering the study, they were greeted by Salvatore's cold gaze from behind his imposing desk, a relic of the past that bore the weight of countless secrets and decisions. His silver hair was slicked back, and his piercing eyes betrayed a lifetime of shrewdness and authority. The silence in the room was palpable, broken only by the faint ticking of an antique grandfather clock in the corner.

"So," Salvatore began, his voice a low growl that sent shivers down the men's spines. "You've come back empty-handed again."

Mr. Smith cleared his throat, trying to steady his nerves. "Mr. Salvatore, we..."

"Enough," he interrupted, raising a hand to silence him. "I don't want to hear any more excuses. Pavlov has given you the runaround twice now. Your incompetence is driving me to drink. Oh... that's right, which I could if only you'd bring me my wine!"

Smith shifted uncomfortably, his eyes darting

around. "We're trying, sir. He keeps promising he'll have the wine, but…"

"But he never delivers," Salvatore finished the sentence, his voice dripping with disdain. "Promises are nothing without results. You get that, don't you? What am I supposed to do with you two? Any ideas? No? I didn't think so."

Unbeknownst to them, two pairs of keen eyes were fixed on their every move. Across the street, Special Agents Morgan and Garcia sat in their car, a video camera and a parabolic microphone aimed at the window of the second-floor study. As they listened intently, the palpable tension in the study was loud and clear through their headphones.

Salvatore stood up, his tall frame casting a long shadow over his desk. "This is your last chance. Get those bottles, or else. Do I make myself clear?"

Smith and Brown nodded vigorously, their faces pale. "*Si, patron.* We won't let you down again."

"Good," Angelo said, his voice softer but no less menacing. "Now get out of my sight."

As the two men hurried out of the study, the FBI agents quickly packed up their equipment. They still didn't have enough to make a case, but were slowly making progress in bringing down Angelo Salvatore's vast and intricate empire.

Back inside the mansion, Angelo returned to his chair, plotting his next move. Failure was not an option in his world, and those who disappointed him rarely got a second chance.

Back at home, Zach was immersed in his review of Vanessa's wines, researching their values on the internet. His initial impression that there were two distinct collections was confirmed by his spreadsheet: the bottles on the racks averaged two hundred and fifty dollars, while those in the thirty-four boxes were worth thousands. He pushed that question to the back of his mind and continued his investigation.

He completed his valuation at nine in the morning on day four and called Vanessa to schedule their next meeting.

"Hello," said Vanessa over the phone.

"Hi, it's Zach. I've crunched the numbers and finished my report. When should I come over to present it to you?"

"I'm at home with no plans. How about now?"

Could there be a better answer? "Today I have a physio session at ten, but I could be there by noon."

"Great. See you then." Zach found himself humming as he got ready to go.

He arrived before twelve and was greeted by Vanessa, again wearing another casual outfit of an Oxford shirt and jeans, with her hair up and looking both seriously attractive and vulnerable. "Since it's cocktail time somewhere," she said as she ushered him in, "would you like Scotch or wine?"

"It's a little early for me. How about we go over my list first and then have a drink? I also brought this," replied Zach, handing her a bottle of 2019 San Pancho Tempranillo. "This is one of their best, and ready to drink, although it will be better next year if you can resist temptation."

"How nice... All right; let's sit at the dining room table where we can spread out the papers."

Zach opened his briefcase and took out two sets of the valuation, each detailing the wines by name, type, vintage, region, and dollar value. They sat kitty-corner from each other, with Vanessa at the head of the table and Zach to her right on the side. Vanessa put on her reading glasses as she started to study the list.

"I have divided them into two sections, first with the rare wines organized alphabetically, followed by the fine wines, also in alphabetical order. You'll see that my valuation is $11.7 million for the rare wines and $1.5 million for the other wines, for a total of $13.2 million."

Vanessa looked up and said, "That's incredible. I had no idea I was sitting on wine worth that much."

"Most of the value comes from the extremely rare bottles in the boxes. As I'm sure you know, wine appreciates with age and can be a very good investment when the right ones are chosen. Which, in this case, you did, or Edward did."

"Yes, he's the expert. He buys and sells it, runs the cellar, and chooses which wines for us to drink. He knows wine. I, on the other hand, like to drink it."

"I'm guessing you know what you like," Zach said.

"Of course I do, but I don't pay much attention to the labels, so I tend not to remember them. Edward always chose the wines that we served." Vanessa paused before continuing as if gathering her thoughts.

"He called me yesterday to come over and get some of those bottles, but I told him my lawyer said nothing is to be removed until the divorce is finalized. You can imagine how he reacted to that bit of news."

"I'm so sorry about what you're going through," Zach said sympathetically. He reached out and took her hand in his. "If there's anything I can do, just let me know."

"No, I don't think that's necessary. I just become a little paranoid sometimes. It's nice to have you here with me. It helps a lot. I just wish... oh, never mind," she replied, looking away with tears in her eyes.

They returned to their review of Zach's valuation for another twenty minutes, which required a lot of attention to detail and proved to be a thirsty business.

"Shall we revisit my offer of a cocktail now?" Vanessa asked, gently covering Zach's hand with both of hers. "I have a ripe camembert and crackers waiting to be appreciated."

"Absolutely. In that event, shall we have one of your reds? Not from the rare boxes, of course."

"All right. Why don't you choose one from the cellar while I organize the cheese and crackers?"

With that, she got up from the table and went into the kitchen, while he went down to the cellar and took his time with the wines on the racks. He eventually chose a 2014 Freemark Abbey Cabernet Sauvignon from Napa Valley that had caught his eye when he was doing his spreadsheet.

He returned, bottle in hand, to the sound of angry voices coming from the kitchen. Turning the corner, he saw Edward from behind yelling at Vanessa, his neck purple with rage.

"I swear, if you don't agree to my terms, you're going to regret it! Your lawyers can't protect you."

"What's that supposed to mean? Are you threatening me now?" Vanessa retorted as Zach put the bottle down.

When Edward raised his right hand, Zach closed the distance in three swift steps. He looped one arm around his neck and pulled him backward, locking his other arm in place to form a rear-naked chokehold. Edward flailed, but Zach held on tight.

"Relax, Edward," he said calmly in his ear, loosening the hold slightly as Edward's struggles waned. "I'm not here to hurt you, but you're going to listen now."

When Edward finally sagged, his shoulders slumping in surrender, Zach guided him to the front door with a firm hand on his shoulder, his voice calm. "You're done for today. Go home and cool off."

Edward cast a final glance over his shoulder, but Zach's unyielding gaze brooked no argument. As the door clicked shut behind him, Zach exhaled, running a hand through his hair.

He returned to the kitchen and embraced a visibly shaken Vanessa. "My hero. Thank you for that," she said, looking up with tears in her eyes.

"Lucky thing I know Brazilian Jiu-Jitsu. Never know when it'll come in handy," he joked, hoping to lighten the mood. Then he showed her the bottle of wine he'd chosen. "Is this okay? It's ready to drink." Vanessa nodded her assent as she dabbed her eyes.

"Where do you keep the corkscrew and wine glasses?" he asked. "Also, do you have a decanter, possibly an aerator?"

"The cupboard on the right has what you need."

Zach opened it to find an impressive array of crystal wine glasses of varying shapes and sizes. Unable to find his favorite – a Cabernet glass – he chose two oversized Burgundy balloons and proceeded with the ritual of cutting the lead, popping the cork, and pouring the wine gently into the decanter.

Acting in perfect harmony, they moved to the living room where they'd first talked with Lilith and continued to get to know each other better. It had been a while since Zach had discussed such wide-ranging topics with someone who truly listened to him.

With Sophie, he usually felt he had, at most, half her attention as she bounced between talking and texting on her phone. She was one of those people who listened by talking and interrupting. Vanessa, on the other hand, did the opposite. She didn't interrupt; she waited until Zach finished before speaking, and when she did, it was to say something on point, to advance the discussion along its natural path. When Zach couldn't wait to make a point and interrupted her, she stopped talking and looked at him, interested in what he had to say. He did the same for her. It reminded him of his university days. He found it refreshing and endearing.

During the next three months, their relationship developed into a deep and mutually supportive friendship. They texted each other daily, sharing their thoughts and experiences. When they did not have anything in particular to discuss, they talked about the weather. No topic was too trivial. They enjoyed the connection. Their text messages became a lifeline for him, a space where they could share daily events and profound reflections alike.

They also talked on the phone and saw each other at Villa Vanessa a few times a week. Zach managed to extend the appraisal process over five weeks and many lunch and afternoon visits. Soon, Vanessa introduced him to her friends, who seemed pleased that Zach was helping to support her with Edward.

One evening, Vanessa threw a magnificent dinner party which was attended by Zach, Sophie and three of her close friends. Zach was instrumental in choosing the wines from Vanessa's cellar to accompany her delicious cuisine and the lively conversation.

"God, that friend of Vanessa's talked my ear off about shopping and decorating," Sophie said when they were driving home. "She's in the middle of getting a divorce and moving to a smaller place. Her attitude was so, how do I say this, *frivole*."

"That was Nicole. I thought she was quite nice," Zach replied casually, but he was really thinking about Vanessa. Thanks to Nicole distracting his wife, he had been able to concentrate on Vanessa the entire evening. He and Sophie hadn't talked from the time they arrived until they left.

As time went by, Vanessa kept Zach up to date about Edward and her upcoming divorce. The lawyers and accountants were busy calculating which assets should be included as community property. Predictably, Edward was trying to exclude the bulk of his assets from the calculation. It was proving to be a long, drawn-out exercise perfected by divorce lawyers. It also kept Vanessa in limbo, unable to get on with her life, as she worried about what Edward might do if things didn't go his way. From Zach's limited exposure to him, he was a three-hundred-pound bully capable of anything.

Zach taught Vanessa about wine, talked about France and his family, and philosophized about life. A recurring theme was how his marriage to Sophie had cooled. Vanessa was sympathetic and supportive, which helped Zach a lot. He was beginning to feel alive again.

Their discussions often ventured into deeply personal territory. Vanessa confided in Zach about her anxieties, aspirations, and the feeling of being trapped in a protracted battle with Edward. Zach, in turn, shared his frustrations and feelings of isolation in his marriage with Sophie. These heartfelt exchanges solidified their bond, transforming it from mere friendship into a vital source of emotional support for him.

Zach believed he was helping Vanessa as she navigated her painful separation from Edward, which was clearly taking a toll on her. He didn't realize the degree to which he'd also come to depend on her, especially for their almost daily chats. Something he lacked at home. He hadn't realized until now how much he missed it.

When Sophie made her annual trip to Paris during spring break to see her parents, Zach used the two weeks to spend time with Vanessa. They'd usually meet at her house for lunch or dinner. Sometimes they would go out to Ernie's Bistro, which was their favorite, and where they could be alone and unseen. It all started on March 25th with a text from Vanessa.

"Nightcap?" It was nine o'clock, and Zach was on the way home after dropping Sophie off at the airport.

"Sure," Zach texted back. "Be there in 15."

"See you then."

Vanessa led Zach into the living room where the gas fire flickered, the lights were dimmed, and soft jazz was playing. They hugged each other tightly for what seemed like forever.

"Scotch?" Vanessa asked as they disengaged to Zach's affirmative answer.

She crossed the floor to the trolley and poured two Dalwhinnie Scotches with ice, then joined him on one of the loveseats.

"What did Lilith tell you about me?" Zach asked.

"Only that she thought you were quite lonely."

"She sees people pretty clearly. Both of us."

"I guess. What are we going to do about it?"

"I think this is the beginning of a beautiful friendship," Zach replied, holding up his Scotch.

Two hours of intimate conversation followed as they continued to get to know each other, which others might have mistaken for lovemaking. One of them did, as it turned out.

Eventually, Zach announced it was time for him to leave, and as they got up, Vanessa looked concerned.

"I may have poured you too much Scotch," she said. "Are you sure you're okay to drive?"

"I'll be fine. I know my way home by heart," he joked. She looked skeptical but deferred to his judgment, although it was clearly unreliable. If she was trying to get him to spend the night, it went right over his head.

After another lingering hug at the door, Vanessa looked at Zach closely and asked, "Do you think you would ever leave Sophie?"

"What we have here is so wonderful; why spoil it?" he replied, then noticed her reaction.

"I guess. Anyway, safe travels."

Zach returned to his empty house and poured himself another Scotch. Had he disappointed Vanessa? Sensing there was unfinished business between them, he picked up the phone. They talked for another hour, although the next day he had difficulty remembering exactly what they'd discussed.

Edward's House – January 31, 2023

Edward watched from his bedroom window as the silver Ram truck pulled up and stopped at the curb. As the two giants lumbered up the walkway, he braced himself for this next encounter. It was eight o'clock Tuesday morning, the day he was supposed to hand over the penalty bottle of wine to Salvatore's heavies. He didn't have it yet. Jimmy had told him to stall for a week.

He went downstairs and opened the front door to be greeted by two scowling faces. The harsh morning light clashed with the somber presence of the two men, who filled every corner of the foyer with menace.

"Mr. Pavlov, how are you on this fine, sunny day?" the one called Mr. Smith asked sarcastically, while Mr. Brown's cold eyes lingered on Edward, silently daring him to defy them again.

"The day has hardly started, but I'm fine, I suppose," he replied, avoiding eye contact, which of course they noticed right away.

"I sincerely hope you have a bottle of wine for us. Mr. Salvatore expects people to keep their promises."

"I'm afraid I haven't been able to locate it yet, but I'm assured I'll have it by the end of the week. If I could have until, say, Sunday…"

"Mr. Salvatore will need more than that," Smith said, his eyes narrowing. "What wine, and where did you find it?"

"My partner Jimmy found more wine in Asia, but it won't be delivered to him until later this week."

"Would that be James Jin-Hie Wong, who lives on Commonwealth Avenue?"

"Yes, yes, that's him. How did you know that?"

"We know a lot, Mr. Pavlov. Don't we Mr. Brown?" Mr. Brown just grunted. "Mr. Salvatore anticipated that you might welch on your debt again, so he instructed us to give you this choice: we can either break one of your fingers or on Sunday, you give us two bottles for our trouble in having to come back here again. How much is your finger worth, Mr. Pavlov?"

"It's definitely worth more to me than the wine. What about this? Would Mr. Salvatore be willing to accept his money back instead and call it a day?"

"That's not how this works. He expects everyone he deals with to make good on their promises. You understand that, don't you Mr. Pavlov?"

"Okay," Edward sighed. "Come here next Sunday before noon, and I'll have the two bottles for you, and hopefully the other six bottles too, for a total of eight."

"Nine."

"Nine?"

"You forget. The deal is that you give Mr. Salvatore one bottle for every month or portion thereof that you are late. Since next Sunday will be February 5, you will owe an extra bottle for February. That's a total of nine bottles."

"Gentlemen, be reasonable. These wines are worth fifty thousand dollars apiece!" Edward pleaded.

"We are being reasonable, Mr. Pavlov. We haven't broken anything yet, have we? See you next Sunday. Oh, and Mr. Pavlov, make sure you have at least two of the bottles then."

Walking back to their truck, Mr. Smith said, "Do you think we should pay Jimmy Wong a visit, Mr. Brown?"

"Let's wait until Sunday, Mr. Smith. I believe we

now have his full attention." As they drove off, they didn't notice the nondescript gray Ford sedan that followed them.

Edward closed the front door, and was unable to stop himself from shaking. What would he do if Jimmy didn't come through by Sunday? He fished his cell phone from his pocket and called him.

"Hello Ed. A bit early to be calling, isn't it?"

"I just met with Salvatore's people again. They offered me a choice: break one of my fingers or give them a second bottle of wine on Sunday. This is going to spiral out of control unless we nip it in the bud now. I'm counting on you, Jimmy, I really am."

"Calm down, my friend," Jimmy replied. "I told you last week I've sourced more wine, but they won't be exactly the same bottles. Do you think they might be willing to take other wines of equal value instead?"

"Let's do this. Give me nine bottles of whatever you can find, and I'll see if I can talk them into it. Better make it ten bottles. I know how these guys think. Every change or delay requires more vig, as they call it."

"Fine. Call me on Friday."

The previous week, Jimmy had met with the Silver Serpent Triad at their headquarters in Chinatown, thanks to his brother Ronald. It was hidden behind an unassuming herbal medicine shop, the air inside thick with the scent of incense, sharp and heady, almost suffocating. Sitting across from Jimmy in intricately carved red rosewood chairs were the Triad's three leaders, each one more menacing than the next.

"It needs to be done cleanly," Jimmy said as he handed over an envelope stuffed with cash.

The main man's lips curled into a thin smile. "The Silver Serpent does not fail," he replied in a voice like cold steel as fingers, covered in tattoos of serpentine scales, took the envelope. Jimmy nodded, swallowing the lump in his throat.

In the early morning five days later, the streets of Russian Hill lay still, bathed in the soft glow of street lamps. Vanessa's grand Spanish Colonial home was wrapped in shadows as the Triad's thief glided like a ghost through the night. He was a small, wiry figure dressed in black, his face obscured by a sleek mask that left nothing visible but the cold glint of his eyes. He approached it from the back, avoiding the motion sensors and cameras.

He crouched by the basement door and held a portable hacking tool near where the alarm panel was on the other side of the wall, and watched as the tiny screen flickered to life. It began overriding the alarm system with a series of quick electronic blips. His fingers danced over the keypad, disarming the security while tricking the system into thinking everything was still fine. The lights on the alarm remained green. The house, once protected, was now vulnerable.

Silently, he picked the lock and pushed the door. It didn't budge, so he pushed harder. Finally, it gave way with a metallic screech against the concrete floor. The air inside the basement was musty, cool, and filled with the rich aroma of old wood and fine wines.

In the wine cellar, he used a small flashlight to locate the cardboard boxes that sat along the wall and picked up the one closest to him, without bothering to examine its contents.

Upstairs, in the stillness of her bedroom, Vanessa stirred. She'd always been a light sleeper, and tonight was no exception. A scraping sound, like a door being forced open, had broken the quiet. Frowning, she reached over, her hand shaking as she picked up the alarm screen on her bedside. It showed something she couldn't quite understand at first. Someone had disabled the alarm.

Her blood turned to ice as she sat up, her heart pounding against her ribs. She forced herself to glance at the screen again, praying it was a mistake. For a long, terrible moment, Vanessa couldn't move. She was frozen, paralyzed by terror. A thousand thoughts raced through her mind. Is it a burglar? Someone here to kill me? Is it Edward? No, he doesn't have the new alarm code.

Her breathing came fast and shallow, and she felt the cold sweat beading on her skin. She wanted to hide, but she couldn't make her limbs respond. She stayed in her bed, the covers clutched tight around her like a flimsy shield.

In the basement, the thief paused for a moment, listening. Silence. Then he turned and left the same way he'd entered, yanking the door shut.

Vanessa squeezed her eyes shut, wishing she could will herself to disappear. What was that? There it was again, the grating sound of a door being shut downstairs. Was the intruder leaving? On shaking legs, she crept over to her bedroom window and looked out to see a dark figure moving swiftly down the street. It looked like he was carrying something, but she couldn't see what it was. He didn't look back as he climbed into a black SUV. Within seconds, he was gone.

Vanessa let out a breath she didn't know she'd been holding. Her heart was still hammering as she stepped back from the window, trying to piece together what had just happened. Someone had broken in, but what had they taken?

The following Sunday morning, the silver Ram

truck arrived at eleven sharp. Edward was ready for them this time with a box containing nine bottles of 1946 Pétrus.

"Good morning, Mr. Pavlov," Smith said, his tone stern and devoid of goodwill. I hope, for your sake, that you have something for us this time."

"Good morning, gentlemen. Indeed, I do. Nine bottles of the finest wine that money can buy."

"That's just great," Smith replied, producing the list of the six wines. "Where's the merchandise?"

"Come into the foyer." As Brown closed the door, Edward showed Smith the box on the floor. He bent down and pulled out the bottles for inspection one by one, comparing them with his list. Edward could see he was having difficulty reconciling what he had with what he was supposed to have.

"I'm confused. These don't match the ones I've got here," Smith said, holding up the list in front of Edward's face.

"That's correct. Mr. Wong was unable to obtain the exact wines, so he substituted equivalent wine. We didn't want to keep Mr. Salvatore waiting any longer, and finding the exact wines he ordered could take months."

"Excuse us while we make a call." They stepped out of earshot and returned two minutes later. "He says, in the spirit of cordial business relations, he'll accept the substitution as long as you add another bottle as compensation."

"We'll agree to his terms. I just happen to have another Pétrus to add to the box," Edward said, retrieving it from the coat closet and handing it to Mr. Smith.

"Thank you, Mr. Pavlov. You're a gentleman. Mr.

Salvatore looks forward to doing business with you in future."

"That's not likely," Edward muttered as he closed the door on them, hopefully for good. Just then, his cell phone buzzed in his pocket.

"What the hell do you think you're doing, breaking in and stealing wine in the middle of the night?" Vanessa screamed into Edward's ear. "You scared me half to death!"

His mind raced: if those ten bottles came from his cellar, then Jimmy Wong was far more sinister than he'd realized.

Later that month, Zach had his annual five-course gourmet dinner paired with wine for his wine group. This year, it was held at La Toque Rouge, a French restaurant on Pier 39 at Fisherman's Wharf. A dozen people were in attendance, including Vanessa.

The restaurant's interior was white shiplap with huge picture windows overlooking the boats moored below. Rose-colored Murano sconces adorned the walls, giving the place a classy look. The setting sun bathed everything in a golden hue, creating an atmosphere that enhanced the occasion.

A long table for twelve people, covered in white linen, waited for them. Off to the side was a small table with the evening's wines, airing in decanters. Zach had brought them to the restaurant earlier in the day and supervised their decanting so they'd be ready to drink with dinner.

As Zach was drinking Champagne with his members, in walked Vanessa looking stunning in a cream-colored Tom Ford evening gown accented with an emerald necklace and matching earrings. Not to mention the intoxicating perfume she had on that seriously distracted Zach for a few beats. "The Vanessa Effect," he thought to himself as he got her a Champagne and introduced her to the others. He reminded himself that Sophie was nearby and not to be distracted or look too interested.

Also new to the group was Dr. Maurice El-Haddad, a friend of Sophie's who she invited to the dinner to even out the table of twelve. Accordingly, he was seated beside Vanessa, where they engaged in the lively conversation of two people who have just met and find they have much in common. Zach glanced at them a few times, feeling a bit... what?

Maurice was a single, seventy-two-year-old professor emeritus of Romance Languages at UC Berkeley who had a charming disposition and a roving eye. He led a comfortable lifestyle and lived alone in a modest condominium in Oakland. Originally from Algeria, he'd immigrated to America from France twenty years earlier, became a citizen and settled in the Bay area. He was very charming and attractive to the opposite sex, two attributes which he employed to full effect. Through the seemingly innocent banter, it didn't take long for him to learn about Vanessa's pending divorce settlement. She would soon be a wealthy woman, and he sensed that she was ready for a new relationship. He found her to be tantalizing and before the evening ended, was formulating a strategy.

From the head of the long table, Zach introduced the wines that he'd selected for the evening before each course. The first was more of the Champagne which they'd started drinking earlier, served with oysters on the half shell and a classic mignonette of shallots, vinegar, pepper and sugar.

"Welcome everyone. In the immortal words of the Greek philosopher and cynic Diogenes, 'What I like to drink most is wine that belongs to others.' He was an irascible, philosophizing beggar. One day, when he was sitting on the ground in the Athens marketplace, Alexander the Great came up to him. The most powerful man in the world. Blocking the sunlight, he offered to give him anything he desired. Diogenes simply rumbled in reply, 'Stand out of my light.' He didn't like Alexander, or Plato, or probably anyone, but he did like wine, his one redeeming feature. A toast, then, to Diogenes.

"First up tonight, we have the Taittinger non-vintage Brut Champagne, which is familiar to most of you. What you may not know is that it's a blend from thirty Chardonnay and Pinot Noir vineyards. Bright, fresh and dry, it has aromas and flavors of citrus and minerals. It's one of my go-to favorites. Please enjoy," Zach concluded, raising his glass again. Through events such as this, they'd become a close-knit group of friends, with the exception of newcomers Vanessa and Maurice.

The second course was a foie gras terrine served with garlic and basil toast points. For this course, Zach had chosen a 2018 Château de Beaucastel Châteauneuf-du-Pape, decanted for two hours. This was followed by an endive salad with goat cheese, oranges and almonds, paired with a 2020 Jean-Marc Brocard Chablis Grand Cru. Judging from the rising volume of the voices at the table, the dinner was progressing nicely.

The highlight of the evening was three Super Tuscan wines from Italy, paired with roasted rack of lamb with a Dijon and panko crust, seasonal vegetables and dauphine potatoes.

"For the main course, we have a special treat: a horizontal tasting of three renowned Super Tuscan wines. Before I describe the wines, let me tell you a little about how they got their name. Of course, they all come from Tuscany in Italy. The term Super Tuscan first appeared in the early 1980s, thanks to renowned Tuscan winemaker, Mario Incisa della Rocchetta. In 1945, he started blending Tuscan grapes, such as Sangiovese, with French grapes, like Cabernet Sauvignon. He did this because there'd been a shift to mass production and deterioration in quality. Chianti became cheap wine;

remember the bottles wrapped in straw with the candles in them? His creation was a revolutionary, bold style of wine that was unlike anything else produced in Tuscany. He called this wine Sassicaia, which was finally released in 1968. It was an immediate hit, and other winemakers in the region quickly followed suit.

"At the same time, Piero Antinori, Rocchetta's cousin, was also experimenting with blending Cabernet Sauvignon with Sangiovese, and in 1971 introduced Tignanello to the world. Then Ornellaia was created in 1985 by Piero's younger brother Lodovico. The rest, as they say, is history: blended Tuscan wines that rival the best of Bordeaux. For this reason, I hope La Toque Rouge will forgive me for serving Italian wine tonight.

"It was not all clear sailing for these new wines, however. Tuscany, which is the world's oldest regulated wine region since 1716, was not about to change its ways to include non-native grapes. Due to its strict DOC (Denominazione di Origine Controllata) regulations that required all the grapes to be local, in the beginning these wines were labeled with the lowly Vino da Tavola, or table wine, designation, despite their quality.

"What followed shows how slowly entrenched bureaucracy changes. In 1992, a compromise was struck whereby Super Tuscans could be labeled with a new, less modest denomination: IGT (Indicazione Geografica Tipica) – an entry level category. Eventually Sassicaia received its own DOC denomination from the Italian government in 2013, as printed on the label. Sometimes it pays to be first.

"We have those three wines here, all from 2014, decanted for two hours and ready to drink. I may have tasted them, but only a little! The Sassicaia is made from the Cabernet Sauvignon and Cabernet Franc grapes;

Tignanello from Sangiovese and Cabernet Sauvignon; and Ornellaia from Cab Sauv, Merlot, Petit Verdot and Cab Franc. They all have intense aromas, strong tannins and deep color. They're more complex and flavorful than Chianti, which is lighter and more acidic. I think you'll find them a nice complement to the next course.

"And remember, as a sommelier, my job is to convince you that spending $300 on fermented grape juice is the best decision you'll ever make."

Before dessert, Zach passed around his silver *tastevin* for inspection and gave a short lecture about its use going back to 1680, similar to the speech given to him and Sophie years before by the sommelier at Alonzo's Ristorante in Malibu. The difference was that, in the ensuing thirty years, the device had gone out of style and wasn't seen anymore. Zach found it a pity, a break with the history he valued, so he reintroduced it for his presentations. He saw Maurice put up his hand.

"Yes, Maurice," Zach said, acknowledging him.

"Zach, please excuse me. As you know, I speak French, and the word "taste" does not exist in that language. How can the word *tastevin* be correct?"

"Thank you for asking. It turns out that *tastevin* comes from 'taster' or 'to taste' in Old French, and from 'tastare' in Vulgar Latin. As I mentioned, the *tastevin* was created in Burgundy in 1680 when Old French was still in use. It survived as 'to taste' in English and 'tâter' or 'to touch' in French. I hope that answers your question, Maurice."

"Very well," he replied, clearly displeased that he had been upstaged in his own field. Zach took a certain comfort from his displeasure since he was feeling a bit jealous as he watched how well he and Vanessa were getting on at the far end of the long table. He couldn't hear what they were saying, but he could read the enthusiastic body language.

For dessert, the restaurant served its specialty – hot Grand Marnier soufflé with crème anglaise. Zach paired this with a 2016 Château Rieussec Sauternes. Espressos and teas followed, and a more contented crowd could not be found in San Francisco at ten o'clock that night.

"That was a most enjoyable dinner; thank you, Zach," Maurice El-Haddad said smoothly as he approached him from the table. Dressed formally in a dark blue suit, white shirt and military tie, he looked positively dapper. Vanessa, who was following behind him, looked like she was on top of the world.

"Thanks for coming. I'm glad you enjoyed it."

"I found the choice of wines especially interesting. In my academic circles, we don't tend to drink much fine wine."

"No, I suppose not," Zach replied, watching Vanessa. "How did you enjoy the evening, Vanessa?" Maurice moved aside to allow her to move forward.

"It was delightful," she replied. "Thank you for putting this on. All these things you do must be very time-consuming. We are happy beneficiaries."

"It is, but I enjoy it, and it keeps my hand in, so to speak, since it forces me to refresh my knowledge when putting together the wines and food."

"Well then," said Maurice. "Good night, and have a pleasant rest of the evening. We'll say good night to Sophie now." Maurice moved over to where Sophie was talking to another couple, with Vanessa on his arm. Zach felt another pang of jealousy as he watched them. More so when he noticed that they left the restaurant together, still talking animatedly. Was she leaning on his shoulder?

The next day, when Zach telephoned Vanessa, she was quite bubbly. "Maurice was very provocative last night."

"Yes, I noticed his arm around your waist as you left together. What did he say?" Zach asked warily. He didn't feel threatened exactly, and what right did he have to even express an opinion, but there was a nagging hesitation given Maurice's reputation as a ladies' man. He didn't know Maurice well, but word gets around.

"He was very impressed with last night. He called me today to invite me out to dinner. I made it clear not to expect anything afterward. He seemed to respect that. Anyway, I'm seeing him again tomorrow," she said lightly as if it were completely normal and nothing to worry about.

"Well, okay; let me know how it goes. From what little I know of him, he never says or does anything without an expectation of a return." He let that sink in for a moment before continuing. "After all, he's just a professor on a tight budget. I have to admit I'm feeling a bit jealous."

"I kind of like that, your feeling jealous, you know?"

"I bet," Zach replied, laughing. "What else is going on today?" They talked for twenty minutes before Vanessa mentioned she had to leave for an appointment. Zach hung up and went about his day, frequently thinking of her and looking forward to their next encounter.

Two days later, Zach was at Vanessa's when the doorbell rang. She answered it, and was handed a dozen red roses, which pleased her greatly from the way her face beamed.

"Who sent the flowers?" Zach asked.

"There's no card," she replied blithely. "Probably Lilith." Zach somehow doubted that but quickly reminded himself it was none of his business.

He continued to see and talk to Vanessa, although less frequently. He could not be certain but sensed that she was pulling away. There were little hints, such as when he invited her to an afternoon wine tasting, and she suggested it would be better if they took separate cars. When he replied that was unnecessary, she relented, and everything seemed normal during the tasting. When he took her home, he walked her to the door where they hugged briefly, but she did not invite him in. He sensed she didn't want him to stay, so he left, feeling confused and concerned.

Cabo San Lucas – April 7, 2023

On Good Friday, Vanessa flew to Cabo San Lucas to spend a week with Lilith in her luxury condominium. She had been looking forward to this trip as it was her first since her separation from Edward. She had a tight group of girlfriends, including Lilith, who'd circled around her, and Zach thought the trip would be a useful distraction. He had joined Vanessa's group of supporters as the only male friend who was helping her to move forward. It was a role he embraced.

Her flight from San Francisco arrived in the afternoon. She disembarked and soon found herself in a never-ending line that snaked from the tarmac into the terminal. This was not her first trip to Cabo, but she'd never seen a line like this before. She made a mental note not to come here during *Semana Santa* in the future.

An hour later, she shuffled into the immigration lobby, where thankfully there were six officers processing the passports. Twenty minutes and a *"Bienvenidos a México"* later, she began the next gauntlet that ran from immigration to the baggage claim area. Another forty minutes after that, with her suitcase in hand, she confirmed to the customs officer that she had no alcohol or tobacco and was then invited to hit the big button. The light turned green for go, which is how the term *"gringo"* originated, courtesy of U.S. Immigration in San Ysidro, and she was mercifully through the two-hour ordeal where tourism and bureaucracy typically clash.

Or so one might think. Next came the hallway with the car rental agencies and timeshare companies who are uber aggressive and descend on the unwary like locusts in a cornfield. An old hand, she marched purposefully with her eyes straight ahead, never hesitating or making eye contact, until she was finally outside in the hot Mexican sun.

"Vanessa! You finally made it!" Lilith shouted from the rickety wooden bar perched on the edge of the pavement. "Join me for a margarita."

Vanessa rolled her bag over to the bar and slipped into the white plastic chair opposite Lilith, who raised her hand and said expertly to the passing waiter, "*Dos más, por favor.*" Then she purred, "So... how was the flight?"

"It was fine, a bit bumpy at times. Oh, and there was this middle-aged guy somewhere behind me who went postal and had to be restrained by the cabin crew. He was shouting and screaming about something. Eventually they wrestled him into his chair and tied him down. It was quite bizarre. Later, the flight attendant told me he was either drunk or on drugs and wanted to open the exit door and get off."

"Since COVID, there's been a noticeable rise in unruly passengers. It's hard to understand; there seem to be so many different reasons. I just hope it stops soon."

They talked and caught up as close friends do until their margaritas were exhausted, then walked over to Lilith's dented white Honda in the parking lot. They continued their animated discussion during the twenty-minute drive down the sun-soaked highway to Lilith's condominium in the marina. Vanessa was always struck by the stark contrast between the azure sea and the arid desert landscape. The marina was filled with luxury yachts and fishing boats, while beachfront bars and restaurants beckoned with the promise of fresh seafood and vibrant nightlife, creating an intoxicating welcome to this Baja California paradise.

Vista Magnifica had two gleaming white marble towers that reached 22 stories into the cloudless blue sky. They took the elevator to her penthouse suite in tower one, with uninterrupted views in every direction since she occupied the whole floor. The style was Mexican modern, with cream-colored marble floors and mostly white furniture. Bright accents were sprinkled here and there, and colorful local paintings adorned the white walls. A home away from home – "cozy" as Lilith would say coyly. The art business had been good to her.

After Vanessa dressed in lighter clothes more suitable for the tropical climate, she joined Lilith outside on her expansive terrace overlooking the blue Pacific. She helped herself to some white sangria from a pitcher sitting on a hardwood serving tray and flopped down on the chaise lounge beside her friend, who put down the paperback she was reading.

"You have no idea how much I needed this," Vanessa confessed. "After a year alone, trying to adapt to a world without Edward, I now find myself with not one but two suitors, and I'm finding it difficult to choose between them."

Swinging her legs into a sitting position on the side of the chaise, Lilith replied affectionately, "Tell me about it."

"You already know about Zach."

"Hold on, he's married."

"That's true, but I told him I love him soon after we met," Vanessa admitted sheepishly. Even with her eyes closed, she could still feel Lilith's disapproving glare boring into her. A few beats passed while Lilith mulled this over.

"Who's the other guy?"

"A man named Maurice El-Haddad. He's a professor emeritus at Berkeley. He's single, and... he's seventy-two."

"How did you two meet?"

"At Zach's annual wine dinner at Fisherman's Wharf in February. He's a friend of Zach's wife."

"A bit old, isn't he?" Lilith probed, cutting to the chase.

"Perhaps, but he's physically fit, and he's steady, and I feel safe with him. He's not out to prove anything, and he doesn't pressure me. We have a... comfortable relationship."

"Does he have any money?"

"He's been very generous with me."

"So, what's the problem?"

"The problem is, I don't want to hurt Zach. I really do love him. He's wonderful, and if he were single, I'd marry him in a heartbeat. We've had so much fun together, and we talk about everything. When I'm with him, I feel like a child again. He's helped me get back in touch with my feelings after the wasteland that Edward left me in."

"Yes, but he's married. So?"

"Yes, he's married," Vanessa sighed. "I just hoped..."

"Look, I know Zach pretty well, and, as unhappy as he may be, he's not the type to leave Sophie."

"God, I hate this. I thought I could be Zach's friend; then Maurice came along, and... Oh well." Vanessa's eyes filled with tears.

"Well, you're here for a week," Lilith said, taking her hands in hers. "Take time to think about it, clear your head, then make a decision. You're going to have to disappoint one of them. Anyway, it's almost six o'clock, and we have dinner in an hour with friends I want you to meet. So, let's get cracking."

Dinner was at El Pollo restaurant on the south coast, about fifteen minutes away by taxi, which Lilith preferred in order to avoid the hassles of finding a parking space. Sitting in the small taxi, Vanessa always found the winding streets, while scenic, a bit jarring on her back as she took in the familiar sights. Coming here was like a journey back in time to a simpler life, far away from the hustle of San Francisco.

Perched on a cliff overlooking the ocean, El Pollo was a local treasure that served home-style Mexican dishes. Its unassuming exterior was a cheerful yellow, with rustic wooden shutters and a hand-painted sign featuring a smiling red rooster. Inside, tantalizing aromas of grilled meats and simmering sauces carried them to their table, set for six with hand-blown glassware on an embroidered tablecloth. Already seated were Lilith's friends, two couples in their late sixties.

Over margaritas served with guacamole and chips followed by dinner of pollo asado marinated in fragrant spices, Vanessa mostly listened to the two couples, expats who had moved here permanently from the States. Like many who made this switch, they were enthusiastic ambassadors. She heard all about the fresh seafood, fruits and vegetables, especially the avocados, limes and mangos, relaxed way of life, sense of community, and Mariachi Bands, amid brief references to the cartels, frustrating bureaucracy, and *mañana* attitude.

"Why did you decide to move here full-time?" Vanessa asked politely when she could finally get a word in edgewise.

"We're tax refugees from California," said Jim somebody who used to do something important. "We still pay federal tax, but here we are free of the state taxes. Makes a difference when you are living on a fixed income."

Tax was not really Vanessa's area of interest, but the company was charming enough and she felt the tension draining out of her. Mexico and tequila tend to do that. As attractive as it seemed, she didn't see herself moving here. San Francisco was her home and always would be. In spite of the good food and good company, she found her mind constantly wandering back to thoughts of Zach and Maurice. She knew she was going to make a callous decision on this trip.

The week flew by, thanks to Lilith, the social coordinator *extraordinaire*. Every day was filled with allotted spaces for sunbathing, shopping, dining in, dining out, cocktail parties, seeing old friends, and meeting new ones. Zach texted her twice, and tried to call her once, but she could not talk to him yet, and ignored his calls. She could not handle the distraction as she sorted through her emotions.

She did take Maurice's daily calls, however. Their relationship was blooming, and she wanted it to progress. He didn't know anything about the complication with Zach. Even if he did, he probably wouldn't have cared. He had his eye fixed on Vanessa. May the best man win, as they say.

"You're going to have to choose what's best for you," Lilith advised her the day before she was due to leave. "No more being a doormat for men. Zach's a big boy; he'll get over it. After all, he's not one of us. He's just a man. He can be replaced. All of us are behind you."

"My problem is we shared so many intimate

moments. We've gone too far down the path. For me to end it now will be a stab in his back. He would never trust me again."

"I'm sure that's true, but both of you should have thought of that before you started. It's not like you're high school students anymore. Here's what you do: tell him you're now with Maurice and slowly work him out of your life. Then block him on your cell phone. I'll do it too, and have Maurice and the girls do it. That will send him a clear message."

Eventually Vanessa realized that she wanted Maurice. It came down to a simple reality: Zach was married and Maurice was not. She was attracted by the idea of being a professor's companion, which would be an entirely new experience for her. She had not gone to college; now she could have an eminent professor on her arm instead. In spite of that, she was confident she could keep up with him. After all, she'd learned loads of things along the way, and she was intelligent. Zach had told her so many times.

Maurice could give her what she wanted – a serious relationship that she could share with her friends. There would always be limitations with Zach, which wasn't what she wanted. She made up her mind to tell him as soon as she returned home and then cancel him quietly when the time was right. A nice clean break, just like Lilith recommended. After all, he's just a man.

Villa Vanessa – April 14, 2023

"Hello?" asked Vanessa on her cell phone.

"Welcome home!" blurted Zach enthusiastically. "How was your trip?"

"It was non-stop. You know Lilith, every day was completely organized; I never had a moment to myself," she said, sounding exhausted.

"I guess that explains why you never replied to my texts. I didn't want to bother you on vacation, as I knew you'd be busy," he said, trying not to let his concern show. "When can we see each other?"

"I'm busy running errands this morning, and then I'm meeting a girlfriend for lunch. I'm free around two thirty, but only for an hour," Vanessa replied, as she wanted to keep this meeting as short as possible.

"How about I drop by then?"

"Perfect, see you soon."

Zach felt his heart skip a beat as he looked forward to seeing Vanessa after the week's absence. In that moment, he felt that everything was going to be okay.

At two thirty, Zach rang the doorbell to be greeted by Consuelo, Vanessa's housekeeper. "*Hola, Señor*," she said. "Señora Vanessa is running a little late. She called me to say that she'll be here in ten minutes. Please come in."

She showed him into the living room, where he stood, unsure of what to do as his doubts returned. Consuelo paid no attention to him and carried on with her work in the kitchen. Zach wasn't used to Vanessa keeping him waiting or being in the house without her.

About twenty minutes later, Vanessa walked into the kitchen, dressed in a dark blue jacket and skirt as if she had been to a formal meeting. This was the first time he'd seen her look so businesslike. They hugged tentatively. Did he detect a certain hesitancy on her part?

"Thanks for seeing me. I missed you," Zach said.

"I wanted to see you too," she replied. "Come, let's sit down."

It had become normal for them to sit together on one of the love seats in the living room, but this time Vanessa positioned herself on the side nearest to Zach, causing him to sit across from her, separated by the coffee table. He felt the distance between them. They proceeded to chat about this and that until Vanessa paused, drew in her breath, and said solemnly, "I've decided to be with Maurice and see where it leads." She watched him closely for a reaction.

After a moment, Zach replied: "I'd be lying if I said I didn't think something was up. I didn't know what it was, but I sensed a change in you. For starters, you didn't answer my calls or my texts last week."

"I know I've hurt you, but you hurt me too," she said and started to cry.

"How did I hurt *you*?"

"You know the answer to that."

"We talked about this and agreed that I'm married to Sophie and would never do anything to hurt her. We agreed to draw the line at friendship and not cross over into an affair."

"I know, but I need more: a man to go out to dinner with, have fun with my friends, watch movies with, share my morning coffee with in bed," she pleaded, recovering from the tears. "I want to be a couple again. Maurice can give me that."

"Did I ever lead you on or give you a reason to think that we would become a couple?" The painful memories of when Sophie broke up with him in college were flooding back. Zach was determined not to give in to them and make the same mistake he'd made before.

"Never. You were always a complete gentleman."

"I don't see a problem here," Zach replied. "We can keep our friendship going. We just need to adjust it so that I don't interfere with you and Maurice. You're too important to me to lose. Are you dumping me?"

"No, I'm not dumping you, but you have a wonderful person to love sitting at home. You should refocus your affection on Sophie, who is as unhappy with the distance between you as you are. Start paying attention to her and you'll see that she will respond. Everybody wants to be loved."

"I've got you to thank for putting me back in touch with my feelings," Zach replied. "That just might work. I'm willing to give it a try. I'll have to see if Sophie is too. I have no idea of what her reaction will be."

"You know that you've helped me a lot."

"We've helped each other."

"I want to give you a bottle from the rare boxes to show my appreciation for the excellent work you did. Why don't we go to the cellar now and you can choose one," she suggested as she continued to deflect his emotional attachment. She'd made the transition in Cabo San Lucas; now she had to help him do the same.

They went down to the cellar, Vanessa leading the way. There, Zach chose one of the 1946 Pétrus, which, at $21,800, was neither the most nor the least valuable of the lot. Then they returned to the living room, where they stood awkwardly looking at each other, neither one sure what to say next.

"I'm afraid I have to meet a friend in thirty minutes, so we'll have to cut this short," Vanessa said.

"Then let's go," Zach replied, ready to end this. Vanessa saw him to the door, where they hugged briefly. That was the last time he would visit Villa Vanessa.

For the rest of the month, he tried calling but always got voice mail. He tried texting but received no reply, although the messages showed as being received. Then it happened: Vanessa, Maurice and Vanessa's girlfriends all withdrew from the wine group chat, and he knew he'd been canceled.

This threw Zach into a spiral of emotions, ranging from denial to depression. He experienced daily heart palpitations and kept waking up at four in the morning with Vanessa on his mind. He was normally a sound sleeper, getting nine hours a night, and sleep was his go-to refuge when he was depressed. Not this time. This was something entirely new to him.

"What's the matter, *chérie*?" Sophie asked him over dinner, having noticed his erratic behavior.

"It's Vanessa. She and Maurice canceled me without any warning. I can't believe she'd do that to me," he said, looking positively miserable.

"Don't interfere. Let her enjoy her time with Maurice. Why does it bother you so much?"

"We became very close friends; I thought we were best friends. Apparently, I was wrong. I'm having a tough time getting her out of my head."

Weeks passed, but the anxiety did not. Zach had to face facts and let time do its work.

Agent Pruno – May 5, 2023

"Agent Pruno! Where the hell have you been?" asked the agent manning the front desk as Zach walked into the district office of the California Department of Alcoholic Beverage Control, known as the ABC, on New Montgomery Street.

"Hey Bob, is there a chance I could see Mitch?" Zach asked.

"He's busy working on the budget and not very happy about it after last year's cuts. Why should I say you're here?"

"Tell him I think I may have stumbled onto a major wine forgery case. That ought to pique his curiosity."

Bob picked up the phone and punched in Mitch's number. "Mitch? Bob at reception. Our old friend Zach is here. Says he has a big wine forgery case for you to crack and wonders if you have a minute to see him. Right. Okay. It's your lucky day. He says to come right up. I imagine he's happy to take a break."

Bob buzzed Zach in, who walked past the glass-walled conference rooms and took the elevator to Mitchell Adams' office on the eighth floor. Although he'd retired as a senior agent eight years ago, he still worked part-time and maintained a close friendship with the chief. As he walked down the hall, he looked at the drab walls decorated with assorted alcohol-related posters and was reminded that he didn't miss it at all.

Mitch was waiting for him at the door to his office, a big smile on his face.

"Hey Mitch, how you doing?" Zach asked.

"Not too bad for a brother surrounded by a bunch of white folks. Come on in and sit awhile. Are you limping?"

"Yeah. A minor skydiving accident in September. I've lost the cane, but I'm having trouble getting rid of this limp after eight months. I'm going to have to teach myself how to walk normally again."

They shook hands heartily, and Mitch waved Zach to one of two wooden chairs facing his functional desk in his rather shabby office. As usual, he was dressed in a brown suit, white shirt, bland tie, and brown shoes. His round wire-rimmed glasses and graying hair completed the image of a career bureaucrat in his sixties. Smart guy though, and fiercely loyal to his people.

Zach didn't think less of Mitch for his chosen career. He knew we all have our parts to play, without which we would have... what? Can you imagine what life would be like without any regulation, with people completely free to do whatever they felt like, whenever they felt like it? After six years on the inside, Zach appreciated what Mitch and his department did for the citizens of California.

Mitch sat down behind his desk and offered Zach a coffee, which he politely declined, knowing how awful it was. They chatted about past cases for a few minutes as they caught up with each other. When the time came for business, Zach put the bottle that Vanessa had given him on the desk.

"What do we have here?" Mitch asked, turning the bottle over in his hands and looking closely at the label.

"As you can see: a 1946 Pétrus. A unicorn by any definition, worth in the neighborhood of twenty grand, and potentially much more to a motivated buyer."

Whistling quietly, Mitch picked up the bottle to examine it more closely. "It certainly looks genuine."

"Looks can be deceiving. Do you remember that case in China a couple of years ago, with the group that put cheap wine in expensive bottles? I don't remember the details, but the gist of it was selling fake wine for thousands that cost much less."

"I do remember that, but that was China where anything can happen. This is California where we keep a tight rein on the alcohol trade. I can't believe anyone would try it here."

"Normally, I would agree with you, but a sixth sense tells me this bottle is a fake." Zach proceeded to describe his meetings with Vanessa (omitting the drinks, meals and hugs), her estranged husband, and the thirty-four boxes of rare wines which he'd appraised at $11.7 million. "That's an awful lot of unicorns in one place. Not impossible, but highly improbable."

"Who does this bottle belong to?" Mitch asked.

"Vanessa Cole gave it to me for appraising their wine collection. I've brought it here for you to check. If it's real, no harm done. On the other hand, if it's fake…"

"Say no more, Agent Pruno. You've always had good instincts. My only regret was that you left us. I'll send it up to the lab rats in Sacramento and see what they can make of it."

They both rose from their seats and walked over to the door, where they shook hands again. "Give my best to Sophie and the kids. Tell her I miss her cooking, especially her coq au vin," Mitch said as Zach started down the hall. He received a raised right hand from Zach in reply.

As Zach left the building, he wondered if his visit was justified or if it was motivated by revenge for what

Vanessa had done to him, as he was still raw from their last encounter. After all, he had no solid proof, unless of course the bottle was fake, in which case all hell was going to break loose.

At ten o'clock ten days later, Zach's cell phone rang. It was a call from Mitchell Freeman at ABC.

"So, Mitch, what's the good word?"

"The short version is this wine is not what it appears to be. When can you come down so I can show you the lab report?"

"I can be there in thirty minutes."

"See you then."

Zach was at his house, a quick drive to New Montgomery Street. When he knocked on his door, Mitch was busy studying the lab report. He waved him in without looking up.

"There's a copy for you," Mitch said, indicating the document on Zach's side of the desk, which he picked up and thumbed to the summary section at the end. It concluded that the wine was probably fake. He then turned to the methodology section to see how they'd reached their conclusion.

Using the latest AI technology, the lab first analyzed the chemical compounds in the wine to determine if it came from Pétrus. While the algorithm determined with ninety-nine percent accuracy that it was from Pauillac, it was only seventy percent confident that it was from Pétrus and forty-four percent certain that it was made in 1946. According to the report, being unable to pinpoint the winery indicated it wasn't genuine. The vintage was harder to determine.

The bottle checked out, and while the cork was recent, that could be explained by the need to replace it every thirty years to prevent the wine from going bad.

It was the next step that clinched it. They examined the label to determine if modern paper had been used. In 1957, the report stated, a chemical called ultrawhite was introduced which causes it to glow under ultraviolet light. This fluorescence was present, proving that the label was later than 1946. The printing process also showed that it was made by a laser printer instead of the traditional printing plate used back then.

"In what world," Zach thought aloud, "would the owner of a genuine Pétrus put a new label on the bottle?"

"Excellent question," replied Mitch, "and one that I propose to refer to the FBI."

"Whoa, whoa, whoa. Do you think this will be enough?"

"No, I don't. That's exactly why I want to give it to them. They're better equipped to get to the bottom of this. I'll need you to file a report to send to them with the wine."

"All right," Zach said as he got up with the lab report in hand. "I'll write it on the way out and get back to you if something more comes my way, although that's not likely as Vanessa has blocked my calls. Don't ask... Oh, and don't forget to warn me before they raid the place. At least ten minutes."

"I'll do my best, but you know the feds don't like others to play in their sandbox," Mitch replied, also standing. "Anyway, thanks for this. Any travel plans?" Mitch asked.

"Actually, we do. We're leaving in June for two weeks in Italy with the kids while the weather is cooler and before the tourists get there."

"That's great. Are the kids doing fine?"

"They are, thanks. They're no longer at USC. Lucas graduated and is now working as a waiter in L.A., hoping for his big break as an actor. His sister decided that acting wasn't for her and changed her major to French, which of course she's fluent in. Two years ago, she moved over to UCLA to do her PhD and follow in her mother's footsteps."

"Are there any significant others in their lives?"

"No, they're still single. This will probably be our last trip together as a family. I mean, just the four of us."

"Say, I was sorry to hear about your parents last year. Car accident, wasn't it?"

"Yeah. Dad was driving on the L.A. freeway when he had a stroke, lost control, and caused a six-car pile-up. They didn't survive the accident. My sister is a lawyer in L.A. and thankfully handling the probate, which should be wrapped up in a few more months."

"My sincere condolences. Anyway, you have a good one, and let me know if you find out anything else," Mitch said, shaking Zach's hand.

"See ya, Mitch, and thanks."

"See ya, Zach."

At reception, Zach obtained a blank report form and completed it in one of the empty interview rooms. On the way home, he thought about his access to Villa Vanessa. Since it had been cut off, he'd just have to let the chips fall where they may. What else could he do?

FBI Field Office – May 18, 2023

Martin Abelman, called "Mabel" by the staff behind his back, was eating a sandwich at his desk on his second day back. His body might be in the office, but his head was still on the beach in Maui, drinking the exotic drinks with those little paper umbrellas. One week was not enough for a family getaway. He doubted much persuasion would be required to convince his wife that, from now on, their holidays should last at least ten days. Well, that was the dream at any rate.

The special agent in charge of the San Francisco FBI field office had been in the position for three years and was respected by the other agents and the staff. At forty-eight years of age, he liked to run a tight ship. He set an example by eating lunch most days in his office, where he used the time to work.

Located in the heart of San Francisco's civic center, the FBI field office sat on Golden Gate Avenue in the city's futuristic federal building, its sleek glass and steel exterior mirroring the cityscape. Inside, the atrium was a vast open space with uniformed guards and state-of-the-art surveillance systems that monitored everyone who entered.

Ascending by elevator to the FBI field office located on the higher floors, there was a marked shift in the ambiance as visitors walked down the corridor lined with photographs and commendations chronicling its history of law enforcement. The reception area opened onto a sprawling workspace filled with cubicles, each one a command center equipped with the latest technology. In the middle was a glass-walled conference room that served as the nerve center for strategy meetings and briefings. Adjoining the main workspace were specialized units, each tailored to specific aspects of the FBI's investigative scope – forensics, cybercrime, counterterrorism.

As Martin Abelman worked through a pile of field reports, his phone rang, offering him a welcome break.

"Hey Marty, Mitch Adams here. How was your holiday?"

"Too short. I can still feel the sand between my toes. What can I do for you Mitch?"

The two colleagues had worked together on a number of cases over the years and had a high regard for each other, which had turned into a solid friendship. When one of them called, the other paid attention.

"I've got something here that might interest you," Mitch said. "One of our former agents, who is a sommelier, brought in a bottle of 1946 Pétrus which our lab analyzed and confirmed is fake. I have the bottle and lab report in front of me, as well as our agent's report detailing where he found it. If you're interested, I'll send them over this afternoon."

"Please do. You know we're always happy to help you booze boys clean up the city. I don't think I've ever had a fake wine case. This will be interesting."

"Okay. I'll shoot it over. Let's get together soon." Mitch hung up and made arrangements to deliver the items to him.

Later that afternoon, after Abelman reviewed the reports from the lab and Agent Pruno, he did a name review on his computer. One of the names was a match: Edward Pavlov appeared in stake-out reports filed by Agents Morgan and Garcia. A bit thin, but worth calling them in to compare notes. Fortunately, they were at their desks and presented themselves to their boss ten minutes later.

"Have a look at these, and let me know your thoughts," Abelman told them as they sat down with their thick file on Angelo Salvatore. Intrigued by the wine's age, the two took turns reading the two reports. Special Agent Morgan was the first to speak, leafing through their file.

"During our investigation of the Salvatore crime family, we followed two of his soldiers to a house in Pacific Heights, which we since determined is rented to Edward Pavlov. Our research indicates he's a successful businessman who is currently going through a divorce. He's also a member of the prestigious Redwood Private Men's Club on Nob Hill.

"Salvatore's heavies showed up at Pavlov's place at eleven o'clock Sunday morning on January 8. This was the first time we'd seen him. They were there to collect six bottles of rare wine that Salvatore had purchased from an associate of Pavlov's, one Hugh Albright, a respected banker. He said he'd have to check with Albright first and they left.

"They returned the following Sunday, and Pavlov told them he had the wine but couldn't get it from the cellar at his home in Russian Hill due to the divorce proceedings. He said his wife told him that her lawyer advised her it was community property, and to keep it until the divorce was finalized. He then asked Salvatore's men for two months to get the wine, and they called for instructions. Salvatore apparently agreed provided that Pavlov gave him one more bottle of wine each month to compensate for the delay. He said he'd do this, and they left.

"Then he drove to a house in Laurel Heights which is registered to James Jin-Hie Wong. Salvatore's men followed him, and we followed them. We were unable to listen to their conversation, but we know Pavlov was rattled by his previous meeting with the boys because he'd gone straight there. He only stayed for ten minutes before leaving. We didn't follow him as our tail was the Salvatore car, which left directly after Edward and returned to Salvatore's mansion. There, Salvatore reamed them out for their incompetence in getting his wine and put them on a short leash to resolve the problem.

"The third meeting happened on Tuesday, January 31. Salvatore's men drove to Pavlov's house to pick up the monthly bottle of wine, but he didn't have it yet. He said his partner Jimmy Wong said he'd found some in Asia and could give it to them the following Sunday. They then gave him a choice: they could either break one of his fingers or he could give them two penalty bottles on Sunday. Not surprisingly, he chose the latter.

"On Sunday, February 5, they returned, Pavlov paid them off with what looked like a case of wine and they left. We don't know the exact contents because the transaction happened inside the house and we couldn't record it. My guess is the box contained the bottles of wine for Salvatore."

"What does your gut tell you?" Abelman asked.

"When it comes to Jimmy Wong, the rat is always closest to the cheese. I'm convinced that Wong is making it and Pavlov is selling it at exorbitant prices, although there are still gaps in our case. Plus, we'd need a different buyer from Salvatore who'd be willing to testify," Morgan concluded.

"I'm happy to hear you say that. Open a new file on Edward Pavlov and James Wong, and when you're ready, obtain search warrants for the three houses and arrive prepared to make arrests. Also, have our lab analyze the wine to verify ABC's analysis."

The two agents returned to their desks, where Carlos Garcia asked his partner: "Do you suppose Edward Pavlov sold any of the rare wine at the Redwood Club?"

"An excellent question, Special Agent Garcia," replied Morgan. "I begin to have hope for you. Why don't we pay them a visit and find out?"

At nine the next morning, they approached a uniformed member of staff who was guarding the front desk at the Redwood Club. His gold embossed name badge identified him as *Henry Newton, Reception*. He was dressed in a gray uniform with navy blue piping, white shirt and a black tie bearing the club crest. Thinning gray hair and reading glasses combined to create the appearance of an immovable fixture charged with the club's defense.

"Good morning gentlemen; what can I do for you?" asked Henry, who'd been with the club for thirty-seven years, and recognized them for who they were – not members.

"I'm Special Agent Morgan, and this is Special Agent Garcia." They held up their identification for Henry to verify. "We're conducting an investigation that may involve a member of this club, a Mr. Edward Pavlov. Have we come to the right place?"

"I can confirm that Mr. Pavlov is a respected member of longstanding," Henry replied proudly.

"Would a member such as Mr. Pavlov put on a private event, such as a dinner party?"

"Yes, we have rooms for such events where the activity might otherwise run afoul of the rules. You understand."

"How would we find out what events Mr. Pavlov hosted or attended, say in the last twelve months?"

"For that, I would have to direct you to our Miss Barnes. If you would kindly take a seat over there, I'll ring her now." They seated themselves on a couch located opposite the reception desk beneath an original oil painting that looked more expensive than their houses and watched Henry make the call.

"Miss Barnes will be with you directly," he said from across the room, then returned to shuffling paper on his desk while he awaited his next opportunity to protect the club.

A few minutes later, a prim young woman with her dark brown hair tied in a bun walked up to them. Dressed in a modest navy skirt and white blouse, she too wore an embossed gold badge with the name *Priscilla Barnes, Social Secretary*. Looking down on them, she said frostily, "Good morning. I've been told you have some questions about our private events. Please follow me to my office."

She led them to the elevator, which took them to the fifth floor. Her office was tiny with just enough room for her desk, filing cabinet and one guest chair. Both chairs had their backs against the walls with hardly enough space to squeeze into them. The two agents elected to stand.

"What is it you'd like to know?" she asked, unconcerned that there wasn't a second guest chair, letting them know they would not be staying long.

"As we mentioned to your man at reception..."

"Henry," Miss Barnes interjected.

"Yes, Henry. As we mentioned to Henry, we would like to know what private events Edward Pavlov has hosted here. We're particularly interested in events featuring wines he has brought into the club."

"I'm not able to help you. This is The Redwood Private Men's Club. We take our commitment to maintain our members' privacy very seriously," she said slowly and distinctly, emphasizing the last three words.

"We appreciate that. As you will appreciate, we can return with a search warrant, which could have the effect of exposing much more private information about your members than we are currently seeking or need. With your cooperation, we can limit our inquiry and potentially save your members from embarrassment," Agent Garcia spoke up for the first time.

"You have my sincere apologies, but my hands are tied. The directive from the top is very clear: members' information is not shared outside these walls. Is there anything else?" she asked, getting to her feet.

"No, Miss Barnes, that will be all for now. You have yourself a nice day," replied Agent Morgan. This was not the first time they'd encountered immovable objects with a zeal for obstructing justice, which only strengthened their resolve. They would return in force, likely to their target's regret.

As they walked down the steps to their car, they discussed whether to apply for a search warrant or a subpoena and decided that Carlos Garcia would spearhead the process of obtaining approval from upstairs and applying to the judge downstairs. "Operation Hangover", as they decided to call their file, was now underway.

The Federal Building – the Next Day

Back at his desk, Carlos Garcia was refreshing his memory about the difference between a subpoena and a search warrant, and which was easier to obtain from a judge. He didn't resent his senior partner for dropping this on him or his advice, spoken with a wry smile, that he look on it as a learning opportunity. Instead, he put his head down and got to work.

He already knew that search warrants are issued to law enforcement, who are authorized to search for the evidence and then seize it without the owner's consent. The judge who issues it must be satisfied that a crime has been committed and evidence of it will be found in the place described in the warrant.

By contrast, he read that *subpoenas duces tecum* are used to demand physical evidence from the person who has it, in this case Miss Priscilla Barnes, Social Secretary of The Redwood Private Men's Club. Obtaining one did not require the probable cause standard of a warrant but wouldn't permit them to enter the club to do the search and seizure themselves. Miss Barnes would be able to control what documents she chose to deliver to them. That could be problematic, depending on how protective of the club and its members she decided to be.

Clearly the search warrant was better, but did they have enough evidence to convince a judge to issue it? They had the bottle, the two lab reports confirming it was fake, and Agent Pruno's report that tied the bottle to Pavlov's wine cellar. Next, they had their own reports where Pavlov confirmed to Salvatore's men that he would deliver the six, now nine, bottles of rare wine. Unfortunately, that evidence wasn't admissible without their cooperation, which was none without having something on them. Last, the bottle they had in custody was a 1946 Pétrus, which matched the bottles delivered to Angelo Salvatore. There were definite gaps in their case; it would all depend on which judge they drew.

An hour later, Terrence Morgan sauntered into the office and casually asked: "So, are we ready to obtain our search warrant?"

"As soon as I get the green light from legal," Garcia replied. "I'll run it upstairs now."

On Monday morning, the two agents received the application for the search warrant and rode the elevator down to see the court clerk. Looking at his roster, he informed them that Judge Walter Wallace was in session, and could hear their motion in courtroom eleven.

Sitting atop the mahogany bench, Judge Wallace looked down on the multitude in front of him. Only his upper half was visible, dressed in traditional black robes and a blue and gold striped bow tie. His ruddy face, thick white hair, keen eyes and quiet voice worked together to both command respect and instill fear as he dispatched motion after motion with impressive efficiency. After thirty years on the bench, he'd seen it all before and was not interested in hearing it again.

They had to wait forty minutes until their turn came, when they moved from the gallery to the table. Morgan rose to present their case. "Special Agent Terrence Morgan, Your Honor, and this is my partner, Special Agent Carlos Garcia. We're here to obtain a search warrant..."

"Thank you, Special Agent Morgan," said Judge Wallace. "I see that you wish to conduct a search at the

Redwood Club. May I assume Mr. Pavlov is a member of this club?"

"He is, Your Honor," Morgan replied.

"Let's see if I've got this correct. You want me to let you go into the Redwood Club and disrupt their operation for all present to see, on a hunch that one or more of their members is involved in forging wine?"

"With due respect to Your Honor, it's not exactly a hunch. We have the bottle of fake wine, we know it came from Mr. Pavlov's cellar, and he's sold more bottles of the same wine to the Salvatore crime family.

"Yes, but you don't know if Mr. Pavlov participated in making it, do you?"

"No."

"Furthermore, you don't have the bottles given to Angelo Salvatore, so you don't know if they're real or fake, and that's before we discuss the admissibility of that evidence."

"No."

"Then I'm not about to allow you to run ragged around one of the oldest and most respected clubs in the city, in the country for that matter, based on a suspicion that you *might* find something. Thank you for your time, gentlemen. Application denied. Next case."

"Never trust a judge with a bow tie," muttered Morgan to Garcia as they left the courtroom.

When they returned, they called their boss and told him Judge Wallace had denied their application. Special Agent in Charge Martin Abelman ordered them to come right up.

"Did you know that Walter Wallace is a longtime member of the Redwood Club?" Abelman asked when they entered, looking none too pleased.

The two partners looked at each other and rolled

their eyes. Talk about drawing the wrong judge. They decided their best course was to remain standing.

"As I see it, you have two choices: either find something more to connect this Pavlov and the club to the crime or issue a subpoena and see if you get lucky with your Miss Barnes. Close the door on your way out."

"I thought that went well," Morgan said to Garcia sarcastically as they walked down the stairs. "How do we break out of this Catch-22?"

"There is a third option," replied Garcia. "We get a wiretap of Pavlov's cell phone."

"That won't tell us anything if he isn't part of the forgery racket. What about that Asian guy he visited on Commonwealth? He was in a big hurry to see him right after the pressure from Salvatore and didn't stay very long. Find out who owns the house, and let's do a preliminary wiretap of both their phones. Meanwhile, issue the subpoena to Miss Barnes."

After a quick Americano at the deli around the corner, Agent Garcia ran a search of the house on Commonwealth and found that it was registered to James Jin-Hie Wong from Hong Kong. Then he found his cell phone number in the California White Pages. He also looked at the U.S. Citizenship and Immigration Services database and determined he was there on a six-month visitor's visa. All this information was online, and in his possession within minutes.

There was no way they could obtain a wiretap approval since wine forgery was not a wiretap crime for which the court would issue the order. However, they could do a preliminary wiretap without approval for thirty days, although they would not be able to use it in court later. This might tell them what they needed to know in order to obtain the search warrant.

At five o'clock, Agent Garcia sent the file back up to legal to issue an application for the subpoena, which they received two days later in time to go back to court for a second try. It was just their luck that they appeared again before Judge Walter Wallace in courtroom eleven, this time having waited their turn in the gallery for about two hours.

"Special Agent Morgan," the Judge said tersely. "I see you're back in my court. I trust that this time you'll have more meat on the bones."

"Yes, good morning, Your Honor. We followed your advice and are here to obtain a *subpoena duces tecum* for the documents described in the draft order before you."

"It says here that you want Miss Barnes at the Redwood Club to produce all documents, lists, records, worksheets, and so on pertaining to any and all meetings, parties, dinners and events which Edward Pavlov organized or attended between January 1, 2022 and May 24, 2023. That could be quite a lot of work for her. Why do you need such a long period of time?"

"Your Honor, as we've said in our affidavit, we believe that Edward Pavlov obtains the wine from Jimmy Wong and sells it to other members of his club. The Redwood Club has confirmed it has private rooms for business meetings and dinner parties where such a thing could happen. Consequently, we want to see records of these events organized or attended by Edward Pavlov since January 1, 2022, so we can interview the members who were there and probably purchased this wine."

"I will grant the subpoena, but I'm shortening the time frame to six months prior to today. So that would be... November 24, 2022 to today. I've changed and initialed the start date. There you go; it's signed. Let's have the next case."

Later that day, the FBI delivered the subpoena to the Redwood Club and started wiretapping Pavlov and Wong. Lists of the six dinners hosted by Pavlov arrived from Priscilla Barnes the next week, showing the names of the twelve members in attendance. Unhelpfully, she did not include any contact details for them which, while annoying, only slowed them down about twenty minutes. They were the FBI after all.

The two agents decided to split the lists and visit the members to see what they could find. They discarded the idea of calling them first since they were members of the same club and would probably circle their wagons at the first hint of trouble. They wanted the element of surprise that comes when one is confronted by law enforcement without warning, thus curtailing the chance to prepare suitable lies.

"Before we visit the club members, let's talk to Agent Pruno who started this whole thing," Terrence Morgan said to his partner.

He dialed the ABC number and asked to speak to Mitchell Adams.

"Mitch Adams."

"Good afternoon, Mr. Adams. Special Agent Terrence Morgan with the FBI. On the line with me is Special Agent Carlos Garcia."

"Gentlemen, what can I do for you?"

"Mabel... err, Special Agent in Charge Martin Abelman, whom I believe you know, has handed us the Edward Pavlov wine fraud file," continued Morgan, who proceeded to recount their dubious progress so far. "We still don't have enough for a search warrant, and we're not sure where the wine is made. We were hoping to meet with your Agent Pruno, who might give us some pointers."

"Unfortunately, he left for Europe with his family today for two weeks, but I'm sure I can arrange to have him call you. He's gone to Italy, so he'll be nine hours ahead. I could text him to call you at nine tomorrow morning, which will be six o'clock his time."

"That'll be fine. Thanks for the assistance."

Florence – June 2, 2023

The text from Mitchell Adams at ABC arrived while Zach was sleeping, and he didn't see it until the next morning. He texted back to confirm that he would call the FBI at nine o'clock their time.

Zach and his family spent the day immersing themselves in the vibrant and historic city of Florence. They began with a visit to Michelangelo's iconic David. The statue, standing an impressive seventeen feet, was a breathtaking example of Renaissance genius. Housed in the Accademia Gallery, it radiated life, capturing David in the moment of contemplation before his battle with Goliath. Every detail, from the tense muscles to his focused gaze, left them awestruck. Particularly the children, Zach was pleased to see.

Following their cultural tour, they meandered through the cobblestone streets, bathed in the warm Tuscan sun, until they found a charming street-side café for a late lunch. Zach ordered his first Bistecca alla Fiorentina, known as steak Florentine at home, which was delicious, and was surprised to learn from the waiter that it was seasoned with only salt and pepper. Sophie and the kids had pasta, which they declared to be the best they'd ever eaten. There was an undeniable magic in eating Italian food in its birthplace.

They returned to their hotel room at four o'clock, lodged in a restored Renaissance-era building. Their spacious rooms featured high ceilings with exposed wooden beams, frescoes on the walls, and large windows that opened onto the busy street below. Sophie and the kids, feeling the day's adventures catching up to them, announced that they were going to lie down until dinner. Meanwhile, Zach caught up on the news on his cell phone, comfortably nestled in a leather armchair by the window until it was almost six o'clock.

"Sophie," Zach yelled through the bedroom door, "I need to make a call to L.A. at six. Why don't you take the kids to the café next door? I won't be more than twenty minutes."

"What's up?" a sleepy Sophie asked, opening the door.

"You remember that bottle of fake wine I gave Mitch? The FBI is now on the case and wants to talk to me."

"Oh, Zach," she sighed, suddenly awake from her nap. "I warned you to stay out of it."

"I'll be fine. They don't know who I really am. They only know me through ABC as Agent Pruno."

"That's what you say, but secrets have a way of coming out." Zach waited for Sophie and the kids to exit their suite so he could talk in private, then made the call.

The FBI telephone rang at precisely nine o'clock in the morning with Agent Pruno on the line. "Good evening, Agent Pruno. Thanks for taking the time to talk to us while on vacation. We'll make this brief," said Terrence Morgan, who gave him the same update he'd given to the ABC chief. "What can you tell us that we don't already know?"

"Not much, really," Agent Pruno replied. "I've spent a lot of time at their home, during which Vanessa told me many things about Edward, to the point where I feel like I almost know him. According to her, he's a three-hundred-pound-egotist and a bully, so his profile fits someone who could be prepared to forge wine if he figured he wouldn't get caught."

"Do you think they know the wine is fake?"

"I can't tell you that with any certainty. I only met him once when I had subdue him before he could hit Vanessa. She never expressed any doubts or concerns about the cases of rare wine sitting in the cellar. She made it clear they were Edward's responsibility and that she had nothing to do with them. But she has proven herself to be an artful deceiver. My guess is Edward is either complicit or willfully blind."

"You say you subdued him?" Morgan asked.

"Yes, it was last January, I think. Edward was incensed that Vanessa wouldn't give him some of the rare wine because her lawyer told her not to. He came over and threatened to hit her if she didn't agree, so I stepped in and restrained him. When he calmed down, I escorted him to the door. That was the only time we met, and we've never spoken."

"I see... Please excuse this next question, but I have to ask: how close are you to Vanessa Cole?"

"I was *very* close," Zach replied. "Apparently a lot closer to her than she was to me. I supported her emotionally after Edward abandoned her, and we spent a lot of time together for about three months. Then Maurice El-Haddad came along, swept her off her feet, and it was goodbye to me."

"I'm sorry to hear that. You called her an 'artful deceiver?' Why is that?"

"She has a dark side which she masks well. She showed all the signs of being a battered woman and transferred those feelings to me. She was very attentive and seductive, in retrospect like she wanted me to replace her husband. Enter Maurice, and for two months she carried on with him without the slightest indication that she was seeing him and probably sleeping with him.

Then she abruptly canceled me and had Maurice and all her friends that I'd met do the same. By my count, she ended eight friendships in one day."

"What made you suspicious about the wine?"

"After you've been in this business long enough, you develop a nose for these things. I found it hard to believe that so many unicorns could be in one place at the same time."

"Unicorns?"

"Sorry, 'unicorns' are extremely rare wines, so rare that the chances of finding one is the same as finding a unicorn."

"Very good. Thank you for your time, Agent Pruno. Go back to your family, and enjoy the chianti and cappuccinos." They hung up, and Morgan looked at Garcia. "How about this? We don't have enough to search Jimmy Wong's house, but we do have enough to arrest Pavlov and his wife for dealing in fake wine. Then we lean on them to cooperate against Wong, Pavlov gives a confession on tape, and we're done."

"We don't know if Wong made it," Garcia replied. "If we arrest them, he might skip town. Better to hold that thought until we interview the club members, see what they say, and how many more fake bottles we can lay our hands on."

Back in Florence, Zach walked down the three flights of stairs to the street and found three happy campers ensconced in Italian caffeine at the café next door. The outdoor seating area was abuzz with the lively chatter of locals and tourists alike, the air filled with the rich aroma of freshly brewed coffee. He sat down and told them about Harry's Bar, where the Bellini cocktail was invented. This intrigued Emma, who'd never tried one, although she'd heard they were rad. They decided to walk to the restaurant along the Arno River, crossing the historic Ponte Vecchio and its quaint jewelry shops.

A classic for over sixty years, Harry's Bar is consistently rated in the top three bars in Italy. The soft lighting from the white sconces perched on hardwood walls, accented with historic artwork and photographs, transported them back to classier times. The presence of bygone days was oddly reassuring, and they immediately felt comfortable as they were seated at one of the tables for four.

Lucas and Emma ordered Bellinis, the classic blend of Prosecco and peach purée, while Zach and Sophie opted for Negronis, the bittersweet cocktail of gin, vermouth and Campari. These were followed with four of Harry's specialties: appetizers of Asparagi gratinati al Gruyère, tender asparagus spears baked with Gruyère cheese, and Tartare di Manzo alla Harry's, a beautifully seasoned beef tartare. For the mains, they enjoyed Vitello Tonnato, thinly sliced veal with a creamy tuna sauce, and Pescato del Giorno, the fresh catch of the day.

They ate family style, as they frequently did when dining out, so everyone could try each dish. Zach paired the appetizers with a crisp Pinot Grigio and the mains with a vintage Brunello di Montalcino, which complemented the flavors of their meal perfectly. Living in the Taylor household, the family was accustomed to having superb wines with their meals. The kids quickly understood that any evening at Harry's Bar was an experience that captured the essence of Florence's rich culinary and cultural heritage, leaving them with memories that would linger long after they left the city.

Soon they were strolling back along the Arno to their hotel. The kids were in the lead immersed in conversation, interspersed with texting on their phones, giving Zach a chance to talk to Sophie privately.

"I've been quite preoccupied with Vanessa's canceling me," he confided.

"I've noticed," Sophie replied, rolling her eyes. "How did the call go with the FBI?"

"They wanted some background on the players. I think they're getting ready to make arrests."

"Let's hope you're not one of them. What did you want to say about Vanessa?"

"As you know, I've been having a difficult time getting her out of my head. During those three months we spent together, we grew very close, to the point where I actually considered her my best friend. I was not that to her, obviously."

"Was she trying to steal my husband?" Sophie asked, defensively.

"Possibly. I wanted a friend, but she wanted more, a replacement for Edward probably. She'd been alone for a year and said she wanted to be a couple again, which is something that Maurice could offer her and I couldn't. It's just that she rekindled feelings in me that I hadn't felt in a long time, which caused me to realize how lonely I was.

"As she was distancing herself from me, which I can see now in retrospect, she made a really good suggestion. She said I should refocus on our relationship. You and me. Is that something that would interest you?" Zach asked tentatively.

"I don't know. I've grown used to the way we do things. What would you change and how? Should we see a marriage counsellor?" Sophie was clearly struggling with all this.

"I don't think we need to do that. I've been

thinking about this almost non-stop lately. It seems to me a good marriage only needs a few critical things: first and foremost, listening to each other. Your paying attention to me when I talk to you, and vice versa. Active listening. Not just talking about work and the kids. Talking about life, philosophy, and, God forbid, politics.

"People who actively listen take in what you say without interrupting and respond with questions because they're genuinely interested in what you're saying. They maintain eye contact, sit still, and wait for people to finish their thoughts before speaking. They use this skill to develop relationships and build trust.

"Next, playing to each other's strengths instead of concentrating on our weaknesses. Giving each other the benefit of the doubt. Taking a deep breath before hurling criticism, considering the other point of view, and hopefully agreeing that our good points outweigh the bad. I once read that a successful marriage only needs to have more positive things happen each day than negative things.

"Then there's supporting each other. Standing together as we tackle life's hurdles, like we do with the kids. We should do this for everything we encounter. And gratitude: starting each day being grateful for being alive and having each other and the kids. There are billions of stars out there, and the chances of us even existing are incredibly tiny. Being grateful that we exist and have this extraordinary opportunity to experience life. It's not about happiness; it's about gratitude.

"I know this will take a long time, but I'm certain we can do it if we put our minds to it. That is, if you want to. I think too much contempt has crept into our marriage over the years. We need to replace it with consideration and respect.

"Vanessa made me realize that the solution was right in front of me. It doesn't require a different person but a different attitude. Even though nudging me back in your direction suited her strategy to get me out of her life so she could carry on with Maurice, it still makes sense. This may be our last chance at happiness. Let's not screw it up. Anyway, that's my speech. What do you think? I'm game if you are."

They walked a few more yards in silence while Sophie collected her thoughts. Did she want this? Was it even feasible? She'd become used to being in a marriage that was now more business than love. They each had their separate lives and careers, and now with the kids gone, they spent more time glued to their cell phones than talking to each other. It seemed like every year their relationship deteriorated a little bit more as they grew apart. She'd accepted this. Did she want to go back?

"That was quite a speech," she said at last. "As you said, it will take a long time for me to get used to the new Zach. I guess all we can do is try and see how it goes."

"Thank you, *chérie*," he said, giving her a peck on the cheek. "Now, let's go explore Italy and our new relationship."

Nob Hill – June 5, 2023

Special Agent Terrence Morgan was on the trail of the second name on his list, William Baxter, the well-known philanthropist. He lived in The Pines, a posh condominium on Nob Hill. Once home to the magnates of the Gilded Age, it now hosted a blend of historical landmarks and modern luxuries. The streets were lined with renovated Victorian mansions, interspersed with upscale boutiques, fine restaurants and exclusive clubs, like the Redwood Club, which was not far away. It was a coveted location for the city's elite, where cable cars trundled up and down the inclines, their bells ringing out a nostalgic melody that echoed through the streets.

The Pines was a tribute to modern luxury amid the historical grandeur. Towering over the historic mansions and landmarks of Nob Hill, the building offered breathtaking views of the city and the bay beyond in this affluent and elegant neighborhood.

At nine o'clock that morning, Morgan ambled up to the concierge in the contemporary lobby, its air thick with exclusivity. The scent of fresh flowers from the elaborate arrangements filled the room, polished marble floors gleamed under the ambient lighting, and a grand chandelier hung from the high ceiling, its crystals refracting light in a dazzling display. He was greeted politely by the concierge, whose observant eyes missed nothing. The staff at The Pines were accustomed to catering to the needs of their affluent residents.

"Good morning, I'm Special Agent Terrence Morgan of the FBI," he said, holding up his ID. "Would you please inform Mr. William Baxter that I'm here."

"Very good, sir," replied the uniformed concierge stiffly, who picked up his telephone, wondering why these FBI types couldn't afford better suits. "Mr. Baxter is in and will see you now. Take the elevator to the fourteenth floor. It opens onto his suite, which occupies the whole floor."

William Baxter was waiting for him when the elevator opened onto an opulent foyer. He was standing on a Persian rug, dressed casually in gray slacks, a light blue button-down shirt, black cashmere sweater, and black slippers. His athletic appearance and full head of silver hair belied his age of seventy-three years.

"Good morning, Mr. Baxter. I'm Special Agent Terrence Morgan with the FBI," Terrence said, holding up his credentials, which Baxter politely ignored.

"Good morning, Special Agent. Come in and sit down. Would you like some coffee?" he asked as he showed him into the adjoining living room which had a commanding western view of the Presidio and the Golden Gate Bridge beyond. On the walls were four original cubist paintings from the twenties that captured the essence of the style nicely, adding just the right touch of sophistication to the room.

"Yes, thank you. I take mine black," Morgan replied. Baxter went through a door, presumably to the kitchen, and talked to someone about coffee, then returned and sat on the opposite couch.

"Now then, what can I do for you?" asked a congenial William Baxter with what appeared to be genuine interest. He was smooth, but that was to be expected from a billionaire.

"We are conducting an investigation that has taken us to your club, the Redwood Club, which has advised us that you attended a private dinner party there with Edward Pavlov and others on the evening of December 18 last year."

"I remember that dinner; it was a week before Christmas. There were twelve of us. We were all Edward's guests. He conducted an auction of rare wines, and I bought one... a 1946 Pétrus I believe."

Morgan's heart skipped a beat. Tamping down his excitement he asked, "Do you still have it?"

"Yes, I'm sure I do. Shall we go to the cellar and check?" William led him down the hallway to a door with a small bronze sign that read *Wine Cellar*. He unlocked the door and switched on the lights to a climate-controlled room with wine racks lining the walls, full of wine bottles with little tags describing their contents. William walked straight over to one of the racks and chose an old looking bottle, which he held out for Morgan to inspect. "This is the one," he said.

"Would it be all right if we brought it back to the living room, and I will fill you in on the details?"

"Certainly. Shall we?"

When they returned to the couches, their coffees were waiting on a silver tray. Baxter placed the bottle on the coffee table, and handed Morgan his coffee in an antique English bone China cup.

"Why all the interest in this wine?" asked Baxter.

Special Agent Terrence Morgan took a sip of perhaps the best coffee he'd ever tasted as he gathered his thoughts. "How well do you know Edward Pavlov?" he asked, answering a question with a question, something that William Baxter would not be caught dead doing, which, come to think of it, is probably why he wouldn't have made a good cop.

"Let's see. I think I met him about eight years ago when he first joined the club. It was at a meet and greet for new members. We found we had a common interest in rare wines. That eventually led to my attending his wine dinners, which he does about once a month."

"Are you a regular at these dinners?" asked Morgan.

"Pretty regular. I try to go to all of them, unless I'm out of town or otherwise engaged."

"So, you've bought other rare wines from Mr. Pavlov."

"Oh yes. I'd say three or four cases."

"Do you still have them?"

"For the most part. They are consumed on special occasions from time to time."

"Could I get a list of the bottles that you purchased from Mr. Pavlov, and that you still have?"

"That might be tricky as I don't have any receipts, but I'll do my best."

"That'll be fine," Morgan said, then paused a moment. "Mr. Baxter, the reason I'm here is because we're conducting an investigation into wine forgery that we believe involves Mr. Pavlov." He watched him closely for his reaction.

"I can't believe Edward would be involved in anything like that," he replied without hesitation or apparent concern. "The ones I've tried over the years have all been superb."

"He may not be. We have another 1946 Pétrus from his wine cellar that we've confirmed is a forgery, and we'd like to test yours to confirm it's genuine."

"Come to think of it, I recall leaving that dinner in December with some doubts about this bottle. Let's see, what was it? Oh yes, it was something Edward said as I was leaving that made me do some research into the rare wine business. There are many articles on the internet about wine fraud. I eventually decided not to be concerned because Edward would ensure a good provenance for his wines which he said, now I remember, he said he has a supplier that buys them from wealthy investors in Asia."

"Does the name James Wong or Jimmy Wong mean anything to you?" Morgan asked next.

"No, I can't say that it does."

"Thank you for your time, Mr. Baxter. You've been very helpful. May I take this bottle with me? Our lab will test it, and we'll return it to you if it's the real thing. If not, we'll need to keep it as evidence."

"That bottle in front of you cost me $100,000, Agent Morgan. What are they going to do to it?"

"They will subject the label to certain tests to see if it was made in 1946, and will insert a needle through the cork and extract a small amount of wine which they'll test to see if it came from the vineyard."

"Fine. Take it, and let's hope its genuine."

"Also, while you're looking for those other bottles you bought from Mr. Pavlov, could you please check your records for payments you made to him. Canceled checks, bank statements, and the like."

"I'll do what I can."

"Please don't discuss this with Mr. Pavlov."

"Naturally," replied Baxter.

When they reached the door, Morgan paused. "Do you remember who proposed Mr. Pavlov for membership?"

"As a matter of fact, I do. Club rules require each person be nominated by two members. In this case, Hugh Albright, the banker, and Judge Walter Wallace."

As Morgan stepped out of The Pines and onto the sunlit street, he took a moment to admire the grandeur of Nob Hill. The air was crisp, a gentle breeze carrying the distant sound of church bells from Grace Cathedral, another of the city's celebrated landmarks. The juxtaposition of old and new, the blending of historical elegance with modern luxury, created an atmosphere that was timeless. It was a setting suited to William Baxter, whose philanthropy and social standing made him a significant figure in the city's elite circles. Morgan knew Baxter was definitely going to bring him one step closer to unraveling the mystery that lay at the heart of his investigation.

Back at the office, Morgan sent off the bottle to their lab, then huddled with his partner who so far had come up with nothing.

Three days later, the bottle and lab report came back: the wine was fake. More importantly, it had identical chemical characteristics to the first one, which meant they were both made by the same person. Armed with this information, they could step up their game with Pavlov's fellow members, who had obviously been sold fake wine too.

They also received William Baxter's list of the other wines he'd bought from Pavlov, which he agreed to hand over for testing, along with bank statements showing his payments. When Morgan went back to his apartment to pick up the twenty-seven suspect bottles, Baxter was visibly unhappy about the Pétrus. He expressed his hope that the others wouldn't turn out to be the same, although he privately suspected this was not going to end well.

Sunset District – June 9, 2023

On Friday morning, Special Agent Carlos Garcia was out tracking down his fourth name. He'd struck out on the first three: two of them were away on business trips, and the third was entirely evasive, said he didn't recall being at any of the listed dinners and asked if he should call his lawyer. Garcia marked him down for special treatment later.

At eight o'clock, he rang the doorbell at Hugh Albright's modest house on Lincoln Way, across from Golden Gate Park. The two-story home was unassuming, with weathered clapboard siding and a roof that bore the marks of years in the coastal climate. A neatly trimmed lawn with a few well-placed shrubs led to the narrow porch, which sagged slightly under the weight of time.

"A bit down-market for a senior banker and member of the fancy Redwood Club," muttered Garcia, noting the peeling paint on the windowsills and the faded welcome mat as he rang the doorbell.

The front door creaked softly as it opened, revealing a cozy, albeit dated, interior that spoke more of comfort than affluence. Before him stood Albright – short, portly and dressed in a dark blue suit. Beside him was a teacup Yorkie on a leash, which immediately attached itself to Garcia's lower right leg.

"Mr. Hugh Albright?" he asked, shaking his leg to release its new appendage.

"The very same. Whom do I have the pleasure of addressing on this fine June morning?" Albright replied.

"I'm Special Agent Carlos Garcia with the FBI," he replied, holding up his credentials, which Albright studied intently. "I was wondering if I might come in and discuss an investigation we think you can assist us with."

"I was just about to take Candy for a walk, and then I must be off to the bank. Do you want to walk with us?" Albright replied. "We can talk as we walk."

They crossed Lincoln onto one of the park's walkways which meandered through lush greenery, lined with towering eucalyptus trees that whispered in the breeze. Sunlight filtered through the leaves, casting dappled shadows on the ground and creating a tranquil atmosphere. Candy was an energetic little thing, constantly pulling her master this way and that as she explored everything in her path. She was on one of those retractable leashes with a spring-loaded handle that allowed her to roam at will, until Albright pulled her back into line.

"What can I do for you today, Special Agent?" Albright asked when they'd settled into Candy's daily routine.

"We are conducting an investigation into wine fraud that involves the Redwood Club and Edward Pavlov. As you're not our first interview, I'll summarize what we know so far and the information we're seeking from you."

"How intriguing," Albright replied. "Please do continue and spare no detail."

"We're looking into a wine fraud operation in which fake wine is manufactured and sold as very expensive rare wine."

Garcia paused to let this sink in and noticed that the rhythm of Albright's walk changed slightly. Candy noticed too, and looked up at him.

"We know Edward Pavlov sold these wines at private dinners held at the Redwood Club. We have lists of the last six dinners that show which members were there. Your name is on all of those lists." This time Albright stopped and looked straight ahead, his mind rapidly reviewing the implications of what he'd just heard.

"You don't think that I...," he said, turning to look at Agent Garcia.

"No, we don't believe that you are anything other than an innocent buyer at this point, but we could use your assistance as we gather more evidence. Would you be willing to lend us the wines that you purchased from Mr. Pavlov for examination, as well as any receipts that show how much you paid for them?"

"That's the least I could do. I assure you, I would never knowingly be involved in anything remotely illegal. I don't have that many bottles, but whatever I have are yours. This represents quite a financial hit. How will I explain this to my wife? She never agreed to my 'wine folly' as she likes to call it. I fear now I'll never hear the end of it. Ah well, let's sally forth back to the house so I can get you that wine."

"Thank you, Mr. Albright, and please don't discuss this with Mr. Pavlov."

"Say no more, sir. My lips are sealed and shall remain so until you say otherwise." Albright drew his thumb and forefinger across his lips to emphasize his goodwill.

As they walked back, Garcia asked, "How do you know Angelo Salvatore?" That stopped Albright dead in his tracks as he visibly went pale.

"Angelo who?" he replied.

"You know, the man you sold the six bottles of Pavlov's wines to."

"Ah, that Angelo. Well, yes, you see, it's like this."

Twenty minutes later, Carlos Garcia was driving back to the office with nine bottles of rare wine and copies of bank statements showing astronomical prices paid for them to Edward Pavlov. "What people won't do when they have too much money," he thought to himself, shaking his head. "He would have done better putting it into his house."

He also had his notes of Albright spinning a somewhat convoluted tale about meeting Salvatore through the bank years ago, and that the subject of wine came up one day during a lunch meeting, where Albright offered to provide him with the six bottles in order to promote more business. He was definitely worried. They might be able to use that later.

Their haul for the week was impressive: thirty-eight bottles of the rarest wines money could buy, plus assorted financial records of payments made to Edward Pavlov. Eventually, they might get around to filing a report with the IRS to see if he'd reported the earnings for income tax purposes. That would wait until they had their crack at him first.

They also had extensive wiretap recordings of both Pavlov and Wong, which didn't contain anything incriminating: Edward continuing to berate his wife for not settling and not giving him access to the wine; Jimmy calling home to check in with his family and tell them how well he was doing.

One recording of Jimmy was promising, however. Two days ago, he'd called Village Wine Traders to order twenty cases of Bordeaux and Burgundies of varying vintages. None of them were rare wines, with an average price tag under a hundred dollars.

"They must have been wines for blending," Garcia muttered as he pulled into the station parking lot.

There was no longer any doubt in their minds that James Jin-Hie Wong, also known as Jimmy Wong, was fabricating wine by substituting cheaper wine and putting it in the correct bottles with forged labels. Two questions remained: did they now have enough to get a search warrant, and was the evidence at his house or somewhere else? They would only get one shot at this, so they had to be right the first time.

The Redwood Men's Club – the Same Day

"Ryan? How are you today?" Judge Walter Wallace said over the phone to Ryan Townhill, a director of The Redwood Private Men's Club.

"Walter, how nice of you to call. How can I help you?" Ryan replied.

"There's something I'd like to discuss with you, and I was hoping we could have lunch today at the Club. Shall we say the Sequoia Room at noon?"

Ryan opened his phone and scrolled to the calendar to confirm he was free. "Certainly. See you then."

As Ryan Townhill walked past reception just before twelve, he greeted Henry with a mock salute.

"Good afternoon, Mr. Townhill. How are you today, sir?"

"Fine, thank you, Henry. You're looking well," he said as he approached the counter.

"Thank you, Mr. Townhill. Can't complain now that you're here." Henry found that a little flattery never hurt, especially when talking to one of the directors.

Townhill made his way through the Victorian main lobby with its huge crystal chandelier to the main dining room where a sumptuous lunch beckoned.

The Sequoia Room had picture windows flanked by royal blue silk curtains that reached to the high ceilings, offering magnificent views of Nob Hill and the vistas beyond. Original oil paintings from past centuries that were worth a small fortune adorned its walls. Its thirty linen-covered tables were served by white-uniformed waiters who hustled back and forth to their stations. Trained to anticipate every need, they moved with the precision and grace of a well-rehearsed ballet. The soft clinking of glassware and the murmur of quiet conversations created a cultured atmosphere befitting the club's refined clientele.

Seated at a prime window table for two was Judge Walter Wallace, deep in contemplation as he studied today's lunch menu like he was reading a legal brief. Water had already been poured, and a 2018 Châteauneuf-du-Pape sat on the table, breathing in a decanter. The Judge was sipping Scotch on the rocks from a Waterford crystal tumbler while he waited for his guest to arrive.

"Find anything interesting?" Townhill asked as he slid into his seat.

"Ryan, hello. They have Dover Sole Meunière today, and they've assured me it was flown in from the UK yesterday, except I already ordered the red wine. So, I think I'll have the saddle of lamb au jus and a small green salad to start." He jotted his choice on the order pad for the waiter and looked up at Townhill. "And you?"

"Let me see," said Townhill, surveying today's offerings. "I'll join you in the green salad, and then I'll have the roast duckling with foie gras." One did not eat at the Redwood Club in order to lose weight.

"Would you like a cocktail, sir?" a waiter asked over his right shoulder.

"What is he having?"

"A double Auchentoshan 12-year single malt with ice."

"One of my favorites. I'll have that too."

After Townhill's Scotch arrived, and while they were waiting for their meals, their conversation strayed onto the latest club gossip.

"Did you see that Hugh has been posted for two months for not paying his dues?" confided the Judge leaning forward, frowning and talking in a low voice so as not to be overheard. One could not be too discreet when discussing other members.

"I recall hearing about that in one of our directors' meetings. I haven't seen him around lately, but I'm not aware of his circumstances. Is he still at the bank?"

"I certainly hope so. At his age, I doubt he would find a comparable position anywhere else, and San Francisco is not exactly the most affordable place to live."

"Plus, he has expensive tastes," Townhill added.

"I know, I know. Let's hope he pulls through. He's a likable chap, our kind of member."

Their conversation continued in this vein through the meal, followed by dessert of apple pie à la mode for the Judge and chocolate truffle cake with whipped cream for Townhill. Over coffee and Cognac, the Judge got down to business.

"Ryan, the reason I called you is because there is something that happened in my court two weeks ago that involves Edward Pavlov, and it may involve you." The gravitas in the Judge's voice made Townhill's ears perk up.

"Oh?" he replied, putting down his snifter.

"Yes. The FBI brought a motion, two motions actually, the first for a search warrant of the Club, which I denied. Two days later, they returned for a subpoena which I had to grant."

"What were they after?"

"They were investigating private dinner parties which Ed reportedly hosted here and wanted the names of the members who attended."

"Why?"

"They said they're looking into a wine forgery scheme and believe he might have sold them rare wines that aren't genuine."

"I don't believe that for a second. Those wines have a sterling provenance. I'm sure Ed has taken every care to ensure that," Townhill replied warily.

"Do you have proof? I mean, there is a lot of wine fraud out there. Did you buy any of this wine at these dinners? Did you take steps to verify that the wine is genuine?"

"I bought a few bottles. Let's see. Ed told me that he basically relied on his supplier, who told him the bottles came from collectors in Asia who were either downsizing their cellars due to old age or had fallen on hard times. I had no reason to doubt him. He said his supplier is well-connected and knows his business."

"Well, the FBI seems pretty sure the opposite is true. They have a bottle of 1946 Pétrus from his cellar that they tested and verified is a forgery."

"Wait a minute; you're just telling me this now?" he asked, suppressing his alarm.

"I know. I'm sorry. Madge and I flew out that night to our place in Tahoe and didn't return until yesterday. What with the travel and disruption, I didn't think of it until I walked into my office this morning. My advice to you is, when the FBI calls you, cooperate with them and tell them everything you know about this affair. It sounds like Ed and his supplier may be the victims of some unsavory characters."

"Thanks, Walt. I will. Thank you for lunch. If you'll excuse me, I want to get right on this."

"Not a problem," replied Judge Walter Wallace. "One more thing, this conversation is strictly *entre nous*."

"Of course, you have my word," Townhill replied as he rose from the table, shook hands, and walked into the men's cloakroom, where he called Edward Pavlov and told him what the Judge had said. A panic-stricken Pavlov immediately called his partner, Jimmy Wong.

"Jimmy? Ed. Listen, we have a problem. I have reliable intel that the FBI is investigating a wine fraud and has subpoenaed my club for names of the members who bought wine at those dinners I hosted there.

"Those documents won't show what they purchased, but they wrote checks to me for millions of dollars, and they probably still have the wine. The FBI's going to test all those bottles to verify if they're real.

"They also have a bottle of the 1946 Pétrus which they acquired somehow from my cellar, which they say is a fake. You know what this means, don't you? Please tell me you didn't know anything about this," Edward said, his distress evident.

"This is not good," Jimmy replied evenly. "I will tidy up here, and you should do the same. We are under no obligation to help the FBI."

"I think we should lie low for a while; do you agree?"

"It appears so. I don't think we should talk on the phone in future, other than to arrange a meeting place. Use a place we both know without mentioning it by name and use a time that's two hours later than when we actually meet."

"Understood. Let's meet soon when we know more," Edward said and rang off.

At the federal building, there were not two happier agents in the field office that day. Having just listened to the recording, they stood and gave each other a high five.

"This time, let's make sure we don't go before Judge Wallace for the search warrant," Morgan said to Garcia, and he meant it.

"This can't wait until Monday," Garcia replied. "Wong might move or destroy the evidence by then. We have to move *now*." They scrambled to prepare the search and arrest warrants to take downstairs for an emergency application.

Just after four o'clock the two agents appeared at the warrant desk and were informed that Judge Moira Hennessy was on night duty.

Twenty minutes later, they appeared before the Judge in her chambers. At forty-four, the middle-aged jurist had already made a name for herself with a series of decisions that were both good law and also left no doubt where she stood when lawbreakers appeared before her. She was a no-nonsense, law-and-order judge who was tough on crime. With her auburn hair tied in a bun, she looked up at them dubiously from across her desk. Her black reading glasses had a sobering effect on the two men, as they shifted their weight from foot to foot.

"Please be seated. Okay, let's have it. What's the emergency, Special Agent...," she said.

"Terrence Morgan, Your Honor."

"All right, Special Agent Morgan. Proceed."

"We are here to obtain a search warrant for the three premises described in the warrant, as well as arrest warrants for the occupants. The first is owned by James Jin-Hie Wong, who is in the United States on a visitor's visa from Hong Kong. This is where we believe he is producing large amounts of fake wine. The second house is being rented by his partner, Edward Pavlov, who we know sells it. The third house is owned by Mr. Pavlov and his common law wife, Vanessa Cole, where this wine is being stored." As Morgan spoke, Judge Hennessy was reading his affidavit.

"Stop right there," she interjected. "It says here that Mr. Wong is fabricating the wine at his house. I don't grant warrants to search people's homes lightly. What is your reason to believe it's being made there?"

"From today's phone transcript, you can see that Mr. Pavlov panicked when he was told about our investigation and called Mr. Wong, who said 'I'll tidy up here, and you should do the same.' We know that there are boxes of this fake wine in Pavlov's wine cellar. It's reasonable to believe that more evidence exists at Wong's house as well.

"We know that Wong supplies Pavlov with the wine, who in turn sells it to a select group of well-heeled collectors. We also know he managed to find nine bottles of *extremely* rare wine within three weeks to bail Pavlov out of his problem with Angelo Salvatore." He let the last name hang in the air for effect.

"Is that the same Angelo Salvatore who heads the notorious crime family?" Now they were getting somewhere.

"The same, your Honor."

"So, you surmise, based on this circumstantial evidence, that Wong is making this wine and Pavlov is selling it. If I grant these warrants, I'm concerned that a clever attorney will move to suppress the evidence, and then what will you have?" asked the Judge.

"That's a risk we'll have to take, Your Honor. If we don't move now, there won't be any evidence left come Monday."

"Very well," she said, signing and handing him the warrants. "There you go. Good luck."

As they took the elevator up to their office, Morgan joked to his partner: "When it comes to making wine, there's a right way and a Wong way." Garcia groaned, shaking his head as he covered his eyes with his right hand.

When they entered the office at five thirty, their team was assembled and raring to go.

Part III
The Fallout

*Every perfect crime has a flaw, and
each flawless lie has an expiration date.*

FBI Field Office – Later that Evening

It was seven o'clock that evening by the time Special Agents Morgan and Garcia finished organizing their eager group into three teams of four to execute the search warrants. Morgan would lead his team at Jimmy's house, with Garcia taking Edward's house. A third team, led by Special Agent Isabella Mancini, was given Vanessa and the wine cellar.

At thirty-one, she was a recent addition to the office, but had already shown she was highly capable. In addition to a law degree from Santa Clara University, she had a Masters in Forensic Psychology from the University of California-Irvine. Although she'd never led a raid, Morgan decided she was the better choice to handle Vanessa Cole.

"Listen up, people," Morgan announced when they were ready to go. "We're playing this by the book. We don't want to give them any ammo to set aside our searches on a technicality. First up, you all know the knock and announce rule, but here's a little refresher. The rule says you must: first, knock on the door; second, announce yourself as FBI; third, inform the target that you have a search warrant; and fourth, give them reasonable time to open the door. If anyone refuses to open the door or allow you in, you may break it down.

"There are cases where searches have been set aside where officers failed to identify themselves or state their purpose, or forced entry without giving the target the opportunity to open the door, or entered before a reasonable amount of time passed. I don't want that to happen here."

"Remind us what a 'reasonable amount of time' is again," some joker from the back asked as everyone laughed.

"Settle down. If there's no answer and the lights are off, wait five minutes. If the lights are on, or if they go on, wait two. Standard procedure: two of you at the front door, and two more at the rear."

They synchronized their watches, and, at eight o'clock, there were knocks on three doors. Edward was the first to answer. Opening the door, he was greeted by the sight of two men in suits, one of whom was holding out a piece of paper.

"Mr. Pavlov? Edward Pavlov?" one of them said.

"Yes," Edward replied, taken by surprise.

"I am Special Agent Terrence Morgan with the FBI. I have a warrant to search these premises," he said, handing it to him. "Please step aside." With that, Morgan and the other agent gently pushed their way past Pavlov into his foyer. They were followed shortly by the other two agents, who had been covering the back in case Pavlov decided to make a run for it.

"I don't understand," a stammering Pavlov said.

"Mr. Pavlov, we're here to gather evidence for our investigation of a suspected wine fraud being perpetrated by you, James Wong and Vanessa Cole. Is any of the wine here?"

"No... I mean, I don't know what you're talking about. Should I call my lawyer?"

"That's your right, sir, but it will not stop us from searching these premises." The other three agents had already spread out and were opening cupboards and drawers. "It would make this go faster if you answer a few questions."

"Like what?" Edward asked suspiciously.

"Like, do you have a computer, and, as I already asked, do you have any of the wine here?"

"My computer is upstairs in the second bedroom, which I use as an office; and no, I don't have any of 'the wine' here, as you put it." Morgan noted that he'd just admitted to knowing about the fake wine.

"Very good," said Morgan. "Please have a seat in the living room and we'll call you if we need you." He left him sitting on the plush gray sofa with one of the agents to keep an eye on him. As Morgan climbed the stairs and entered the office, Pavlov called his lawyer, who told him not to say anything and that he'd be right over.

"Good news is we have his Dell Laptop," an agent said to Morgan as he entered the room. "Bad news is, no papers yet showing any wine transactions."

"Keep looking while I contact the other teams to see how they're doing," Morgan replied, and called Special Agent Mancini. "Isabella, what've you got?"

"Mrs. Cole is being cooperative. She answered the door promptly and welcomed us in. She says she knows nothing about any of this, and doesn't have any documents. We're in the wine cellar now removing the boxes of rare wine that Agent Pruno identified."

"How many did you find?"

"Twenty-three, and we also found a document that might prove interesting. It's a valuation of the cellar made six months ago by a sommelier by the name of Zachary Taylor. Mrs. Cole says she hired him to appraise it for her divorce."

"Where is Mrs. Cole now?"

"She's in the living room with one of the agents."

"Good work. I'll see how Carlos is doing." His call to him went unanswered after ten rings. Not a good sign.

At eight o'clock, Agent Garcia knocked on the

door of Jimmy Wong's house. The lights were on, but nobody opened the door. The seconds ticked by, and nothing happened.

Inside, Jimmy heard the knock and quickly moved to the living room, where he furtively peeked out of the window with a view of the front door. He saw two men in cheap suits who looked either like religious fundamentalists or police. In either case, he was not buying what they were selling.

Without hesitating, he raced upstairs where he grabbed his passports and ready cash, then made his way down to the basement, grabbing a windbreaker along the way. "Too soon," he whispered to himself, as he took the stairs two at a time. He'd started the clean-up process, but most of the incriminating evidence was still there. Nothing he could do about that now. Better to save himself and live to fight another day.

He opened the rear basement door silently and peered out. By the back stairs leading up to the kitchen door he could hear two men talking. They hadn't noticed the basement door below grade, hidden from their view by a hedge. He had the element of surprise. "Attack them where they are unprepared, appear where you are not expected," Sun Tsu, author of *The Art of War*, skillfully counseled him from 2,000 years ago.

Wong moved with cat-like stealth up the concrete stairs, his footsteps barely whispering against the hard surface. He crouched behind the thick hedge, his eyes scanning the dimly lit yard. His fingers brushed the ground, grasping a small rock. With a calculated flick of his wrist, he sent it sailing over the men's heads. The rock landed with a conspicuous rustle in the bushes on the far side of the yard.

As he anticipated, the two men jerked their heads to the right, their attention diverted by the sudden noise. This was the moment Wong had been waiting for. He launched himself from his crouched position, sprinting the five yards separating him from his targets. The first agent barely had time to process the shadow descending upon him before the flying kick connected squarely with his back. The impact sent the agent sprawling to the ground, gasping for breath.

Landing nimbly on his feet, his body coiled like a spring, he pivoted smoothly to the second agent, who was starting to turn back toward the commotion. With precision and speed, he delivered a debilitating finger jab to the agent's throat. The man's eyes widened in shock as he crumpled to the ground, choking and incapacitated.

In less than two seconds, both agents were down. Wong didn't waste a moment. He dashed across the yard to the garage, his movements fluid and efficient, and slipped into the driver's seat of his Porsche 911. The car's engine roared to life with a ferocious growl. He shifted it into reverse gear and tore into the back lane, tires screeching against the pavement. From the moment he left the basement to the instant he sped away, less than twenty seconds had passed.

At the front of the house, Garcia heard the commotion in the backyard, followed shortly by two disheveled agents who limped from around the back.

"What happened to you two?" Garcia asked them.

"He surprised us," one of the agents replied. "He came out of the basement door while we were watching the kitchen, and attacked us from behind. As we were picking ourselves up, we heard a car speed away from the garage."

"Did you see the license plate or type of car at least?"

"No, it was hidden by the garage and the fence," the agent said sheepishly.

"Let's break it down!" Garcia said to the agent holding the battering ram, who moved forward. With one solid hit, the door splintered open. In the excitement he didn't notice his cell phone vibrating in his pocket.

Garcia's men proceeded to search the place and soon discovered the locked door to the basement. "Knock it down," Garcia ordered. The door gave way and two agents disappeared down the stairs.

"Agent Garcia," yelled the agent from the basement. "You'd better get down here!" Garcia went down into the basement, and knew immediately they'd hit the jackpot. A few minutes later, having left two agents there to catalog and remove the evidence, he called Morgan.

"Operation Hangover is a go, repeat operation hangover is a go. We have everything here that we need, except Jimmy Wong," Garcia said to Morgan.

"Where's he?" Morgan asked.

"The two rookies guarding the back door let the Kung Fu Panda get away. They say he surprised them from behind; used martial arts. I'll put out an APB."

Annoyed, Special Agent Morgan returned to the living room, hauled Pavlov to his feet, spun him around and cuffed him. "Edward Pavlov, you're under arrest. You have the right to remain silent. Anything you say can and will be used against you in court. You have the right to talk to a lawyer for advice before we ask you any questions. You have the right to have a lawyer with you during questioning. If you cannot afford a lawyer, one will be appointed for you. Do you understand?"

Pavlov didn't reply. He just looked down at the floor. Like most people who have never been arrested before, he was in a mild state of shock and disbelief. How was this happening?

An hour later, Pavlov's lawyer walked into the living room. "Alexei Zakharov, here to see my client."

"Make it brief, counsellor," replied Morgan. "He's under arrest for wine fraud. His next stop is the county jail, where he'll spend the night, and longer if he can't arrange bail."

Zakharov sat beside Pavlov on the couch and talked to him in hushed tones, again reminding him not to talk to anyone, and advising him he would retain the best criminal lawyer in the city to take his case. He explained that, at this late hour on a Friday night, he'd have to spend the weekend in jail, but assured him that bail would be arranged on Monday. That required an application to a judge, hence the wait. It was a favorite trick of police to arrest you on a Friday night, he said, so you'd have to spend the weekend in jail. He estimated the judge would set bail in the fifty-thousand-dollar range. Since he already had Pavlov's power of attorney and his banking information, he could handle all the details. Then he left, his dejected client holding his downturned head in his hands.

Now furious that Wong had escaped, Morgan called numerous television stations and news outlets, informing them of the allegations and that they would escort Pavlov from his house at ten o'clock. Calls like that tended to have the same effect as pouring fish food into a goldfish bowl. A feeding frenzy resulted, which was exactly what Morgan intended.

At ten o'clock precisely, they opened the door and Morgan frog-marched Pavlov, who he was holding by the arm, his handcuffed hands in front of him for all to see. A flurry of lights went on and cameras rolled amid shouted questions from the press. This "perp walk" was now an ingrained part of law enforcement, used regularly to lower the accused's chance of a fair trial.

"Let's see how his lawyers explain this away to the jury," mused Morgan about his orchestrated media frenzy as they navigated the crush between the house and the street.

The remaining agents also left with their booty, which only amounted to Pavlov's Dell laptop computer. They'd found no rare wines or records showing any transactions pertaining to the wine business. "Slim pickings," Agent Morgan thought sullenly as he guided a grim Edward Pavlov to the rear seat of his car, making sure to protect his head as he slid him in.

The others had fared better, in spite of Wong's escape. They had custody of twenty-three cases of fake wine from Vanessa's house, the wine-making paraphernalia from Jimmy Wong's house, and Vanessa herself, who was earnestly pleading her innocence. Come to think of it, so was Edward, but that came as no surprise to anyone.

On the Lam – Later that Night

As Jimmy Wong headed east on Geary Boulevard, his mind was racing. He needed to change his license plate and was looking for a quiet side street where he could make the switch. Just before Japantown, he turned right and pulled up to the curb behind a line of cars.

Popping the hood, he put on a baseball cap that he kept behind the driver's seat, then got out and looked around to confirm nobody was watching. With a screwdriver from his toolkit, he exchanged his license plates with those of the car directly in front.

The next order of business was to find a telephone store and buy a burner phone, since the cops were listening to his conversations. He removed the battery and SIM card from his cell phone in case they were tracking his movements. On second thought, he walked over to the nearest storm drain and dropped the triad through the grate to a satisfying splash.

Five minutes and a few blocks later, he stopped at 24 Hour World Mobile, where he purchased the dumbest cell phone he could find, plus a prepaid SIM card. Back in his car, he took stock: the Porsche would be known to them, if not now, then soon, but not the license plate. That would buy him a little time, but he needed to ditch the car quickly.

Next, he had about thirty thousand in cash and two passports: one from Hong Kong with the name James Jin-Hie Wong, and the other from Macau with the name Juan Jiao-long Huang. The one thing he'd done right in the last six hours was to wire all the money to his company, Grand Fortune (Hong Kong) Limited. Its bank account was at a regional Chinese bank in Hong Kong, beyond the reach of the U.S. authorities. Too bad he didn't have time to clear out the basement.

He had to move fast, before they started watching the airports. Maybe they already were. His destination was Hong Kong, but how to get there without being caught in the process? He needed a private jet. Executive airports tended to be more accommodating and less nosy, based on the incredible assumption that only the rich and honest used them. Yes, a long-range jet that could reach Hong Kong without refueling, to avoid the risk of arrest while stopped in Hawaii. Time to make a call on his new cell phone.

"*Wái?*" a voice answered on the other end.

"Brother, it's Jimmy," he said urgently. "I need your help."

"What is it this time, little brother?" Ronald, his oldest brother, groaned. Ronald well knew his unstable younger brother's antics, and was anticipating that, whatever it was, it would most probably disrupt his day. It was after eleven o'clock Saturday morning in Hong Kong, and he was just about to leave with his family for a family dim sum lunch at their favorite restaurant. His wife was glaring at him, her eyes urging him to get going. He did not have time to talk.

"I need you to arrange a private jet to bring me home, not later than tomorrow, and make sure it's a non-stop flight."

"Can't you handle that from your end?"

"It's difficult to explain, and right now we don't have time. Trust me, it's urgent," Jimmy said gravely. "Also, I will use my Macau passport. You know the name."

"Fine," Ronald sighed. "I'm just going to an appointment right now, but I'll see what I can do and call you back at this number, okay?"

"Thank you, brother. Enjoy your lunch," Jimmy said as he ended the call, not naive enough to believe Ronald had a business meeting on a Saturday morning.

"Urgent private jet. Non-stop. Macau passport." Ronald shook his head as he and his family headed out to their lunch.

Sitting in his car, Jimmy was contemplating his next move. He decided to hole up in a motel near the San Francisco Airport where the executive airport was located, likely where the private jet would be. With nothing to do in the meantime but keep out of sight, he restarted the car and drove toward the airport, using only side streets.

On the outskirts of the airport, he found a suitably seedy motel. When he checked in with his Macau passport, he was asked if he wanted the room by the hour or the day, which spoke volumes about his choice. He booked a single room for one day, hoping his brother would come through for him quickly, then drove his car over to room 8. When he opened the door, the first thing he noticed was the mirror on the wall at the head of the bed, and another on the ceiling. Functional.

Jimmy was dressed and lying on the bed when the call came in at ten o'clock Saturday morning. His brother explained that, after numerous phone calls, he finally found Stellar Jet Charters with a long-range jet that was available to fly that afternoon, but at a price: $310,000. He needed to be at Hayward Executive Airport, which was a few miles from his motel, by two o'clock. Ronald confirmed that Stellar had received his wire and that the flight would be non-stop.

With four hours to kill, Jimmy decided to have a late breakfast at a chain restaurant across the street. When he returned to the motel, he moved his car a few blocks away to a quiet lane, removed the license plates and dropped them through the grate. Then he walked six blocks away and called a taxi, which arrived quickly. He instructed the driver to take him to the executive airport and arrived in plenty of time to do the paperwork and board his flight.

The pleasant lady at the Stellar Jet Charters desk helped him with the forms, copied his passport and informed him that his crew of three would be flying a Gulfstream G-650 with a range of seven thousand nautical miles.

"What is the distance to Hong Kong?" Jimmy asked.

"Let's see," she replied, tapping on her computer. "A little over six thousand nautical miles."

"So, the flight will be non-stop."

"Correct. You're all set. The waiting area is over there. Help yourself to coffee or tea."

If Stellar Jet Charters was in any way suspicious about why a Chinese national named Juan Jiao-long Huang was traveling alone, at an exorbitant price, non-stop to Hong Kong on short notice, they didn't show it.

At one thirty, he boarded the plane and settled into his seat, while the attractive flight attendant brought him a bottle of water. This was not his first time on a private jet, so he knew what to expect. "So far, so good," he thought, as he took a sip.

"Good morning, Mr.... err, Huang," came a voice with an Australian accent over the intercom. "I am Captain Michael Harris, your pilot today. With me is my copilot, Richard Jones. You've already met Christine in the main cabin. Our flight will take approximately twelve and a half hours, which should put us into Hong Kong at one thirty Sunday afternoon local time. We've been cleared for takeoff, so please buckle up and enjoy the flight. Bon voyage."

As the jet climbed into the wild blue yonder over San Francisco, Jimmy started to relax, realizing he'd successfully escaped to China, a country without an extradition treaty with the United States. He wondered how Edward would handle whatever his government had in store for him.

Geary Street – June 10, 2023

At five feet eight inches and 180 pounds, Lawrence Taube, Esq. cut an imposing figure in his tailored three-piece suit. After five o'clock most days, he could be found drinking Woodford Reserve Double Oaked Bourbon and smoking a Cuban cigar in his storefront law office on Geary Street. Brimming with memorabilia and Americana, it was a treasure trove of vintage posters, antique typewriters, and shelves of legal books, interspersed with quirky trinkets. Each item told a story, which he often used as props to entertain and impress clients and colleagues alike.

At sixty-two, with long silver hair down to his shoulders, Lawrence Taube used his withering stare to bend both opponents and clients to his will. His presence bordered on mythic, and stories of his courtroom exploits were legendary among the legal community. He relished these tales, often embellishing them for dramatic effect.

When he was holding forth, cigar in one hand and bourbon in the other, he habitually lamented that his role model, Clarence Darrow, caused cigars to be banned in court. One of the greatest criminal lawyers of all time, Darrow was a courtroom master who knew how to distract the jury at the right time, particularly during the prosecution's closing arguments. He'd insert a wire in his cigar so that the ash became longer and longer, causing the jury to focus on it instead of the prosecution.

It didn't matter to Lawrence if the story were true, only that you believed it. In court, he'd often mimic Darrow's tactics, weaving intricate narratives that captivated juries and confounded prosecutors. He even had a framed photograph of Darrow on the wall, which he treated like a shrine, often tipping his hat to it following a particularly clever legal maneuver. "Those were the days my friend," he'd say to his long-gone hero.

Known as a ferocious criminal attorney, the "Lion of Union Square" possessed a comprehensive knowledge of the law coupled with a courtroom presence that few could match. He was, in short, a fixture of the San Francisco legal scene, feared by his opponents and respected by his peers. It was Lawrence Taube that Alexei Zakharov called Saturday morning to get his client, Edward Pavlov, out of the County Jail.

"You're in luck, Mr. Zakharov," Taube replied. "I've just finished a major drug case that went five weeks in court. It was an exhausting contest, but we were victorious. Have you told your client not to talk to anyone while in County?"

"I certainly did, and I'm confident he understands why."

"Excellent. I'll have one of my associates visit him today, and we'll arrange bail on Monday. My retainer is fifty thousand dollars. Can I assume that I can look to you for payment of that and the bail?"

"Yes, I have access to his funds," Zakharov confirmed. "I'll send over a bank draft Monday morning."

Taube hung up and summoned one of his junior associates to handle the bail application. All four members of the firm were working that Saturday in order to catch up on the files that had been neglected during the lengthy trial. The atmosphere was electric, a mix of exhilaration from their recent win and anticipation of the challenges ahead. Twenty minutes later, Danny Glickstein was on his computer scheduling his visit to Edward Pavlov at the County Jail for later that afternoon.

"Good afternoon, Mr. Pavlov," Danny said as he was brought into the interview room. "I work for your attorney, Lawrence Taube, and I'm here to answer any questions or concerns you might have, and prepare an affidavit about you for the bail application."

"When will I be able to get out of here? It's not the most pleasant place, and the company leaves much to be desired."

"I'm sorry about that. Bail applications are made to a judge. Since it's the weekend, we can't go before one until Monday. We'll do everything in our power to get you out of here on Monday afternoon."

"That's two more days! You mean I'll be cooped up with these drug addicts and drunks in that communal cell with only a bench to sit on until then?"

"I'm afraid so. My advice is to keep to yourself, don't make any new friends and above all, don't talk to anyone."

"Will I get bail?" Pavlov asked, subdued.

"The burden of proving you should stay in jail is on the prosecution, so yes, you'll get bail. Now, let's get down to business, shall we? For this affidavit, I need to show that you're an upstanding citizen and not a flight risk. Let's start at the beginning. What's your full name, address, age and occupation?"

Danny efficiently took him through his career, marriages, family, charity work, club memberships (the Redwood Club was a big plus), to establish his ties to the community. His methodical approach reassured him, and he took a small measure of comfort in recounting his life's accomplishments. After they were finished, he called for the guard to take Pavlov back to his communal cell, and returned to the office to prepare his affidavit while the facts were still fresh. He returned to the County Jail the next day, where he had Pavlov sign.

The bail hearing was set for two o'clock on Monday afternoon before Judge Moira Hennessy. Lawrence Taube and Daniel Glickstein were seated at the counsel table when Edward Pavlov was led into court, looking disheveled after two and a half days in jail, and seated beside them. His appearance was a stark contrast to his usual polished look, a visual representation of his sudden fall from grace. Taube rose to address the court.

"May it please the Court, Lawrence Taube for Mr. Edward Pavlov." The prosecutor stopped reading the file and jumped to his feet to introduce himself.

"Good afternoon, Mr. Taube. How nice to have you in my court again," Judge Hennessy said, with just a hint of sarcasm. "What do we have today?"

"Your Honor, as you'll see from his affidavit, my client is an American citizen and a highly respected businessman who has lived most of his life here in the city. He has children and other relatives here. He gives generously to charitable organizations and belongs to various clubs, including The Redwood Private Men's Club. In short, Your Honor, he's not a flight risk. We ask that he be released on his own recognizance with the usual undertakings to appear in court."

The prosecutor was on his feet again. Stanley Stossel Jr. was a diminutive man of fifty-three, dressed in a serviceable suit. His head was bereft of hair, and he wore black horn-rimmed glasses in a futile attempt to look serious. He looked positively disorganized as he shuffled his papers, probably because he was overworked and underpaid, and definitely malicious. Despite his unassuming appearance, he was known for

233

his tenacity and unrelenting pursuit of criminals. He yearned to see them all behind bars.

"Your Honor, Mr. Pavlov stands accused of making and selling millions of dollars of fraudulent wine to his friends at this club of his. He was in a long-running conspiracy with his Chinese partner and his wife. I see no redeeming features that support releasing him at all, and certainly not without bail."

"Thank you, gentlemen," Judge Hennessy said. "Bail will be set at fifty thousand dollars. Next case."

Taube turned to Pavlov. "We'll arrange for the money to be paid into court, and have you out of here and home in time for dinner. In the meantime, relax. You're in good hands."

Pavlov was taken back to his cell, where he sat on his section of bench and kept quiet. He was surrounded by more tattoos than he'd ever seen. They were the dregs of society who were content to leave him be, sensing that he was not one of them. Three days sitting upright on a bench, with your back against a concrete wall, in the same clothes, was no fun. No fun at all.

"What am I going to do?" he thought, leaning forward with his head between his hands. The grim reality of his situation had set in as he began to realize he might not get out of this.

By six o'clock, he was sitting in front of Lawrence Taube in his eclectic office. "Your buddy, James Wong, escaped. They're mad as hell about it," he said pointedly. "They've decided you're the mastermind and want you to take the fall. Your persecutor – which is exactly what he is – is a piece of work. Stanley Stossel will ensure you're toast, unless we pull a rabbit out of a hat. Do we have a rabbit, Mr. Pavlov?"

"I don't know about that," he replied, still shaken

by the last seventy-two hours. "In my defense, I didn't know the wine was fake. Can they even prove that?"

"Allow me to explain how the justice system works. Next year is an election year, so the District Attorney wants to look good. This is a big case that will get a lot of press coverage, he'll make sure of that. The media are a bunch of scandal-mongering muckrakers who love to exaggerate news to sell papers. They'll be all over it, and paint you as the villain.

"At this juncture, the prosecutor has only charged you with one count of fraud, which carries a maximum penalty of five years. When he gets around to filing the indictment with the grand jury, he will have piled on a bunch more charges, which will run you the risk of spending up to twenty-five years in prison. Also, he'll freeze your bank accounts and assets, and look for restitution for the money that your purchasers lost from buying the wine."

"Can he do that; I mean add extra charges to increase the penalty?" Edward asked.

"The prosecutor has complete discretion over what charges he wants to lay. Typically, he'll overcharge you with crimes that don't apply in order to coerce you into pleading guilty. I'm sure you've heard they win ninety-seven percent of their cases in federal court, but that's because ninety percent of the time defendants plead guilty. Defendants typically take the plea bargain to avoid what's called the 'trial penalty', where the prosecutor asks for a harsher sentence because you put him to the trouble and expense of a trial, or so the story goes. It's a very effective system to eliminate your right to a fair trial.

"Stossel is a small man with a big chip on his shoulder. He wants to win at any cost. In his mind, you're already guilty and deserve to be put away for as long as he can get from the court. He'll use all of these tricks, like the charge bargaining and the trial penalty, in order to make the mountain as steep and risky as possible for you to climb.

"Then there's your wife. What is she going to say about all this? Will she testify against you? Does she have the ability to sink you?"

"I get the picture. What should I do?"

"Nothing for now, but make sure you have access to funds to live on and keep our retainer going. *Capisce*?"

"Yes. Is my retainer with you safe?" Pavlov asked.

"Nooo, not anymore. We're one of the first places they'll look. You'll have to be cleverer than that. Good news is, the prosecutor is still putting his case together, so you have a little time. We need to consider every possible move they might make. We'll contact you when we have something solid to discuss. In the meantime, try to relax and know that you're in good hands."

Pavlov left Taube's office, his mind knowing the next steps were critical. He had to trust his lawyer. As he walked the familiar streets of the city, everything felt different. The looming court case cast a shadow over every aspect of his life, altering his perception of freedom and security. The stakes were high and the path ahead fraught with uncertainty.

For his part, Lawrence Taube was pondering the complexities of the case. The thrill of the courtroom, the rigor of legal strategy, and the sheer will to win were what drove him. This case, with its high-profile nature and intricate details, was exactly the kind of puzzle he loved. The Lion of Union Square was ready to roar again, whether in the courtroom or behind closed doors.

Mission District – June 14, 2023

"Mr. Zachary Taylor?" the man in the drab suit asked, flanked by an equally fashion-challenged partner. They had emerged from a nondescript gray Ford sedan which was sitting in front of Zach's house, and parked themselves on the sidewalk, blocking him and Sophie as they exited their Uber from the airport.

"Yes," replied Zach, taken by surprise, putting down the heavy suitcases he was carrying. One thing about Sophie, she did not travel light.

"We're with the FBI and have a warrant for your arrest." The special agent proceeded to identify himself and his partner (they were the two newbies who'd let Jimmy Wong escape a few days earlier) and read Zach his rights. At first, he was too dumbfounded to react, then he felt the other agent take his arms from behind and lock handcuffs on his wrists.

"What's this all about?" he barely managed to ask.

"You are charged with conspiracy to commit fraud in connection with a wine forgery ring, along with James Wong, Edward Pavlov and Vanessa Cole. Let's go."

"Sophie," he said as he was being led to the car, "go inside and call Mitch. Tell him I've been arrested. He'll know what to do!" Sitting in the car on the way downtown, he thought, "Thank God the children weren't here to see this."

Luckily for Sophie, it was not yet noon on Wednesday morning when she called Mitch Adams' private cell number. He answered after the third ring.

"Mitch? It's Sophie. Yes, I'm fine. We had a great time, thank you. Mitch, please stop talking and listen;

this is urgent. We just got home, and Zach was arrested by two FBI agents regarding the James Wong wine fraud thing. I warned him about this, but he said it would all be fine. But it's not fine; it's a disaster. They've taken him downtown. This is my worst nightmare. Can you do something, please? And fast? I don't want him to have to spend the night in jail like a common criminal. God, this is humiliating."

"I've got you, Sophie," Mitch replied. "Say no more. I'll call you back." With that, Mitch hung up and called Martin Abelman, his counterpart at the FBI.

"Hey Marty," Mitch said, "We have a bit of a situation here, and I could really use your help."

"Ask and you might receive," Abelman replied, feeling witty. "What's up?"

"I hear you've made arrests in Operation Hangover."

"That's correct. We nabbed two of them Saturday night, but the main actor flew the coop. This morning, we arrested the fourth member of the group. He's being brought here for interrogation as we speak."

"Is his name Zachary Taylor?"

"Yes, it is. We stumbled onto his name when we did the search of the wine cellar where the forged wine was kept. We found his appraisal of the wine, which implicated him as part of the conspiracy. Mrs. Cole gave us his details, but he was out of the country. He just returned today."

Mitchell Adams let out a long breath to calm himself before he continued. "He's one of us."

"Excuse me?"

"Just like I said, he's one of us. Your men just arrested Agent Pruno! Zachary Taylor is Agent Pruno. I understand that mistakes happen, but I'd appreciate it if you could correct this one as soon as possible." What happened next was a string of expletives from Abelman, an apology of sorts, followed by a promise to release Agent Pruno pronto.

Sometimes bureaucracies do not operate at peak efficiency. On this occasion, when the two agents arrived at headquarters with their prisoner, there'd been a shift change, and the new duty officer failed to tell them to take Zach upstairs. Instead, they took him to an interview room, eager to develop the case and earn kudos for themselves. Especially after they'd let Jimmy Wong escape.

"So, Mr. Taylor," the first agent said. "May I call you Zachary?"

"I'm usually called Zach. Only my mother called me Zachary, when she was mad at me."

"All right, Zach. Tell us about your activities at Mrs. Cole's house, let's see, in January."

"There's really not much to tell. I met Vanessa in early January, and she asked me to appraise her wine collection, which I did over the next few weeks." Standing behind his interrogator, the second agent was glaring at him and flexing his fists as if getting ready to leap over and pummel him into a confession.

"Did you also see her socially?"

"We went out for dinner a few times. I enjoyed her company. She'd separated from her husband a year earlier."

"Did you two connect romantically?"

"Not at all. We were friends, that's all."

"She says she fell in love with you."

"She may have, but it was only a friendship." The menacing agent at the back yelled at him at this point.

"She says the reason you prepared the appraisal

was to verify the prices she and her husband were selling the fake wine for! Come on, admit it. You were in it with them." His face was now a few inches from his. Zach could smell coffee on his breath as he screamed at him.

"That's not true," Zach replied evenly. "If she said that, she's just trying to save herself by shifting the blame onto me. Please call your supervisor. I'm sure this can be sorted out."

Over the next forty minutes, they did their level best to extract a confession from him. They played good cop, bad cop; they withheld water; they set the temperature as high as possible; they threatened him with violence. Despite the discomfort Zach was feeling, he knew they only had his wine appraisal and Vanessa's testimony the night she was arrested, which wasn't a lot. They were fishing for more.

There was no point in Zach telling them he was Agent Pruno, since they probably wouldn't know who that was, or more likely, wouldn't believe him. No, he'd just have to wait until Mitch got through to Morgan and Garcia, so they could connect the dots. This was hardly the tightest spot he had been in as an undercover agent.

"Have those two rookies arrived yet with Zachary Taylor?" Abelman asked the duty officer at reception over the phone.

"Yes sir. They're in interview room three," he replied, unaware that anything was amiss.

"I want you to go there right now and tell those nitwits to bring him here immediately! Are we clear?" If Abelman were a cartoon character, smoke would be coming out of his ears.

Back at interview room three, the agents were put off their stride by a knock at the door. Opening it, they were informed by a concerned looking officer to go immediately upstairs with their prisoner, which they found rather odd, since standard procedure was to interrogate suspects as soon as possible. Exactly what they were doing.

As they emerged from the elevator, Morgan and Garcia were waiting for them. They knew instantly from their scowls that something was wrong.

"Follow us," was all Morgan said, and they walked with Zach in tow, still in handcuffs, down the hall to another meeting room. Special Agent in Charge Martin Abelman was seated at the head of the conference table.

"Sit," he said as they entered, "and take those handcuffs off Mr. Taylor." When they were seated and confused, he continued: "Gentlemen, and I use the term loosely, please say hello to Agent Pruno."

"Christ almighty," Morgan swore quietly, while he gathered his thoughts. "Mr. Taylor, I'm so sorry. We didn't put two and two together because, of course, we didn't know your real name when we talked to you in Florence last week."

"Thanks guys. It's okay. Call me Zach," he replied. "How did you find out?"

"I received a call an hour ago from Mitch Adams at ABC," Abelman interjected.

"Right. I might need a little help explaining this to my wife, who predicted something like this was going to happen. She's probably climbing the walls right now. Would you please call Mitch and ask him to tell her that we're good?"

Once that was cleared up, they ordered in sandwiches and discussed the case, including how they could continue to use Zach undercover to gather more evidence. After reviewing what they'd collected so far, they concluded they could use his help persuading Vanessa to cooperate, and also helping them locate the money, so they could freeze it pending the final outcome of the case. Restitution to the victims was a priority. Zach was unsure how to do either, and he told them so, given that Vanessa had canceled him six weeks earlier.

The meeting came to an end, and the agents took turns apologizing. His time in the interview room had been pretty rough and took him back to his undercover work, something he'd thought was behind him.

"I'm getting too old for this shit," he thought to himself as he was escorted to the street, where the taxi that the FBI had paid for was waiting.

When he arrived home, Sophie greeted him with open arms and a bottle of Veuve Cliquot Champagne. No recriminations, no "I told you so's" – just gratitude that her husband was home and safe. They walked into the kitchen where their kids were standing by the counter, which was a surprise as they'd said their goodbyes earlier at the airport.

"Hey Dad," his daughter Emma said, as she came up and hugged him. His son, Lucas, was standing beside her. They looked both happy to see him and concerned at the same time.

"Didn't I just spend two weeks with you in Italy?" Zach asked facetiously.

"We know, we know," replied Emma, rolling her eyes. "Mom called us and told us it was important for us to come over now and stay for dinner, and be together as a family today. She didn't tell us why, but said it was important. We're here for you, Dad. Whatever it is, we've got your back."

Edward's House – June 18, 2023

It was Father's Day, and Edward Pavlov was looking forward to going to his daughter's house for a family dinner. All his kids and their families would be there, excluding Vanessa and his ex-wife. On second thought, maybe he should swear off women altogether, since he didn't seem to have much luck with them. Anyway, he was in the kitchen washing a few dishes by hand when the doorbell chimed. He opened the door to find the sun blocked by his two least favorite thugs.

"Hello, Mr. Pavlov," the one called Mr. Smith said. "Do you have a moment?"

"Will this take long?"

"Not if you have $920,000 handy."

"I don't understand. I thought our business was completed," Edward said warily.

"We thought so too, until Mr. Salvatore read about your arrest, and the problem with the wine you sold him. As you can imagine, he was quite upset."

"Don't you mean he's upset with Hugh Albright? After all, that's who sold him the wine."

"Ah, yes, Mr. Albright. First, he says he doesn't have that kind of money, and looking at his house, we're inclined to believe him. Second, he says he's a victim too. He says he bought many bottles from you over the years, so he's also out of pocket *mucho dinero*. Turns out, he's one of your creditors, just like Mr. Salvatore. Who'd have thought they'd have so much in common?"

Smith grinned briefly, then fixed Edward with an icy stare. "This is no laughing matter, Mr. Pavlov. Mr. Salvatore wants his money back, and he wants it now."

"How did $460,000 get to $920,000?" Edward asked matter-of-factly, failing to see any humor in this situation.

"As you know, Mr. Salvatore is an extremely fair person. You've had his money for six months, and he's entitled to a profit. Ten percent per week is normal, but given the circumstances and the large amount involved, he's willing to be reasonable. And he'll keep the wine as a memento. So, when can he expect payment?"

"I don't have it on me. I'll have to make a few calls..."

Sensing he was being evasive, Smith cut him off. "Listen, don't take too long. As we told you before, Mr. Salvatore is not a patient man. We'll return at six o'clock tomorrow night to pick it up. Oh, and Mr. Pavlov, make sure it's all cash."

The two hulks turned on their heels and drove off in their Ram 1500 pickup truck, followed by a nondescript gray Ford sedan from the FBI motor pool. The agents inside had recorded the conversation.

"I think it's time we paid Mrs. Pavlov a visit, don't you Mr. Brown? Let's drive over to Russian Hill."

Fifteen minutes later, they were talking to Vanessa at her front door and making her feel extremely anxious. The events of the past few days had taken their toll on her, and she was on the verge of snapping.

"What do you expect me to do about it?" she demanded, her voice rising.

"Please, Mrs. Pavlov. Try to remai..."

"I'm not *Mrs. Pavlov*. My name is Cole, Vanessa Cole. I'm not married to that bastard, never was, and we're separated. Have you got that?"

"Got it. Your hus... Your former partner has been a bad boy, and now owes our client $920,000, which he has until six o'clock tomorrow to pay. You look like an intelligent woman. I'm sure I don't have to explain the consequences if he fails to pay up."

"All right, fine. I'll call him; and don't come back."

"If the money is paid, I'm sure you won't see us again. If not, well... Anyway, you have a nice day." As they left, Vanessa was already dialing Edward on her cell phone as she closed the door. Her hands were shaking uncontrollably.

"Pick up, pick up!" she whispered as it rang for the fifth time.

"Hello, Vanessa," Edward said, contemptuously.

"What the hell, Ed? First you get me arrested, and now two jumbo-sized guys just came here looking for $920,000! They say you have to pay them by six tomorrow, or else. It's bad enough we're going through this separation business, but now this? Tell me, what are you going to do about it? I'd like to know."

"Christ, Vanessa. This has nothing to do with..."

"The hell it doesn't! Have you seen the size of those guys? Just being near them freaked me out. They're not the kind to take disappointment lightly. So, I repeat: what are you going to do about it?"

"Okay, okay. Enough. They want cash. There's enough in the lock box under the floor in the wine cellar. I'll come over this afternoon and get it."

"But the lawyer told me not to give you anything because it's community property."

"Vanessa! Now's not the time. We're literally talking about life and death here! Please get with the program."

"What's in it for me?"

"Fine. If you'll do this, I'll sign whatever you want, and we'll be done with each other."

"How much is in the lock box?"

"I don't know. I guess about three million."

"All right; but this time you have to tell me the combination. I won't touch the rest without talking to you first."

"Suit yourself. I'm having dinner with the kids. I'll drop by on the way there, at around five."

Vanessa's welcome was colder than usual, and Edward could see she was suffering from the strain of all this. They walked silently down to the wine cellar, where he crossed to the far corner and lifted some of the floor boards, revealing a medium-sized cavity containing a steel lock box measuring two by three feet. He entered the combination and methodically removed bank notes worth a million dollars, counting out loud. Vanessa could see there were lots more where those came from, and asked what the combination was. Edward sighed, and told her. The events had overtaken their petty squabbles.

Edward put the money in a sports bag he had with him, replaced the floor boards and left. There was nothing more to say except "thank you" and "goodbye".

At six o'clock the next day, as Edward was handing over the sports bag with the cash, the FBI was watching.

"Should we move in on them now?" Special Agent Carlos Garcia asked his partner Terrence Morgan.

"And charge them with what?" Morgan replied. "All I see is three men settling a misunderstanding. We may not like Angelo Salvatore or his methods, but we can't let that color our judgment of what's going on here. Our chance will come."

Little Italy – June 19, 2023

While Edward Pavlov was surrendering his sports bag full of cash, Angelo Salvatore was sitting down to dinner with five of his trusted associates at Cucina Italiana, a restaurant where the community gathered to enjoy hearty, home-cooked meals. Tonight, it was providing a discreet setting for Angelo and his *capos* to convene. This meal was less about sustenance: it was a ritual of camaraderie and respect, reinforcing the bonds that held the family together.

Nestled in the heart of Little Italy, the restaurant exuded Old-World charm with its warm, rustic décor and flickering candlelight. Its walls were adorned with vintage family photos and colorful murals depicting scenic Italian landscapes. The soft hum of conversation and the aroma of fresh herbs and garlic filled the air, which enhanced the sense of authenticity and tradition, and kept its loyal customers coming back for more.

As they helped themselves to the antipasto of cured meats, cheeses, marinated vegetables and olives, the men discussed business and shared stories, their laughter mingling with the clinking of glasses. The Chianti, with its deep, robust flavors, complemented the savory notes of the dish. The atmosphere was surprisingly relaxed given the business they were in, and the iron will of the head of their family. That could all come to a halt if he should become suddenly displeased with anything or anyone.

On a sideboard, one of Jimmy's fake wines was breathing as a special treat. Although he'd not tried any of them yet, Angelo figured it was worth the gamble.

After all, how bad could it be if they were selling for fifty thousand dollars apiece? It was also an occasion for celebration, since he expected at any moment to hear from his dense soldiers that he was $920,000 richer. Right on cue, his cell phone chirped.

"Boss?" said Mr. Smith. "The chickens are in the roost." Angelo killed the cell and turned to his guests, a big smile on his face.

"*Benvenuti a tutti*," he announced, clinking his wine glass with a fork. "Tonight is a special one for me as we've just closed an important business deal, which some of you know about." He raised his glass in the direction of Hugh Albright, who acknowledged him by tipping his head slightly and holding up his wine glass.

Unbeknownst to everyone involved in *Operation Hangover*, Hugh and Angelo went way back. In fact, they had first met in high school, and worked on and off together for some forty years. The opportunities for them to collaborate were dwindling as the myriad of money laundering laws increasingly choked the banking industry. Doing commercial transactions these days was like navigating a veritable minefield. That, of course, made this wine transaction all the sweeter. In addition, the ten percent commission that Hugh would receive from Angelo would help take the sting out of his fake wine purchases through the years. Friends looked after each other, after all.

Besides Angelo and Hugh, in attendance were two senior members of Angelo's organization, his *consigliere* who handled his legal affairs, and his accountant who took care of the books. Altogether, they were the executive committee of the Angelo Salvatore crime family, responsible for the major decisions that could not be handled at the individual level.

"My friends, I have a special wine to share with you tonight in honor of the occasion. It's breathing behind me, which is more than I can say for some of our former associates..." He waited until the laughter died down. "Seriously, this wine was purchased at great cost, and I'm told it is one of the finest that money can buy. It's very hard to find as there are not many of them left." He held up the bottle so everyone could see it was a 1946 Pétrus. Well, not really, but he was not about to tell them that. His transaction with Hugh to purchase the wine didn't involve the other members, so they were in the dark about the fraud. He signaled the waiter, and took out a card with notes about the wine.

"We will serve it now, and I welcome your opinions." He put on reading glasses and consulted his card. "This wine is from Bordeaux in France, and is over seventy years old. Pétrus is one of the great estates, and has been labeled the most expensive wine in the world. It has been called 'wondrous', 'spellbinding' and 'timeless' by wine critics. I trust you'll agree. Please raise your glasses in a toast to good food, good wine and good friends. *Saluti*!"

Angelo sat down and looked around the table as the goodfellas tasted and talked animatedly about the wine. He waited patiently for the bravest to voice an opinion. Something each of them knew to do only with utmost caution, and as little as possible. You never wanted to be the nail that sticks out of the coffin and gets hammered down. Hugh, not being Italian and therefore largely unaware of the risks, was the first to go.

"Without a doubt, one of the finest wines I've ever had the opportunity to drink. It hasn't suffered one jot from its old age, much like our esteemed host." Much applause and compliments directed at Angelo followed.

"My first taste immediately transported me to another world, another universe, where perfection reigns supreme. It is an outstanding wine from a great vintage. The bouquet is simply breathtaking, and the flavors are to die for... please forget I said that." Hugh quickly realized from the solemn faces staring at him that it was time for him to sit down, but as he did, the room burst into peals of laughter. There was not a dry eye in the room when the *consigliere* went next.

"Signore Salvatore, it is an honor to be in your company and to share this excellent wine with you. I agree with Mr. Albright that it's the best I've ever tasted. From the perfumed aroma to the refined and balanced taste, I wouldn't say no to trying some more." He sat down to backslapping by one of the *capos*, who rose to speak.

"Don Angelo, as you know my experience with wine rarely strays beyond Italy, but I have to say, this wine rivals, perhaps exceeds, the best I've had from Tuscany and Veneto. It's not every day any of us have the chance to drink a classic like this, so old and yet so fresh and alive. Thank you for including me."

"Don Angelo," said the other *capo*, "I too am grateful for this chance to experience what the French can do with their grapes when they get it right. I've never tasted a wine this delicious. *Bravo e grazie.*"

The accountant, who knew what the wine's cost but didn't know about the fraud or today's collection from Edward Pavlov, got up to say the final words of praise. "Gentlemen, without a doubt, the finest wine I've had the privilege to drink, and the finest to be had anywhere. I would drink it all day, if only I could afford it. Thank you so much for including me, Don Angelo. From the bottom of my heart."

Dinner was then served, starting with a creamy risotto garnished with shaved truffles. This was followed by chicken cacciatore, its tender pieces nestled in an aromatic tomato sauce, studded with bell peppers, mushrooms and olives. The savory aroma filled the air, mingled with hints of garlic and fresh herbs, promising a rustic, homey delight with each bite. Cloth napkins were affixed to everyone's collars to save their shirts from any splatter of sauce, an old school nod to practicality over politeness.

The evening continued until ten o'clock, when they all departed for their homes, the memory of drinking a historic wine still fresh in their minds. Angelo was pleased that the Pétrus had been so well received. "Is a wine still fake if people accept it as the real thing?" he mused as he was chauffeured to his nearby mansion in his vintage black Cadillac limousine.

Not far behind, the FBI B team followed Angelo in their Ford sedan, since Morgan and Garcia were busy across town watching Pavlov's house. "When are we going to catch a break in this case? I'm getting really tired of this endless watching and waiting," the agent sitting in the passenger seat said.

"Be patient," his partner replied. "Salvatore will make a mistake soon enough, and when he does, we'll be right there."

"It's over." It was Vanessa calling on WhatsApp.

"Hello, Vanessa," replied Zach. "I see you kept my number after blocking it," he said, an iciness in his voice revealing memories that he'd tried to bury. It didn't make his new assignment of obtaining her cooperation any easier.

"Maurice dumped me. He said he doesn't want to be involved with my legal problems. He's such an academic and a coward. I wish I'd never met him."

"I can't say I'm surprised, given what I heard about him. When someone betrays your trust like that it tends to destroy the relationship; but you already know that."

"Ouch! Can we meet at Ernie's and talk? I really need to see you."

"Fine. I'll see you there at four."

Later, as Zach was about to leave his house, he texted Sophie: "Meeting Vanessa for a drink. All good. Back by 6." Then he drove the twenty minutes to Ernie's, where he sat at a corner table with a clear view of the entrance. It had been two months since he last saw Vanessa, and he'd not expected their paths to cross again. The bitterness of how she ended their friendship still lingered, a raw wound not yet healed. Vanessa had walked out of his life, leaving an emotional trail of chaos and confusion. Her sudden call brought it all crashing back.

When she walked in, Zach's eyes narrowed as he nursed a glass of Dalwhinnie 12 on the rocks. Vanessa looked as stunning as ever, her brown hair cascading to her shoulders, her eyes sparkling. She wore a sleek, black dress that accentuated her figure, no doubt a calculated choice to appear vulnerable and alluring.

She approached the table with a tentative smile, her demeanor a mix of contrition and seduction. "Zach," she began, her voice soft. "Thank you for agreeing to meet me."

He took a slow sip of his Scotch, allowing the silence to stretch uncomfortably before responding. "You said it was important. I'm here. Let's talk."

She sat down, smoothing her dress and looking around nervously. "Maurice and I are finished. Apparently, my legal problems scared him off."

Before Zach could reply, Ernie was by his side. "Haven't seen you two in here for a while," he said warmly. "What can we get you, Vanessa?"

"A double Macallan 12 on ice for me, please Ernie," she said, not looking up. Sensing now was not the time to linger, Ernie beat a hasty retreat for the bar.

Zach arched an eyebrow, his gaze unwavering. "Helping you is the last thing from my mind right now."

Vanessa winced at his words, a fleeting expression of genuine hurt crossing her face. "I'm sorry I hurt you. I really am. But right now, I need your help. You know about the charges against me. We're in this together. I didn't know the wine was fake, Zach. I swear."

He leaned back, crossing his arms. "And why should I believe you? The last time we spoke, you were busy with Maurice and I was left dealing with the fallout."

"I didn't mean to hurt you," Vanessa replied quietly. "When we met, I was vulnerable and lonely. I'd been drifting, single and alone, for over a year. You were lonely too. We offered each other shelter from the storm, but eventually I realized I needed more than you were willing to give. You made it clear you weren't available. I needed someone who was." She lowered her eyes.

"And Maurice came along. Did I do or say anything to make you believe that we would become lovers, or that I would leave my wife?"

"No, never, you never misled me, I always admired your discipline. But your friendship wasn't enough for me. We had a situationship with no progress, no future. We hardly went out, weren't a couple, didn't do things with my friends. I found it too confusing to have both of you in my life at the same time. I wanted a serious relationship."

"I thought about that a lot in those two months after you moved on. I thought we had something special which could co-exist with my marriage. During our time together we talked about everything. I thought I knew you. Were you ever straight with me?"

"I loved you and hoped you'd understand," she replied solemnly.

"Was it really love, or was it more about getting me to leave Sophie?" Zach asked to no reply.

"Please," she implored, her voice breaking. "I don't have anyone else to turn to. Edward is not going to help me, and his partner Jimmy Wong has fled to Hong Kong. I'm stuck, Zach. I need you to help me."

Finally, there it was, the real reason for this meeting. Zach studied her, conflict evident in his eyes. Vanessa had a way of weaving herself into people's lives, creating a tapestry of dependency and manipulation. Despite his better judgment, a part of him still felt drawn to her, a magnetic pull he couldn't quite shake off.

He took a sip, savoring the rich, complex flavors. "Let's get to the point, Vanessa. What exactly do you want from me?" he asked, his tone measured.

She nodded, her expression turning businesslike. "I've been thinking about our strategy. We need to present a united front, show that we were both duped by Edward and Jimmy. The more cohesive our story, the better our chances. And I need your expertise. You appraised my wine cellar. If you testify that neither of us knew the wine was fake, it could help my case. They respect your opinion in the wine community, Zach. Your word carries significant weight."

He sighed, running a hand through his hair. "It's not that simple, Vanessa. My own reputation is on the line. Associating with you again, after everything... it's a risk." He sensed it was not yet time to reel her in.

"I know, I know," she said quickly, reaching across the table to touch his hand. "I'm desperate. I'll do anything to make it right. Please, Zach."

He pulled his hand away, the gesture as much for himself as for her. "Why should I believe you won't disappear again when things get tough?"

She hesitated, a flicker of something unreadable in her eyes. "Because I need you. More than ever." Their eyes locked, a silent battle of wills playing out in the charged space between them. Vanessa's desperation was palpable, a tangible force that tugged at Zach's resolve. He wanted to believe her, to think that she was capable of change, but the scars of their past interactions ran deep. He quickly reminded himself that this wasn't why he was here.

"Okay, here's what you have to do," he said finally. "First, after you tell them you didn't know anything, you have to say that I also didn't know about the fake wine and wasn't involved in this alleged conspiracy, that you only hired me to appraise the wine collection for community property purposes."

"All right."

"Next, you need to tell them everything you know about Edward's involvement with Jimmy Wong, and also where all your assets are located, because they'll want to get their hands on them to compensate the victims. That may be enough to keep you out of jail. If you do this, I'll tell them you didn't know the wine was fake."

"All of it? Fifty million dollars?"

"The amount will depend on how much the prosecutor calculates that people lost. It's up to him."

Vanessa was silent for a few seconds while she mulled it over. Suddenly, her face lit up with a mix of relief and triumph. "Thank you, Zach. I promise you won't regret it."

As she leaned back, sipping her Scotch with a calculating glint in her eye, Zach could not shake the feeling that she would try to draw him into another one of her webs. Vanessa was a master of manipulation. Only this time, everything would go according to his plan.

FBI Field Office – June 21, 2023

"Good morning, Zach," said Special Agent Terrence Morgan on the phone. "What have you got for me?"

"I met with Vanessa and had a frank discussion about her situation. She's ready to cooperate fully. She'll tell you about Pavlov and Wong, and also where all the jewels are located. She should be calling you soon to arrange a meeting."

"That's excellent news. God knows we need it, since Jimmy Wong skipped town with his millions. The prosecutor is fuming. I wouldn't want to be working in his office right now."

"Just to confirm, she didn't know the wine was fake."

"Got it. I'll do my best to convince the prosecutor. Talk to you soon." Morgan hung up, and sat back to wait for Vanessa's call.

Later that morning, Vanessa Cole sat in the sterile waiting room of the FBI field office, her heart pounding despite her best efforts to remain calm. The beige walls and nondescript furniture only increased her unease as she awaited her fate. The reality of her situation had settled in, but there was no turning back now. She took a deep breath to steady her nerves. This was her only chance to avoid prison and clear her name.

Earlier, Zach had called her to say that he'd spoken to Special Agent Morgan, explained her position, and vouched for her innocence. He told her to call Morgan, and added that he expected her to do the same for him when she met him today. She was happy they were patching things up, and was looking forward to starting again. She really did love him.

"Mrs. Cole?" A tall, stern-faced agent called out from the doorway. Vanessa stood, smoothed her skirt and walked toward the agent. She followed him down a corridor until they reached a small conference room. Inside, two agents waited – one older who appeared sympathetic, and the other younger with an intense, focused gaze.

"Please, have a seat, Mrs. Cole," the older agent said, gesturing to a chair. "I'm Special Agent Terrence Morgan, and this is Special Agent Carlos Garcia." Vanessa sat down, her hands clasped tightly in her lap. She felt the weight of their scrutiny, like they were assessing her every move.

"Mrs. Cole," Morgan began, "on the night you were arrested, you told our colleague that you were unaware of the fraudulent nature of the wine stored in your cellar. Is that correct?"

"Yes," she replied nervously. "As I told your Agent Mancini, I think that was her name, Edward never told me anything about it. I never suspected it was anything but the real thing. The few bottles I was allowed to drink... Well, that makes it sound like I drank the whole bottle. The few times I tried a glass, I thought they were superb and exactly what they were supposed to be."

"All right. I'll say this plainly. We could use your help to bring your husband, Edward Pavlov, to justice. His partner, Jimmy Wong, fled to Hong Kong where we can't touch him."

Vanessa nodded, swallowing hard. "I understand. I'll do whatever I can. I didn't know the wine was fake, and I want to help make things right."

Morgan exchanged a glance with Garcia before continuing. "We appreciate your desire to cooperate. Our goal is to convict your husband and seek reimbursement for the buyers who were defrauded. We know you and Edward have substantial assets, paid for with stolen money, and we could use your help to identify and locate them."

Vanessa's mind raced. She could reveal the location of the hidden stash of cash in the wine cellar, as well as the various bank and brokerage accounts. She knew all about their financial status, and the profits from the wine business, since she'd done the books, not Edward. While he tried to keep his business dealings secret, ironically, he'd trusted her to do the accounting. Now, she'd use that knowledge to her advantage.

"I can help with that," she said, her voice steady. "For starters, there's two million dollars hidden under the floor of the wine cellar. I assume you already know about our other assets, the house, the vacation home in Tahoe, the bank accounts, Edward's business."

Both agents leaned forward, their interest piqued. "Will you lead us to this cash?" Morgan asked.

"Yes," Vanessa replied without hesitation. "But I want something in return." She knew this was her chance.

Morgan nodded. "What's that?"

"I'd like to keep the house and furnishings... and five million dollars," she replied, avoiding eye contact.

"We can do that, subject to the court's approval. In the meantime, the prosecutor is prepared to reduce your charges significantly. Instead of jail time, he'll recommend a fine of fifty thousand dollars."

Vanessa felt a wave of relief wash over her. This was her way out, her chance to reclaim her life. "I agree," she said. "I can take you to the money now. When do we sign the papers?"

"They'll be ready when we return. First, we need to take your statement about everything you know about Edward, Jimmy and the wine business."

The drive to Vanessa's home was tense and silent. She sat in the back seat of the nondescript FBI car, her eyes fixed on the passing scenery. Memories of happier times with Edward flooded her mind, but she pushed them aside. This was about her survival, and, she admitted to herself grudgingly, about doing the right thing for the people who'd been deceived.

When they arrived, Vanessa led the agents down to the musty wine cellar. She walked straight to the far corner, knelt down and carefully lifted the floorboards, revealing the hidden compartment and steel lock box inside, which she opened. "There," she said, pointing to the neatly bundled stacks of cash.

Morgan and Garcia exchanged a look of satisfaction. "Thank you, Mrs. Cole," Morgan said. "This is very helpful."

She stood back and watched as they methodically extracted the money and documented everything. It felt surreal, as if she were watching someone else's life.

An hour later, they were back at the FBI office, where Vanessa signed the documents to formalize her agreement. The relief she felt was tempered by the knowledge that Edward would soon be facing the consequences of his actions, even if he'd been unaware of the full extent of the fraud. She'd lived with him for twenty years before he suddenly called it quits. It was a bittersweet ending to all that they'd gone through.

"You've done the right thing today, Mrs. Cole," Morgan said as they concluded their meeting. "Your cooperation will make a significant difference to the people who lost money."

Vanessa nodded, her eyes misting over. "I just want to put this behind me and move on with my life," she said softly.

"You will," Garcia assured her. "This will be a new beginning for you."

As she left the office, Vanessa felt a strange sense of liberation. Walking with a newfound determination, she fished her cell phone from her purse and called Zach.

"It's done," she said. "When can I see you?"

"I'm a little busy at the moment," Zach replied, thinking furiously how to get out of whatever it was she had in mind. "How about I call you tomorrow?"

"All right, I'll go, but don't wait too long."

"*No problema*," he said with relief.

After they hung up, Morgan called Zach to tell him about the deal Vanessa wanted, which they agreed seemed doable. Then he called Stanley Stossel, and told him the same thing. He agreed sulkily, which is to say, he did not object too strenuously. Carving out the house and five million dollars could be tricky, he said, depending on the value of their assets versus the amount of restitution required for the victims. At the end of the day, it was up to the judge.

Victoria Peak – June 24, 2023

Jimmy Wong, sometimes known as Juan Jiao-long Huang, was seated opposite his father in his wood-lined den. Between them sat a Georgian partners' desk, complete with a jade green leather inlay with stamped gold borders. A relic of past colonial times, it was both reassuring for its sense of history and terrifying for the power it projected. Being back in Hong Kong, Jimmy was feeling decidedly uncomfortable as he fought to contain the squirming little boy inside.

His father ruled a vast empire based on their Macau casino, which over the years had expanded into real estate holdings, currency exchanges and escort services, to name only a few. Now seventy-five years old, Raymond Kai-Li Wong was still a powerful man, firmly in control of his family business empire. Dressed in a black silk suit from his Hong Kong tailor, white shirt and blue paisley bow tie, he observed his son with disdain as the smoke from his cigarette curled around his head.

"You said you had something to tell me, so speak," he said to his youngest and most fragile son.

"Yes, father. I have returned to live in Hong Kong, and work in the family businesses, with your approval," Jimmy replied, trying to avoid eye contact.

"What has caused you to come back? I thought you liked it in America."

"My plans did not work out, and I was forced to leave. I humbly request permission to work in whatever capacity you choose for me."

"What happened?"

"Despite my best precautions, my *Gweilo*

partner was indiscreet. He caused an investigation by the FBI to occur, which resulted in his arrest two weeks ago. I would have been arrested too, but I barely escaped, thanks to my brother. I've been thinking about our businesses, and I'm sure I can be a valuable asset, although I don't want to return to the casino and its sad memories," he said, thinking of Mei-Ling.

Wong senior already knew about his youngest son's problems in San Francisco, and how he'd escaped in a private jet. He was proud of his eldest son, Ronald, who'd saved Jimmy with his quick thinking. What should he do with this impetuous, troubled boy? At least he had the presence of mind to transfer the money to China before leaving.

"What do you propose?"

"I could take over the management of our escort service division. I am told we have an immediate need for a dozen girls from Thailand, and I thought I could, with your permission, fly to Bangkok and bring them here. I've already arranged the flight, and contacted our agent there, who is finding the girls for me to interview as we speak."

"Very well," sighed his father. "You have shown an ability to manage people. You have my permission, but I will be watching you closely. You may go now."

Two days later, Juan Jiao-long Huang, better known as Jimmy Wong, was walking down the long corridor in Bangkok's Suvarnabhumi Airport toward immigration. Leaving China was a calculated risk, but one he decided to take. They needed more hostesses in Hong Kong, and Thai girls in their twenties were preferred for their beauty, warmth and grace.

As he walked, three airport cameras took his photograph, which was instantly analyzed by facial recognition software that had been installed in 2019. He finally reached the front of the long line, and presented his passport to the uniformed officer.

"*Sà-wàt-dee mâi pêuan mueng Thai,*" the officer greeted him routinely in Thai, scanning his Macau passport and staring closely at his computer screen. Although Jimmy didn't speak Thai, he knew it meant "Welcome to Thailand".

"Good afternoon," Jimmy replied casually.

"Please sir, wait here," the officer said, then walked over to a nearby door. He disappeared inside, then returned two minutes later with two more officers.

"Please come with us, sir," one of the two new officers said, gesturing toward the door, which opened onto a labyrinth of small offices. The corridors were narrow, the walls made of dark hardwood on the bottom half and clear glass above, offering glimpses of tense encounters happening in adjacent rooms. The air was thick with the scent of disinfectant.

They escorted him to one of the offices, a small sterile room with a utilitarian desk and a chair on either side. The soft hum of the air conditioner added to the clinical atmosphere.

"Please, sit," the officer instructed, his voice pleasant but carrying an unspoken command. As Jimmy sat on the hard wooden chair and glanced around, he noted the neat stacks of papers and a computer screen displaying a government logo. The officer sat opposite him, his expression neutral but his eyes keen, scrutinizing every flicker of Jimmy's unease. The second officer remained standing between Jimmy and the door. Although their expressions remained placid, they both had heavy black pistols on their belts.

Outside the glass walls, other travelers were

being similarly scrutinized, some looking as bewildered and anxious as Jimmy felt. The glass of the upper walls allowed for an unsettling level of visibility, creating a fishbowl effect where privacy was an illusion.

The officer's questions came methodically, probing into Jimmy's travel itinerary, his reasons for visiting Thailand, the contents of his luggage. Each answer Jimmy provided felt like it was being weighed, measured and scrutinized for any sign of discrepancy. His mouth felt dry and his palms damp as he forced himself to remain calm and composed.

Minutes stretched into an indeterminate span of time, the tension in the room mounting. The standing officer's presence was a constant, silent pressure, his vigilant gaze unwavering. Finally, after what felt like an eternity, the seated officer leaned back.

"Sir, are you James Jin-Hie Wong?"

"No, I am Juan Jiao-long Huang, as you can see from my passport," Jimmy replied, pointing to his passport sitting in plain view on the desk in front of him. He tried to steady his breathing, focusing on the officer's words rather than the pistols or the oppressive stillness of the room. The officer's voice, though even and controlled, seemed to reverberate off the glass and hardwood, amplifying the sense of confinement.

"Our facial recognition software has identified you as Mr. James Jin-Hie Wong. I regret to inform you that Interpol has issued a Red Notice against this person, which requires us to detain you while proper procedures are followed. We are very sorry for the inconvenience. Do you have anyone you would like to call?"

"Yes, if I could use my cell phone, I'd like to call my brother." They handed over his phone, and he called Ronald in Hong Kong, explained his situation, and asked for help. Ronald, for his part, sounded very concerned, and promised to retain local legal counsel without delay. "My brother says he will have a lawyer call this number within the hour."

"Very well. Please come with us." They showed Jimmy to a small, bare room, with bars on the window looking into the office area. "We will keep your cell phone. When your lawyer calls, we will talk to him and arrange for him to meet you. That is, provided he calls you soon and can meet you before four o'clock today. If he does not do this, you will be transferred to the police jail, and he can meet you there tomorrow."

As he was waiting, in a race against time, Jimmy's mind was spinning. He knew that U.S. immigration had digital copies of his face and fingerprints, which he gave them when he obtained his visitor's visa. They obviously used that information to file the Red Notice. It was bad luck that he didn't know about the facial recognition at the airport.

Knowing what he did about the infamous Bangkok Remand Prison, he realized he was between a rock and a hard place. If he fought extradition to the USA, he would spend months, perhaps years, in that overcrowded hellhole, where he'd have to sleep on a blanket on the dirty floor over the legs of other prisoners. The food was terrible to inedible, group showers consisted of scooping water over yourself from a large collective basin, and medical care was non-existent. The inmate lying next to you could be sick or dying, or even dead, since the guards did not check regularly. Death from disease and suicide was a regular occurrence. Having the highest number of inmates in Southeast Asia, they placed you in leg irons for the first three months to stop you from committing suicide.

Jimmy shivered as he thought about what lay ahead. He had to move fast and get out on bail.

After three hours, the two immigration officers returned with another man in a suit, who introduced himself as an official from the Chinese Embassy.

"Wong," he said. "I spoke to your brother, Ronald. I am here to start the process to have you released on bail. We have lawyers who know how to do this. In the meantime, I have arranged for you to be turned over to the Royal Thai Police who will keep you in custody until the bail hearing by the court. That way you will avoid going to the Bangkok Remand Prison."

"Thank you so much. How long will it take?"

"To obtain bail? Your lawyer will know, but I'd estimate less than two weeks. Because this is an extradition case that will be brought by the United States, the lawyer will push the U.S. Embassy to file its case. There needs to be a case before the court in order for you to apply for bail. The FBI maintains an office there, so they move quite fast in cases like these."

Upon entering the police station, Jimmy was overwhelmed by the humid air and stench of sweat and decay. He was processed and placed in a cramped holding cell with other detainees, whose dejected looks said it all. His questions about his medication went unanswered as nobody spoke English or Cantonese.

The next day, a man in his early forties wearing a dark suit visited Jimmy. He introduced himself as Mr. Lin, a Thai lawyer specializing in international cases.

"Mr. Wong, I have been briefed on your situation by the Chinese Embassy," Mr. Lin said, his English polished and clear. "We need to prepare for your bail hearing. It is crucial that we present you as a reliable individual who is not a flight risk."

"Before we start, Mr. Lin," Jimmy interrupted, "I should explain that I'm bipolar, and they haven't allowed me to take my medication, which was in my suitcase."

"I will look into that as soon as we finish here."

"Okay, but don't take too long. It's wearing off, and I'm beginning to feel anxious."

"I quite understand. Now, let's get back to the matter of your release. Tell me about yourself." Jimmy explained his business background, his extensive travels, his family in China, and of course his problem in California and the red notice. Mr. Lin listened intently, taking detailed notes. "We have a good chance," he concluded. "The court will consider several factors, including your ties to the country, your character, and the charges. The embassy's support is a great help."

The days leading up to the bail hearing were desperately lonely, since the other prisoners in the cell kept to themselves and only spoke Thai, referring scornfully to Jimmy as a "*farang*", which he knew meant "foreigner". Most of the time he sat in a corner of the cell, his knees pulled up to his chest, and thought about how he was going to get out of there.

Three days had passed since Jimmy last received his bipolar medication. The guards had stolen it, Mr. Lin reported, and left to find replacements. "What's taking him so long?" Jimmy screamed, causing the other prisoners to whisper among themselves and cast wary glances in his direction. His hands shook as he rubbed his temples, the absence of the drugs gnawing at his sanity. He felt the mania building, a tidal wave of agitation he couldn't control.

Without warning, Jimmy sprang to his feet, his eyes wild. He launched himself at the nearest inmate, his martial arts training taking over. He moved with precision and ferocity, striking with lethal accuracy. The cell erupted into chaos as the prisoners tried to defend themselves, but they were no match for Jimmy's manic strength and skill. Shouts and screams echoed off the grimy walls as bodies collided and fell.

"Stop him!" one of the inmates shouted in Thai, but the others were too terrified to intervene. Jimmy's mind was a whirlwind of rage and fear, as he struck out blindly, his fists and feet connecting with flesh and bone, leaving a trail of broken bodies and blood in his wake.

The commotion drew the attention of the guards, who rushed into the cell with wooden batons. Swinging with brutal force, Jimmy felt the first blow across his back, a jarring pain that broke through his mania. As he turned to face his attackers, another blow caught him across the jaw, sending him sprawling to the floor. The guards didn't stop, beating him relentlessly, while he curled into a protective ball. Only when he lost consciousness did they stop.

When he awoke, he was alone in a small, dimly lit cell. Solitary confinement. His body ached, and he could taste blood in his mouth. Time lost meaning in the isolation, and the walls seemed to close in on him until, finally, the heavy door creaked open. It was his lawyer, Mr. Lin, holding a small package.

"Jimmy, thank God I found you," he said, his voice filled with relief. He handed him the package containing his precious medications. With trembling hands, Jimmy took the pills and swallowed them, feeling a flicker of hope for the first time in weeks. "We'll get you out of here very soon," Mr. Lin promised. "You must hold on a little longer."

As the medication kicked in, Jimmy felt the

chaos in his mind recede. Closing his eyes, he sat back against the cold wall of his cell and took a deep breath.

After an agonizing nine days in solitary, Jimmy was escorted to a modest courtroom with wooden benches and digital displays. There was a raised platform where the judge sat, with a giant portrait of the king on the wall behind him.

Mr. Lin stood beside Jimmy as the Judge entered and the room fell silent. The prosecutor, a stern-looking woman, stood and introduced the man seated beside her, an FBI legal attaché who represented the American government in its quest to extradite Jimmy back to the United States. She outlined the charges and emphasized the severity of the allegations and the risk of his fleeing if granted bail. All of this occurred in Thai, with Mr. Lin quietly translating for Jimmy.

Mr. Lin then stood and presented Jimmy as a respectable businessman from a good family in Hong Kong, with no history of criminal activity. The embassy's involvement was highlighted to reinforce his reliability.

The Judge, a middle-aged man with a stern look, asked several questions, probing Jimmy's background and the nature of his travels. Finally, he announced his decision: bail was granted, but Jimmy would have to surrender his passport and report to the local police station twice a week. Payment of two million bhat, the equivalent of fifty-five thousand dollars, was also required, which Mr. Lin promptly paid.

Jimmy's knees nearly buckled with relief. It wasn't complete freedom, but he was away from the suffocating walls of his cell. Outside the courthouse, Bangkok buzzed with afternoon life as neon lights reflected off the slick, rain-soaked streets. Mr. Lin placed a hand on Jimmy's shoulder.

"This is only the beginning, Mr. Wong," he said, his voice steady. "It is important that you report to the police station every Monday and Thursday before noon. If you don't, the court will revoke your bail and place you in prison until your trial. You do not want this to happen."

"I understand," Jimmy replied as they parted. He hailed a three-wheeled tuk tuk to take him to meet Somchai, their local agent, who by now should have received his other passport in his real name from Ronald. There was much to do, and only a few days until his first visit to the police station.

Lawrence Taube's Office – June 26, 2023

Edward Pavlov sat across from his lawyer, Lawrence Taube, in his eccentric office on Geary Street. His junior, Danny Glickstein, who'd done most of the legwork, was there too. He was feeling the pressure of the past weeks, and the ambiance of the room only amplified his unease. The ever-present law books were a tangible menace, their spines cracked and worn, representing years of legal battles. The soft hum of the air conditioner amplified the oppressive mood.

Taube, with his rotund features and unwavering confidence, sat across the mahogany desk, his hands steepled in thought. He was studying Edward with a mixture of sympathy and determination. Edward could see the reflection of his disheveled self in the polished surface of the desk, a reminder of how far he'd fallen.

"Edward," Taube began, his voice measured and calm, "we need to discuss the plea agreement. This is a critical juncture in your case, and you need to understand what's at stake. For starters, Vanessa signed a plea deal last week. We don't know the details, but if I had to guess, it will be a fine and no jail time in exchange for her cooperation. She's going to tell them everything she knows about you and the wine business, and trade your fortune for her freedom. This will be her way of throwing you under the proverbial bus."

Edward's heart raced. He'd been dreading this conversation. He should never have involved Vanessa. "As I said before, Lawrence, I didn't know the wine was fake. Jimmy's the one who made it. I was just the face, the salesman."

Taube sighed, leaning back in his leather chair. "I understand, Edward, but the circumstantial evidence against you is substantial. You sold millions of dollars' worth of fake wine. The emails, the transactions, the testimonies; they all paint a damning picture. The prosecution has ten witnesses, all scions of society and members of your club for God's sake, who are out millions of dollars thanks to you. They're out for blood."

Edward clenched his fists, frustration boiling over. "How many times do I have to say it: I'm innocent! I trusted Jimmy. How was I supposed to know the wine was fake?"

Lawrence Taube leaned forward, his eyes locking onto Edward's. "Innocent or naive or willfully blind? The cards are stacked against you, Edward. The prosecutor, Stanley Stossel, is only willing to cut a deal because Jimmy Wong escaped to Hong Kong, where there's no extradition treaty."

"I thought we had a treaty with Hong Kong."

"There used to be one, but we canceled it in July 2020, after China imposed its new national security law, which undermined Hong Kong's civil liberties. Remember the mass protests in the streets? Anyway, without an extradition treaty, Stossel's hands are tied. He wants someone to pay for this, and you're the only one left."

"What about that sommelier friend of Vanessa's?"

"You mean Zachary Taylor? They didn't charge him, which tells me they decided he was not part of the conspiracy, so there's nothing for us there. No, it all comes down to you."

"Wait a minute. If they don't have Jimmy, how can they prove I knew the wine was fake? He's charging me with conspiracy, but doesn't he have to prove the underlying crime? I understand they can prove the wine was forged, but for me to be guilty of conspiracy, don't they have to show I intended to sell fake wine?" Edward said, desperation evident in his voice.

"As I said before, are you innocent or willfully blind? Do you realize there have been twenty-seven separate news articles about you so far which leave little doubt about your guilt, courtesy of the DOJ and the servile press? The DOJ believes if they repeat their allegations long enough, everyone, including the jury, will believe them. This will only get worse.

"Will a jury decide that you knew what was going on? Beside the bad press, a great deal of money changed hands. That'll sway them against you, for sure. The decision is yours, but I recommend you take the plea."

Edward swallowed hard, the reality of his situation sinking in deeper. "What's the deal?"

"One count of conspiracy to defraud, which carries a maximum of five years. Stossel will recommend one year in federal prison plus restitution. One year is a win considering the scale of the fraud."

"One year?" Edward's voice cracked. "That's still a year of my life gone. My reputation, my business..."

Lawrence Taube nodded sympathetically. "It's a tough pill to swallow I know, but consider the alternative. If we go to trial and lose, which may well happen given the evidence, you could face five years behind bars, and more if he piles on extra charges. You could be looking at ten to fifteen years by the time he finishes. Do you really want to take that risk?"

Edward stared at the desk, the enormity of the decision overwhelming him. The thought of spending a day in prison was terrifying enough, but the prospect of a lengthy trial with an uncertain outcome was worse.

"I don't know if I can do it. Admitting guilt for something I didn't do…"

Taube's expression softened. "I totally get it, Edward; but sometimes you have to weigh the risks. Think about your family and your future. A year in prison, with a chance to rebuild your life afterward, is better than losing everything.

"There's also the matter of my fees, which will cost you up to two million dollars if you choose to fight. With your assets frozen, how will you afford that?"

Edward nodded slowly, the fight draining out of him. "All right. Let's do it."

His lawyer gave him a reassuring smile. "Good. We'll arrange a meeting with Stossel to finalize the plea agreement. Then it's off to court."

Their encounter with Stanley Stossel took place in a conference room at the federal building. Mustering all the charm of an annoyed eel, he greeted them with a curt nod, and wasted no time getting to the point.

"Mr. Pavlov, Mr. Taube. After lengthy talks with your counsel, I'm prepared to offer you this plea deal," he said, looking at Pavlov: "One year in federal prison, plus restitution. Given the circumstances, this is an exceptional offer, which is only available today. If you leave this room without reaching a settlement, we'll increase the charges in the indictment. Something you do not want to occur."

Edward glanced at his lawyer, who gave a subtle nod. "I understand," Edward said quietly.

Stossel's gaze was unwavering. "You're making the right choice, Mr. Pavlov. This is your chance to accept responsibility and move forward."

Edward felt a pang of resentment, but kept his emotions in check. "I accept the deal."

"Very well," Stossel replied, his tone final as he pushed the plea agreement across the table for them to read and sign. When the signed agreement was slid back into his hands, he simply said: "Good. We'll see you in court. You're free to go, Mr. Pavlov, but make sure that you're available for your court appearance, when your plea will be finalized."

Courtroom number seven was a grand yet intimidating space, with its high ceilings and polished wooden pews. Edward stood beside Lawrence Taube at the defendant's table, his heart pounding in his chest. Judge Moira Hennessey, who Taube explained was known for her stern demeanor and no-nonsense approach, presided over the proceedings.

"Mr. Pavlov," she began, her voice echoing through the chamber, "it says here that you have agreed to plead guilty to one count of conspiracy to defraud. Is that correct?"

"Yes, Your Honor," Edward replied quietly.

Judge Hennessey's eyes bore into him, assessing his sincerity. "Mr. Stossel and Mr. Taube have both recommended a sentence of one year in federal prison, plus restitution. I disagree. Given the severity of the crime, and the very substantial financial losses incurred by the victims, I find their recommendation to be insufficient."

Edward's breath caught in his throat. He shot a panicked glance at Taube, who remained composed but visibly tense, his eyes fixed on the Judge.

"Therefore," Judge Hennessey continued, "I am imposing a sentence of thirty months in federal prison."

Edward felt the ground suddenly shift beneath him. Thirty months. The words reverberated in his mind. This wasn't how it was supposed to go.

"Is there anything else? In that event, court is adjourned," Judge Hennessey declared, striking her gavel.

As the courtroom emptied, Edward turned to Taube, his face pale. "Thirty months, Lawrence. How can they do this to me?"

Taube placed a reassuring hand on his shoulder. "Never fear, Edward. We'll get through this, one step at a time."

As he was led away, the reality of his situation began to sink in. He'd agreed to plead guilty, betting on the joint advice of counsel and leniency from the Judge, only to find himself facing a harsher sentence. Why didn't Taube tell him she could ignore their recommendation and render whatever decision she liked? So much for the famous prowess of the Lion of Union Square.

While Edward awaited his formal sentencing and transfer to federal prison, his emotions fluctuated between panic and dread. He spent the time wrapping up his business affairs and making arrangements for his family. The finality of each conversation felt like another nail in the coffin of his former life.

On the day of his sentencing, Edward found himself back in court before Judge Hennessey. "Mr. Pavlov," she began, her tone as stern as ever, "you have been found guilty of conspiracy to defraud. You have admitted your guilt, and now it is time for you to face the consequences of your actions."

Edward stood motionless, every word cutting deep and fueling an inner fury.

"I hereby sentence you to thirty months in federal prison, to be followed by another three years of supervised release. I'm also ordering that you pay restitution to the victims in the amount of twenty million dollars." An audible gasp from the members of his family reverberated through the courtroom.

The finality of her words hit Edward like a slap in the face. He felt a sense of detachment, as if he were watching the scene unfold from a distance. The gavel came down with a resounding thud, sealing his fate. He'd played the game, trusted the system, made a deal, and been screwed, he thought as he was led away in handcuffs.

As he was led away, he cast one last look at his family and held up his two thumbs to let them know he'd be back.

Bangkok – July 5, 2023

Jimmy's tuk tuk navigated its way haphazardly through the crowded Bangkok alleyways, the air thick with the scents of street food and exhaust fumes. His destination was a featureless building in the heart of the Patpong Red Light District, where he hoped to find Somchai, their local agent. He entered it through a narrow corridor lit by flickering fluorescent lights. At the end of the hallway, he knocked on a steel door, which opened almost immediately to reveal Somchai's smiling face. He was a small man who exuded a quiet confidence, despite missing a couple of his front teeth.

"Wong, welcome, nice to meet you," Somchai said, stepping aside to let him in. The room was decidedly modest with fading travel posters of Thailand on its white walls, and a large wooden table and chairs dominating the center.

"Good to meet you too, Somchai," Jimmy replied, shaking his hand firmly. "Are the girls ready?"

"Yes, they in next room. Before we proceed, we must discuss matter of work permits," Somchai said in his broken English, a frown replacing his smile as he got down to business. Jimmy nodded, understanding where this was going. "Cost of tourist visas gone up, need more money."

Jimmy nodded thoughtfully. He couldn't afford to alienate this man. "Please explain."

"Girls enter on tourist visa. With correct connections, we maybe convert to short-term work permit. It is delicate matter that needs incentive paid to right places."

Jimmy considered this, tapping his fingers on the table. "We need to ensure the girls understand the risks and what's required of them. This business relies on their discretion."

"Agreed," Somchai said, standing up. "Meet them now?" Jimmy followed him to an adjoining room where six young women sat nervously. They were dressed modestly, their makeup understated. Each of them had been chosen by Somchai's team for their looks, charm and ability to blend into the upscale districts of Hong Kong.

"Ladies, this is Wong," Somchai introduced Jimmy to the girls in English. "He is respected businessman from Hong Kong, and if you impress him today, you work in most luxurious city in Asia."

Jimmy smiled warmly in order to put them at ease. "Hello, everyone. I'm here to answer any questions you might have about the work and the requirements."

One of the girls, a petite woman with long, straight hair, raised her hand. "What kind of work will we be doing exactly?"

"You'll be working as escorts," Jimmy explained. "Your role is to provide companionship to wealthy clients. This includes attending events, dinners, and sometimes more personal activities. It's important that you be professional and maintain their confidentiality and confidence at all times."

Another girl asked nervously, "What about our safety? How will we be protected?"

"We take your safety very seriously," Jimmy assured them. "We will provide security when necessary, and have strict protocols to ensure you'll always be safe. If you ever feel uncomfortable, you can contact us and we will come immediately." The questions continued about various aspects of the job, from salary to living arrangements. Jimmy answered each one patiently. By the end of the session, the girls were chattering eagerly with each other, their initial apprehension eased.

"They seem like a good group," Jimmy remarked to Somchai after they returned to the main room.

"They are," he agreed. "I handle all arrangements for visas and travel. When you pay me?"

"When you provide Hong Kong with a detailed statement showing the girls' names and ages, and the amounts required to transport them. I have another matter I need to discuss with you. I want to leave Bangkok in the next few days, and need a guide to take me across the border into Laos. No border control. Can you arrange this?"

The next day, Jimmy met Somchai, who told him they'd take the night bus north to Chiang Rai, where a smuggler named Tran would guide him across Laos to the border with China. From there, he could use his Hong Kong passport to enter China, then fly home.

"Must be very careful in Laos. Jungle many dangers – snakes, border patrols, drug smugglers," Somchai said gravely. His usual happy smile had gone. Jimmy nodded his understanding as he was given his bus ticket, along with a backpack containing essentials for a trek through the Laotian jungle. He opened it and noted the contents: a GPS device, map of Laos, water bottle, energy bars, first aid kit, bug repellant, plastic rain jacket, and a few extra lightweight clothes. Everything a guy needed for a romp through the jungle filled with all manner of deadly threats, Jimmy thought grimly.

Their journey began on the night bus from Bangkok to Chiang Rai, the northernmost province of

Thailand. It was modern, long and sleek, equipped with reclining seats designed for the long journey ahead. The road north was a ribbon of asphalt stretching through the heart of Thailand, passing through towns and endless rice paddies. As they approached their destination, the landscape began to change, flat plains giving way to rolling hills and dense forests.

After eleven hours, Chiang Rai emerged from the morning mist like a scene from a painting. Known for its serene temples, it was a stark contrast to the frenetic energy of Bangkok. Here, the air was cooler and the pace of life more measured. As they descended from the bus, Tran waved at them frantically, and rushed over to greet them. He was a grizzled Laotian with years of experience etched into his face. His calculating eyes never stopped scanning their surroundings as he leaned in close, his voice a low mumble.

"Leave now. Follow me and only do what I say. Okay?" Jimmy nodded. He'd heard the stories and knew the risks, but he had little choice in the matter. He was now in the Golden Triangle where the borders of Thailand, Laos and Myanmar converged, shrouded in peril. It was infamous for opium cultivation and drug trafficking, with powerful cartels wielding influence over the area's remote, mountainous terrain. Lawlessness ruled, with corrupt officials and ruthless drug lords maintaining a tight grip on the local populace. Venturing into the Golden Triangle risked encounters with them, as well as venomous wildlife – a lawless frontier where violence was commonplace and survival was uncertain.

With Somchai back on the bus to Bangkok, Jimmy and his guide took a minivan to Chiang Khong, a small border town perched on the banks of the Mekong River. Wide and muddy, it served as the natural boundary between Thailand and Laos. The official border crossing here was at the Fourth Thai-Lao Friendship Bridge, but Tran had other plans.

"Tonight, cross river by boat, no soldiers, no questions," Tran explained, holding up his thumb as they disembarked from the minivan.

Notorious for their harsh methods, the Lao border patrols were vigilant and ruthless, showing little mercy to those they apprehended. Those unlucky ones who were caught faced brutal interrogations, often in sweltering conditions where physical abuse and psychological torment were common. Corruption was also rampant, meaning that freedom came at an exorbitant price, if it came at all.

At midnight, Jimmy and Tran crouched low, concealed by the dense undergrowth on the river's edge, and watched as a small boat drifted slowly toward them. The boatman, an old Laotian man with a face carved by years of sun and river winds, nodded once, a silent signal that all was ready. Jimmy's heart pounded in his chest as he made his way down the slippery bank, his steps careful but quick. The boatman offered no greeting, only a curt gesture for them to get in.

The boat rocked gently as Jimmy settled himself on the wooden bench beside Tran, his eyes scanning the dark waters around them. As the boatman pushed off from the shore with a long pole, the town of Chiang Khong began to fade into the mist. The Mekong was wide here, its currents deceptively strong, and the journey across frightfully slow.

Tran kept his eyes peeled, knowing they were entering the most dangerous part of their crossing. Laotian border patrols often set up ambushes along this stretch, waiting to catch illegal crossings. Jimmy's pulse quickened with each passing minute, the tension coiling tighter within him.

As they approached the halfway mark, the boatman suddenly veered toward a cluster of small islands, barely more than sandbars in the river. Jimmy's confusion was met with a sharp glance from the old man, a silent command to remain quiet. The boatman's instincts were sharp, honed from years of navigating these treacherous waters. He knew the patrols preferred the open stretches, where their visibility was unhindered. The islands offered cover, albeit minimal, but in this cat-and-mouse game, every little bit helped.

Jimmy crouched lower, his senses heightened. The murmur of the river was louder here, the whispers of its secrets carried on the breeze. Suddenly, he heard the unmistakable sound of a motorboat off in the distance. Jimmy's breath caught in his throat. The patrol was near.

The boatman, without missing a beat, steered them toward a narrow channel between two islands. The foliage here was denser, the shadows deeper. The hum of the patrol boat grew louder, then began to fade as it moved past, unaware of the small, hidden vessel nestled among the reeds.

As they neared the Laotian side, the boatman slowed their approach, guiding them toward a secluded cove. Jimmy scanned the bank, looking for any sign of danger, but all he could see was jungle that loomed before them, thick and dark.

When the boat bumped the shore, Jimmy and Tran disembarked quickly, then turned back to the boatman, who merely nodded before he disappeared back into the river's mists. Jimmy took a deep breath as they began their trek inland. The jungle enveloped them almost immediately, its dense vegetation a stark contrast to the open expanse of the river.

Every step was a cautious calculation. The thick jungle was alive with the symphony of nocturnal creatures, their calls piercing the night air. Tran moved with purpose, sticking to the path he knew, his calloused hands brushing aside leaves and branches. His goal was to reach Pak Beng, a small town to the southeast, a waypoint on their journey deeper into Laos. From there, they could catch a bus north to China.

The path was narrow and winding, often disappearing altogether under the thick undergrowth. Tran's eyes constantly scanned their surroundings, every rustle a potential threat. Hours passed in a blur of green and sweat, until eventually they reached a small river, its dark waters reflecting the moonlight. Tran pointed to a narrow wooden raft hidden among the reeds. "Cross here," he said softly. "Stay low, keep quiet."

Jimmy climbed onto the unsteady raft, and seated himself in the middle. Tran pushed off from the bank with a long pole, guiding them silently across the water. The river's gentle current carried them downstream, the soft lapping of water against the raft the only sound.

Halfway across, Tran suddenly tensed and fell on his stomach, signaling Jimmy to do the same. On the far bank, the beam of a flashlight cut through the darkness, sweeping across the water. Jimmy held his breath as the light passed over their prostrate bodies, thankfully too high to see them. The flashlight moved on, and they reached the opposite shore safely. Jimmy clambered onto solid ground, his legs shaky from both the raft ride and the tension, and they pressed on into the jungle.

An hour later, accompanied by chirping cicadas

and the occasional rustle of unseen creatures, Tran motioned for them to stop. "Rest here," Tran said, his voice a low murmur. "This area usually quiet, but stay alert. Jungle unpredictable."

He handed Jimmy a small packet of food, which they ate in silence, each lost in his own thoughts. Suddenly, a distant sound pierced the night, an unfamiliar noise that didn't belong to the jungle's natural symphony. Tran stiffened, his eyes narrowing as he listened intently. Jimmy followed suit, his heart pounding in his chest.

"Smugglers," Tran whispered, his voice barely audible. "They close. Must be quiet."

Jimmy's heart pounded in his ears as the sounds grew closer, loud voices and footsteps trampling the underbrush. They crouched low, their breaths shallow and controlled. Jimmy glanced at Tran, whose face was a mask of concentration and... was it fear he detected?

The smugglers emerged from the shadows, their figures barely discernible in the dim light. Jimmy could make out the glint of weapons in their hands, their movements purposeful and menacing. The air was thick with tension, every second stretching into an eternity.

Without warning, a shot rang out, shattering the fragile silence. Tran's body jerked violently backward, a spray of blood arcing through the air as he tumbled to the ground. The sound echoed in Jimmy's ears, a deafening roar that drowned out everything else.

Time seemed to slow as Jimmy watched a crimson stain start to spread across Tran's chest. Panic surged through him, and with a desperate burst of energy, he bolted into the jungle, adrenaline propelling him forward as bullets whizzed past him.

The smugglers shouted behind him, their voices

a chaotic mix of anger and surprise. Jimmy's heart pounded in his ears, his breaths coming in ragged gasps as he sprinted through the darkness. Branches whipped against his face, leaving stinging welts, but he didn't dare slow down. The terrain was unforgiving, roots and rocks threatening to trip him with every step. He stumbled but quickly regained his footing, his mind focused on survival.

He could still hear the curses and shouts of the smugglers behind him, the sound of their heavy boots crashing through the underbrush. Jimmy's legs burned with exertion, his muscles screaming for relief. Suddenly, he burst into a small clearing and stumbled to a halt. Ahead of him was a steep ravine, the drop-off perilously close. Jimmy glanced around, searching for another way out. The sounds of his pursuers were getting closer.

In a desperate move, he scrambled down the side of the ravine, clinging to roots and rocks to slow his descent. He slipped and slid, the rough ground tearing at his clothes and skin. At the bottom, he paused to catch his breath, his body trembling with exhaustion and fear.

He knew he couldn't stay there, and forced himself to move, limping through the undergrowth as he searched for a safe place to hide. After what felt like an eternity, he found a dense thicket and crawled inside, making himself as small and inconspicuous as possible.

Jimmy waited, his heart pounding in his chest, as the sounds of the pursuit grew louder and then began to fade. The smugglers were moving on, their search widening. Barely daring to breathe, he stayed hidden until he was certain they were gone. When he emerged from his hiding place, his aching body was covered in dirt and scratches, but he was alive.

He took a deep breath, the humid air filling his

lungs, and glanced around. The dense foliage seemed to close in on him from all sides, the map of the jungle he had studied so thoroughly now a blur of confusion. He needed to find a river which would lead him back to civilization, and safety.

Suddenly, he heard an unmistakable click. He froze, the blood draining from his face. It was the sound of a gun being cocked. Jimmy turned slowly, his eyes searching the shadows. His heart thudded in his chest, the pulse of life pounding in his ears.

Ten feet away, a smuggler emerged from the shadows, a malevolent grin spread across his face. The man's eyes were cold and unfeeling, a predator's gaze locking onto its prey. His gun was pointed directly at Jimmy, the barrel a black hole promising oblivion.

Jimmy's mind screamed at him to run, to dive for cover, to do anything to escape the fate that awaited him. But his body refused to move, paralyzed by fear and the grim certainty of what was to come. He raised his hands slowly, a futile gesture of surrender. The smuggler's grin widened, a silent admission of Jimmy's helplessness.

"Please," Jimmy managed to whisper, his voice barely audible over the pounding of his heart. "I have money. Take it all. It's yours."

The gunshot shattered the jungle's eerie silence, a deafening roar that echoed through the trees. Jimmy felt a searing pain in his chest, a burning sensation that spread like wildfire. His legs gave way and he crumpled to the ground, the world around him spinning. The smuggler approached and stood over him, the gun still smoking in his hand. There was no remorse in the man's eyes, no recognition of the life he'd just extinguished, as he checked his pockets and took his backpack.

Ernie's Bistro - July 6, 2023

With her legal problems behind her, Vanessa seemed to take her renewed alliance with Zach as a sign that she could slip back into her old habits. She'd call or text at all hours, her messages a mix of gratitude and thinly veiled attempts at drawing him back into her web. Zach kept his responses curt and professional, determined not to let her personal charm cloud his judgment again. Sophie was adamant that he drop her for good, and he'd managed to avoid seeing her in person since their last meeting at Ernie's two weeks ago.

One afternoon, as Zach sat in his office preparing a presentation, papers strewn across his desk, his phone buzzed with a message from Vanessa: "Drinks at Ernie's? I need a break."

He sighed, rubbing his temples. The temptation to decline was strong, but he knew that maintaining a semblance of cordiality was the more appropriate way to go. Reluctantly, he replied: "OK. 4 pm."

"Are you serious?" Zach's inner voice nagged. It had taken him months of interrupted sleep with headaches and heart palpitations to finally get her out of his head. Did he really want to start that farce all over again? She was only coming back because she wanted a man in her life again after Maurice dropped her like a hot potato at the first sign of trouble.

"Maybe yes, maybe no," Zach replied quietly to himself, which he had been doing a lot lately. He knew he still had powerful feelings and loyalty for Vanessa, even if misguided. In the right circumstances, would he be able to forgive her? He didn't know, but he still believed, on a philosophical level, that talking things out was important. Even if it led nowhere, at least it cleared the air, helping them to move forward.

When Zach arrived at Ernie's, Vanessa was already there, a bottle of Robert Mondavi Napa Valley Cabernet Sauvignon breathing on the table. She greeted him with a warm smile, but there was an undercurrent of tension in her eyes. "Thank you for coming," she said, pouring him a glass. "I know this isn't easy for you." As Zach took his seat, he tamped down the mild anxiety lurking inside him. "How are you doing through all this?" she asked tentatively.

"As Groucho Marx said, 'I've had a wonderful time, but this wasn't it'. That's a pretty accurate assessment of the emotional rollercoaster I've been on lately." He decided not to overplay the victim, and leave out the heart and sleep problems that plagued him in the first two months. "I heard your settlement with the prosecutor went through."

"Yes, what a relief that was. I get to keep the house and five million, and since it's a court order, there's nothing Edward can do about it. In addition, the judge only ordered twenty million in restitution, so there should be more for me when the divorce is done."

"Sounds like you're a rich woman. You were extremely lucky they believed you weren't involved."

"Oh, but I was."

"I beg your pardon?" Zach said, sputtering his wine mid-drink.

"I kept the books, and I knew all about Edward and Jimmy. I met him many times. Sometimes he would bring a box of his wine to the house."

"Did you know it was fake?"

"Neither of us knew for certain, but of course we

suspected. You'd have to be a blind idiot not to realize the odds of finding that many rare wines were unlikely to impossible." Zach paused to let her words sink in before continuing.

"Do you realize, if the prosecutor finds out about this information you withheld, your plea bargain will be canceled, and you'll probably go to jail?" Vanessa's smug expression dropped when she heard this, but she recovered quickly.

"You're not going to tell them, are you?" she purred. "After everything we meant to each other. Besides, what difference would it make? The real culprits were Edward and Jimmy, not me." She had a point. Would justice really be served by reopening the case? "Also, I was the one who broke the case."

"How do you figure that?"

"Why do you think I gave you that bottle of Pétrus, Agent Pruno?" Her words hit Zach like a ton of bricks. Nobody was supposed to know about his undercover work. Nobody.

"How did you find out?"

"When I was signing the documents at the FBI, I caught sight of Agent Pruno's report about my bottle of wine. I didn't know for sure it was you until now."

"Why did you do it?" Zach asked, thoroughly confused.

"I thought it would speed up the divorce settlement, force Edward into a situation where he had to settle, which it did. I have you to thank; you gave me the confidence to do it. Let's not talk about that anymore. I'm much more interested in talking about you. How are you feeling?"

"How am I feeling?" Zach replied after collecting his thoughts. "The fairest conclusion I reached was that

I was looking for a friend, while you wanted a lover. When Maurice came along, you quietly moved me aside. When I called you on it, you denied it, and then a month later you canceled me." Now they were both looking intently into each other's eyes, looking for a reaction.

"What I see here is a betrayal of trust and what it did," he continued, looking into his glass. "Because we got so close to each other, clearly too close, I trusted you deeply, and that became the foundation of my friendship with you. Then you met Maurice, who swept you off your feet, and for two months you pursued the affair with him, all the while hiding it from me. After that, you handled me by slowly reducing my access to you, presumably so I'd eventually decide to walk away."

"I'm sorry I did that, but I didn't know how to tell you," Vanessa replied, avoiding eye contact. "I couldn't tell you because I didn't want to hurt you more than I already had."

"You didn't hurt me as much as you betrayed me. It's too bad you trusted me so little. Instead, one day, I found out that you'd blocked my cell number and WhatsApp, which sent a pretty clear message that I was canceled. You even had Lilith and your other friends do it too. I could never do that to someone. I know what it's like to be heartbroken. Perhaps you learned some bad habits from your husband."

"I wanted to keep you in my life, but I just couldn't deal with my feelings for Maurice and you at the same time. I had to make a hard choice between the two of you," Vanessa said, tears welling in her eyes.

"Do you remember what you said to me at our last meeting?" Zach asked to no reply from Vanessa. "You said 'I've decided to be with Maurice'. You didn't want to tell me the truth to my face, so you used Maurice as an excuse. He'd come along and seemed like a better deal. I became inconvenient. I'd served my purpose and could be replaced, without any consequences for you.

"In any event," Zach continued, "the lesson I've learned is that when you betrayed my trust, all the certainty we had disappeared, leaving me confused and heartbroken. It reminds me of the drama of high school and college, which I thought was behind me. The whole thing seems so childish."

"Do you think we can be friends again?" Vanessa asked, again searching Zach's eyes, hoping for a positive reaction.

"I'm no therapist, but it doesn't take much to see that this kind of betrayal, which has so completely destroyed our friendship, would be difficult to recover from. You walked away, and if things had worked out with Maurice, we wouldn't be having this conversation now. You're lonely and single again, facing an uncertain future. What am I to you, really?"

"You're everything that I loved about you before. I admit I was foolish. Could I have another chance?"

"We also have the not so small matter of Sophie. She's loved and supported me through this, and we're rekindling our marriage, as you encouraged me to do. I'm no longer lonely and looking for something beyond Sophie. Slowly she's beginning to trust me again. That's about the only good thing to come out of this mess."

"I'm glad. She's a beautiful, strong and intelligent woman, and I'm so happy to hear that's working."

"I have you to thank for helping me make up with her, even though it was part of your plan to ease me out of your life. You did me a great favor," Zach said. "Anyway, it would be tricky to say to her that we're friends again. I can hear her reaction now. Something like 'Are you completely crazy?' comes to mind. She witnessed my distress and sorrow during those first two months. I'm curious, though: how did you explain my sudden disappearance to your friends, who you told to block me?"

"I told them you wanted to have an affair with me, but you were a married man," Vanessa replied casually as if the answer was obvious. "They knew what I'd been through with Edward, and were very supportive."

"So, you lied to me about Maurice, and then you lied to your friends about me."

"Yes, but doesn't everyone?"

"The difference between us is that you'll lie to get what you want. It always amazes me how casually people deceive each other, and then justify it to themselves as if it didn't matter," Zach said. "I thought you were different. I was certain we were close friends, but now I realize that your friendships are only on your own terms. At our last meeting when you told me about Maurice, I made a classic mistake. I criticized you when I said you lied to me, because I stupidly thought I could trust you. That gave you all the justification you needed to cancel me. Not only you, but you made sure that your entire retinue of friends, including Lilith, canceled me too. In one fell swoop you made me the bad guy, ruined eight friendships, erased any memory of me, and all because you didn't want to deal with the truth. And here I've done it again." Zach made a show of gently slapping his palm against his forehead.

"You told me from the beginning that you weren't willing to be a couple with me!" Vanessa said with tears in her eyes, her voice rising. She was clearly very upset, and Zach felt himself being pulled toward her.

"Right," Zach said, glancing at his watch, eager to

leave. "Let's get together again next week and talk some more."

"Please don't go," she pleaded.

"Vanessa, you've been through a lot, and I care about you. I really do. Soon you will meet someone new, and put all of this behind you. I'll text you." Zach got up, and Vanessa extended her hand, which he took. He held it for a moment, then pulled away and left with many conflicting emotions. As he walked out of the restaurant, he found himself humming the song "It was great fun, but it was just one of those things."

When he arrived home twenty minutes later, he found Sophie making dinner in the kitchen. It smelled delicious. "A wise person once said the way to a man's heart is through his stomach," he said, as he came up from behind and wrapped his arms around her.

"Must have been a woman," she replied, turning her head to kiss him. "What man knows how to cook, and keep house, and raise children, and..."

"All right, all right! I get the point."

"*Très bien*. How did the meeting go with Vanessa?"

"We cleared the air, and agreed to meet again next week. She's been through hell, but in time she'll recover and find someone new to love. Who knows; maybe Maurice will take a renewed interest in her now that she's a free woman."

Sophie hesitated for a moment before she replied. "I doubt that, if what you told me is true about her having to turn over all her money to the prosecutor. She was much more attractive to him when she was rich. You know that I think?"

"I'm all ears."

"I think you should really stop associating with

people who didn't go to university. Look at Vanessa and her soap opera with Lilith and her friends. None of them went to college according to you."

"You make an interesting point. It didn't work out so well for Maurice either, or Edward for that matter, who married her, then he went into business with Jimmy Wong. Let's discuss this further. Why don't I pour us some wine?"

"What an excellent idea, and one which you know something about."

Epilogue

Judge Walter Wallace, dressed in his gown and one of his trademark bow ties, heard a soft knock on his door, and looked up to see his secretary hovering there.

"Yes, what is it, Nora?" he asked gruffly. He did not like to be interrupted when he was writing a judgment.

"Judge Hennessy was wondering if she might have a moment of your time," Nora replied timidly.

"Oh, very well. Send her in." A heartbeat later, Judge Moira Hennessy swept into his office as Nora stepped aside and sat down opposite him.

"Good morning, Judge. I'll be brief," she said, pushing a single piece of paper across his desk.

"What's this?"

"It's your resignation, effective at the end of this month, in order to give you time to tidy up any outstanding matters, and allow for a smooth transition of your caseload."

"I don't understand. I still have two years to go on my term."

"This will spare you the notoriety and embarrassment of a judicial inquiry into why you tipped off an accused fraudster who was being investigated by the FBI."

"I did no such thing," Wallace protested.

"I believe you know Edward Pavlov, who is a member of your club. I'm informed you proposed him for membership."

"Yes, I do, but I never warned him about the FBI."

"No, you didn't; but you did warn another club

297

member, Ryan Townhill, a club director, knowing he would then call Mr. Pavlov. That was a clever approach to give you plausible deniability, I'll give you that. In this case, however, it didn't work. Please sign. You'll be doing yourself a favor."

"How do you know all this?"

"Mr. Townhill's conversation with Mr. Pavlov was recorded by the FBI, who had wiretapped his phone."

Knowing he was defeated, an ashen Judge Walter Wallace picked up the Montblanc pen that his wife Madge had given him on his sixtieth birthday and, with a sigh, signed away what remained of an otherwise stellar career. "This is so unjust," he said to nobody in particular. "After all these years and so many exemplary rulings, to be forced out like this." He avoided looking at her as he handed her the signed document.

"Thank you, Judge. It's the right thing to do, for everyone concerned." With that, Judge Hennessy grabbed the paper and departed as abruptly as she had entered. She had promised to be brief after all.

Upstairs in the federal building, the FBI had not yet amassed enough evidence to touch Angelo Salvatore, his *capos* and soldiers. Their surveillance teams continued to watch and listen, waiting for the break they knew would come in the end. They did however notice he had stopped investing in rare wine. Go figure.

As for James (Jimmy) Jin-Hie Wong, also known as Juan Jiao-long Huang, Special Agent in Charge Martin Abelman closed the file with a memo that the suspect was at large in China and beyond their reach. The file would be stored and be available to be reactivated should Jimmy ever resurface in a friendly jurisdiction. The FBI is a persistent organization.

At Edward's rented house in Pacific Heights, a

letter arrived that he didn't read, since he was otherwise detained. It was from The Redwood Private Men's Club of San Francisco, politely informing him that his membership had been canceled, and inviting him not to reapply. His private club life was at an end; he was now unclubbable.

If anyone could be called a winner in this fiasco, it was Hugh Albright: he was reimbursed seventy percent of what he paid for the bogus wine, which he got to keep; and he had his share of the $920,000 paid by Edward to Angelo, plus the $400,000 that he originally received from Angelo. Edward, being otherwise occupied for the next thirty months, had never asked him for it. Hugh somehow doubted he ever would.

When Zach walked into ABC headquarters on New Montgomery Street, he was again greeted heartily by the agent at reception as "Agent Pruno". "Not anymore, Bob" he replied. "From now on, I'm just plain Zachary Taylor, American citizen." Then he climbed the stairs and knocked on Mitch Adams' door.

"Come on in, Zach," boomed his sturdy voice, as Zach opened the door and sat down. The two old friends had a bond between them like no other.

"It's time, Mitch."

"Oh? Time for what?"

"Time for Agent Pruno to retire permanently, along with skydiving. No more temporary, unofficial assignments."

"Do I detect Sophie's deft hand in this? Is she still pissed about you being arrested?"

"She'll get over it. In truth, I need to make a clean break and move on. We've done a good job over the years to keep demon liquor out of the wrong hands. But now it's time."

"Can you imagine this city without any controls at all? You wouldn't be able to drive down the streets because they'd be littered with unconscious citizens," Mitch said, laughing.

"That we definitely wouldn't want. The Statue of Liberty doesn't say 'Give me your inebriated.'"

"Speaking of which, look what arrived from our friends at the FBI," he said, waving a hand toward the far corner of his office. Zach turned his head to see the twenty-three boxes that were seized from Vanessa's cellar. "They said the case is done. They don't want to store them, so they gave them to us. Any idea what we should do with them?"

Zach walked over and took out a bottle. It was the 1961 Romanée-Conti with large red letters "FORGED" stamped diagonally across the label. "You know, I never tried one of these. Do you suppose it's any good?"

"Why don't we open it and see? I've heard the buyers gave them high praise." Zach did not need more encouragement. As if by magic, he produced a corkscrew and opened the bottle on Mitch's desk.

"I don't suppose you have a decanter or any wine glasses here..."

"That I don't, but I do have these," he said, producing two mugs.

"Mugs it is," Zach replied, pouring a little into each. "What shall we toast to?"

"How about, 'To our wives and girlfriends, may they never meet!' Mitch proposed, holding up his mug."

"I think it's a little late for that," Agent Pruno replied sarcastically. He took the first sip, then looked at the chief liquor cop, his eyebrows raised.

"When you grin like that, I know I'm either about to taste liquid gold or utter regret."

"This is superb!" blurted Zach. "No wonder Jimmy got away with it for so long. This bottle's worth at least a few hundred bucks."

"Well then, there's at least twenty-eight thousand dollars' worth sitting over there. Just don't sell it to anyone."

"You're kidding. That's for me?"

"You bet. Consider it our going away present." They continued enjoying the wine and reminiscing until it was gone. "All right Zach, let's get you on your way... but don't forget your friends," Mitch said, concern suddenly crossing his face, as he moved around his desk to show him out.

"Of course. We'll even keep coming to your house for weekend barbecues," Zach replied, with a big smile.

"Well, that's okay then. Who needs you around here when I can have you over, eating my food and drinking my booze, provided you bring one of those special bottles." They both chortled and, with nothing more to say, they embraced, and Zach left to return home, his car brimming with wine.

Across town, Vanessa answered her front door to find Sophie standing there. "Sophie, what a pleasant surprise," she said ingenuously to hide her shock. "Come in."

"I'm only here for a bit; could we have some tea?"

"Of course. Come in the kitchen. I have mint, green..."

"Green would be great, thanks."

"Do you take cream or sugar?"

"No *merci*... I mean, thank you. Old habit."

They adjourned to the living room with the tea, which Vanessa dutifully poured into their cups.

"On second thought, do you have milk?"

"Sure," Vanessa replied, standing up and walking back to the kitchen."

Over tea, they talked about the case, Sophie saying how sorry she was that Vanessa and Zach had to go through it all, and how they should get together soon. Vanessa didn't tell Sophie the true extent of her role in the swindle, since Zach had thankfully pointed out it could cancel her plea agreement.

She also did not tell her about the ten cases of rare wine that she removed from the cellar before the FBI arrived, which she'd intended to use as leverage over Edward in her divorce. "That was a lucky move, and one that will materially help my retirement plan," she was thinking, until her reverie was suddenly interrupted.

"Did you want to steal my husband?" Sophie asked bluntly, looking intently at Vanessa.

"No, I never..." she replied, trying to avoid her stare. "I want you to know he was always a gentleman, and made it clear he would not leave you."

"Are you in love with him?"

"I'd be lying if I said no. We became very close, and I hope that we can all be close again, as friends." Sophie paused to mull this over before continuing.

"As a result of all of this, I've realized how much I love Zach, and what I'd do to safeguard him and my family. I've decided I would do anything to protect them."

Vanessa suddenly felt quite dizzy and a little sleepy; probably still decompressing from the stress, she told herself. "Oh my, I suddenly don't feel well," she said to Sophie.

"Do you need any help?"

"I think I can manage," she said, feeling more disoriented by the second. "Thanks for dropping by. I'm sorry, but I really need to lie down."

Sophie made a hasty exit as Vanessa stumbled to the bedroom to lie down. She felt quite weird, like her body was floating, and before long she could not keep her eyes open. She was found by her daughter the next day, but she was long gone. The chief medical examiner ruled it an accidental fentanyl overdose.

In the fall, Zach and Sophie returned to Paris to visit the Café du Chat Noir. They sat at the same marble-topped table where they had met before, sipping Chablis and eating their *crêpes jambon fromage* as they watched the world go by. They talked about the long and winding road they had followed since that day in 1988; how her parents were now in their eighties, the kids had grown up and moved out, their friends had changed, and they did not have to work anymore.

"It's still hard to believe Vanessa is gone," he said, his voice tinged with sadness. "Such a tragic end. I never would have guessed she was using drugs."

Sophie's fork paused mid-air, her eyes flickering briefly before she resumed eating. "Yes, it was shocking," she replied, looking past Zach to the street, her tone oddly detached.

Authors Notes

The Sommelier is a work of fiction. The names, characters, places, and events are fictitious, and any resemblance to actual persons, living or dead, businesses, companies, events, or locations is entirely coincidental. The author is referred to as "we" in these Notes as this book is the product of a group of people who wrote, edited, and contributed to it. Daniel Llewellyn Shaw is our pen name.

Visitors to Paris will search in vain for the Café du Chat Noir on the Left Bank, where Zach and Sophie met for lunch in 1988, and then returned in the Epilogue. As far as we know, UCLA does not provide recent graduates, like Peter Mosley, to act as liaisons with overseas institutions.

There is no Stanley's Fine Wines on Santa Monica Boulevard, where Peter Mosley and Zach both worked. The same goes for Bean & Co. down the street and Alonzo's Ristorante Italiano in Malibu. San Pancho Winery in Napa is also a figment of our imagination, unless it has come into being since this book was written.

Also, Edward Pavlov couldn't have met Jimmy Wong at Sutter Street Auctioneers because it does not exist. Nor will you find Villa Vanessa on Lombard Street on Russian Hill, as no such house exists. The same is true for the other featured homes which we scattered around San Francisco.

Likewise, we made up the American Institute of Sommeliers, of which Zach is a past president, and Ernie's Bistro in San Francisco, which was frequented first by Zach and Lilith, and later by Zach and Vanessa during their short but ill-fated romance. Small wonder with a host like Ernie, who effortlessly enhances the dining experience and makes all the difference when choosing a place to go.

The same is true for La Toque Rouge French restaurant on Pier 39 at Fisherman's Wharf; our apologies to them again for serving Italian wines, although in our defense, they *were* Bordeaux blends. If we have failed to mention any other restaurant in these notes, rest assured it was also made up. They were all made up.

There also is no Redwood Private Men's Club in San Francisco where the wine auctions occurred, or Stellar Jet Charters at Hayward Executive Airport, which Jimmy used to make his daring escape back to Hong Kong.

The California Department of Alcoholic Beverage Control, known as ABC, exists and has an office in San Francisco. Its mandate is to regulate the alcohol business in California, which includes investigating alcohol-related crimes such as wine forgery. Its peace officers primarily work in plainclothes and partner with law enforcement. It does not, however, have a division chief named Mitchell Adams, nor an Agent Pruno (which, like hootch, is slang for prison wine) among its ranks. It also didn't participate in *Operation Hangover*, which, as far as we know, never occurred.

Fifty years ago, aspiring law students were taught to plead facts, not evidence, when drafting criminal complaints. Not so today, where prosecutors include everything and the kitchen sink in order to tip the case in their favor, leaving little room for any reasonable doubt by a jury already well-versed in the lurid details designed to persecute the accused.

Tricks like the "perp walk," where the law frog marches the accused past a tipped-off press, followed by exaggerated criminal complaints that are reported in the news, add materially to the prosecution's chances of success. Journalists at most pay lip service to the legal principle that a defendant is innocent until proven guilty by adding a sentence somewhere that the accusations repeated in their fervid articles are unproven. The expression "closing the stable door after the horse has bolted" comes to mind.

Today's prosecutors, with their discretionary charging power, engage in "charge bargaining" where they overcharge defendants in order to coerce them into pleading guilty. A further incentive to plea bargain is the "trial penalty," whereby they can expect a harsher sentence if they don't settle and instead put the prosecution to the time and expense of a trial.

As stated by the National Association of Criminal Defense Lawyers in July 2018: "The 'trial penalty' refers to the substantial difference between the sentence offered in a plea offer prior to trial versus the sentence a defendant receives after trial. This penalty is now so severe and pervasive that it has virtually eliminated the constitutional right to a trial. To avoid the penalty, accused persons must surrender many other fundamental rights that are essential to a fair justice system."

In the decision *Missouri v. Frye*, 566 U.S. 134 (2012), the Supreme Court acknowledged that ninety-seven percent of federal convictions now come from guilty pleas, stating that plea bargaining "is not some adjunct to the criminal justice system; it is the criminal justice system."

This undermines the fundamental balance in

criminal law, put so famously by Sir William Blackstone in 1783, "It is better that ten guilty persons escape than one innocent suffer." That is why an accused is supposed to be considered innocent until proven guilty.

In the United States today, not so much. The number of people in prison has increased five hundred percent in the last forty years; in 2023, they numbered two million people. Although America has five percent of the world's population, it has twenty-five percent of its incarcerated people, the highest rate in the world. These statistics are the result of a persistent erosion of the protections traditionally afforded to the accused to ensure a fair trial.

On the subject of wine fraud, truth can truly be stranger than fiction. In December 2013, Rudy Kurniawan was sentenced to ten years in prison for an audacious scheme of counterfeiting rare and expensive wines, which he sold for many millions of dollars. When the FBI raided his house in Arcadia, California, they discovered two hundred old bottles in the process of being reproduced, nineteen thousand forged wine labels, and other paraphernalia used to create his fake wines. The prosecutor called him the "biggest and most successful wine counterfeiter in the world."

According to winefraud.com, the estimated value of counterfeit Kurniawan wines still circulating in the market is around $550 million. It pegs the total of all fraudulent wines in circulation at $3 billion. As Rudy might have said, "People taste what they want to taste. That's why I never worried too much."

Decades before Kurniawan's case, a smaller, but no less audacious scheme was orchestrated by German promoter Hardy Rodenstock. He claimed to have discovered bottles of wine once owned by Thomas

Jefferson, selling them at auction for around $500,000 each. Subsequent chemical analysis established they could not have been made before 1945, which was one hundred years after his death.

Despite being widely exposed as a fraud, Rodenstock was never formally charged. He consistently denied any wrongdoing, and proving that he'd knowingly sold counterfeit wine, as opposed to being misled himself, proved legally challenging. Unlike Kurniawan, he managed to evade prosecution and lived freely in Germany until his death in 2018.

Wine fraud is not limited to faking extremely rare wines. The bigger problem is using cheaper wine to fill thousands of bottles of a more expensive brand. This has happened in China, where police seized over forty thousand bottles of fake Penfolds and Lafite wines in 2022.

Various companies around the world are addressing the problem. Chai Vault, led by wine-fraud expert Maureen Downey, advertises that it is "the first anti-fraud solution for wines and spirits that allows potential buyers to know a bottle is authentic and view provable provenance, before purchase, without physical proximity to the bottle." For a fee, it authenticates wine, both at the time of production or later by the bottle, and enters the certification in the blockchain for easy digital access and tracking as wines change hands.

Domaine Leflaive, which makes the Montrachet Grand Cru mentioned in this book, equips its bottles with RFID chips that can be read with a cell phone to authenticate them.

Until wine authentication is widely adopted by producers, the best advice is to buy uncertified wines from a reputable source.

Wine fraud is as old as the Tuscan hills. Pliny the Elder, who died in 79 AD during the eruption of Mount Vesuvius, lamented the widespread production of counterfeit Roman wine. "Not even our nobility ever enjoys wines that are genuine," he wrote in his *Natural History*. Since then, water has been added to increase volume, chemicals to enhance sweetness, expensive labels put on lesser bottles, and cheaper wine blended with more expensive ones – you get the picture.

The principle of *caveat emptor* (buyer beware) applies as much today as it did then.

Zach and Sophie Taylor will return in:

The **Art Thief**

16226999R00171